First of Tomes

The Tomes of Kaleria: Tome 2

Honor Raconteur

Raconteur House

Published by Raconteur House
Murfreesboro, TN

FIRST OF TOMES
The Tomes of Kaleria: Tome 2

A Raconteur House book/ published by arrangement with the author

Copyright © 2020 by Honor Raconteur
Cover by Katie Griffin
Chinese Vintage Dragon Elements on classic red background. by poppindx/Shutterstock; Set of traditional oriental chinese golden rectangle frames on pattern red background for decoration. by shlyapanama /Shutterstock; Brushed Painted Abstract Background. Brush stroked painting by Hybrid_Graphics/Shutterstock; Gray industry wall by mxbfilms/Shutterstock

This book is a work of fiction, so please treat it like a work of fiction. Seriously. References to real people, dead people, good guys, bad guys, stupid politicians, companies, restaurants, cats with attitudes, events, products, dragons, locations, pop culture references, or wacky historical events are intended to provide a sense of authenticity and are used fictitiously. Or because I wanted it in the story. Characters, names, story, location, dialogue, weird humor and strange incidents all come from the author's very fertile imagination and are not to be construed as real. No, I don't believe in killing off main characters. Villains are a totally different story.

All rights reserved.
No part of this book may be reproduced, scanned, or distributed in any printed or electronic form without permission. Please do not participate in or encourage electronic piracy of copyrighted materials in violation of the author's rights.
Purchase only authorized editions.

For information address: www.raconteurhouse.com

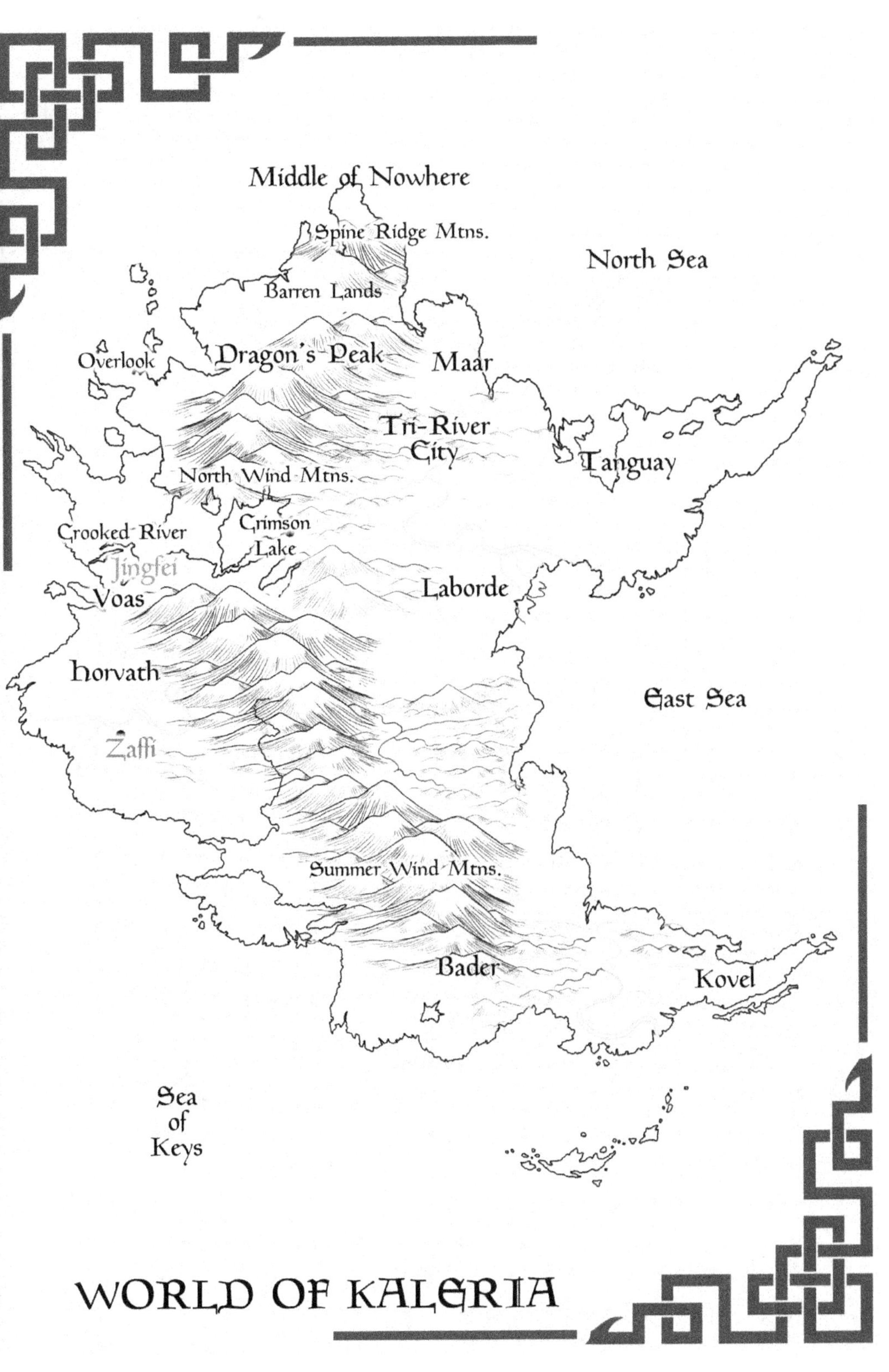

Middle of Nowhere
Spine Ridge Mtns.
North Sea
Barren Lands
Overlook
Dragon's Peak
Maar
Tri-River City
Tanguay
North Wind Mtns.
Crooked River
Crimson Lake
Jingfei
Laborde
Voas
Horvath
East Sea
Zaffi
Summer Wind Mtns.
Bader
Kovel
Sea
of
Keys
WORLD OF KALERIA

Prologue

Something seized her, a strong force that tapped into her stomach, and yanked sharply. Mei Li had precisely enough time to gasp and flail madly before the light disappeared altogether. Stars and shadow wrapped around her, as if she'd stepped into a galaxy, only she had no time to gather her bearings as she sped through it. In a blink, she was through it, and a patch of ground rushed up to meet her.

Mei Li felt disoriented, much like a drunk who couldn't find either equilibrium or balance, and she landed with a thud against hard-packed dirt, grass tickling her nose. Gasping, she flopped onto her side, struggling to catch her breath. She panted for a moment, eyes blind to her surroundings. Was this what a fish felt like, when thrown onto the bank? Winded, disoriented, and weak? She had more sympathy for their plight if that was the case.

The weakness quickly passed and she struggled up to her knees first, getting a good look around. Nothing looked familiar. Not that it said much, as Mei Li hadn't really traveled much in her life. She'd been all over the modern world, but she knew the world's geography and landscape had changed a great deal through the years. She could be anywhere in the world and not be able to recognize it. For that matter, how much of the land had changed over the years? So much so that she, a modern woman, wouldn't deem it familiar?

She looked to the road nearby, hard-packed red clay and wide, with wagon ruts in it. That was promising. Mei Li was a very firm fan of roads, seeing as they led places. The area was lovely, rolling green hills dotted with trees and what looked like farms in the distance. And the weather was fair, that was also good, barely a cloud in the blue sky. At least she wouldn't have weather to contend with.

All good points, but it didn't solve her immediate question: just when and where was she?

Dusting herself off, she got to her feet and started walking east. She kept up a good pace, because without knowing her location, she had no idea of where she could rest for the night. It would behoove her to make tracks as quickly as possible. Still, Mei Li paced herself. She knew she didn't have the stamina to run all day. Or even a quarter of it.

As she walked, her ears perked up. Was that...it sounded like the sounds of battle ahead. Not with clashing swords, per se, although something metal was striking hard. Mostly incantations, and yelling, and substantial thuds as heavy objects hit the ground. What was going on ahead? And did she want to get into the middle of it?

Frowning, Mei Li picked up her pace. Better to know what it was and avoid it than to blindly strike away from the road. She didn't want to go cross-country if she didn't have to.

As she rounded a bend, going down a slight hill, the scene came more sharply into definition. There was indeed a battle—right in the middle of the road, no less. Three mages, one warrior, and something that looked very fierce and straight out of a nightmare.

Mei Li shielded her eyes with a flat hand as she ran, the sun at the perfectly wrong angle to mess with her vision. When she finally got in close enough, she groaned in realization. Not that she'd ever seen this particular beast in person, but she'd read of it. It was the manifestation of the Red Lantern, a powerful, fiery beast that was part lion, part fire, and mostly rage. Red Lantern was supposed to light the path toward Heaven, but being denied that privilege, it went mad and instead sought to destroy the gates leading onto the path. It now wanted to destroy any road it saw.

But hadn't that been sealed...oh dear. Oh no. Surely she wasn't that far into the past?! No, calm down, Red Lantern did escape its seal once, about two thousand years ago. It was possible she was there instead of at the first sealing, which was over five thousand years ago.

Mei Li had no chance to speculate or ask questions. The group was formidable, but they hadn't figured out how to subdue Red Lantern yet, and it was growing fiercer with every attack. Someone kept throwing wind attacks against it, and that only fueled its ferocity. Groaning at the idiocy, Mei Li rushed forward, rummaging in her pack as she did so, praying Shunlei had put in talismans—bless that man, he had. Her hand closed over the thin strips of paper and yanked four out.

"Not wind!" she called as she ran up to the group. "Earth or water, but not wind!"

One of the mages, a woman with singed brown hair, turned sharply to stare over her shoulder. "You know how to subdue this?!"

"I do!"

"Tell us how!"

Mei Li came to a stop, sliding a bit on the slick grass, and panted out, "Follow my directions. I need a four over four—"

"A what?" the burly soldier with the fur around his shoulders demanded impatiently.

"A mage in each directional corner!" Sand and stars, they didn't know what a four over four meant? Just how modern of a term was that?

The mages tried to follow her direction, but of course

Red Lantern could hear her shouting as well as they could, and the fiery beast moved to counteract them. He bellowed fire at them, and the mages were quick to cover the warrior with their own shields, protecting everyone from being set aflame. Mei Li quickly used one of the talismans in her hand to create a rough and ready protective shield, and the fire flared harmlessly around her, although it had been a near thing.

Her heart beat loudly in her ears as she panted for breath. Battling things with people she didn't know wasn't ideal, but there wasn't much she could do about that. Withdrawing long enough to come up with a strategy wasn't feasible in this situation. And it didn't solve her problem of how to get a talisman above Red Lantern's head. Unless she figured that out, they'd not be able to seal it, much less subdue.

One of the warriors turned his head, spotting something in the sky, and abruptly cursed. "Dragon incoming!"

Mei Li's heart lifted in relief. With a dragon's aid, they might win this yet without losing someone in the process.

Everyone else cursed as well, looking alarmed, and they put up defensive barriers over their heads as if...no, surely not. Were they actually preparing defenses against a dragon?

Just how far back in history was she?! Dragons hadn't been humanity's enemy in thousands of years. Over four thousand years, in fact.

With their attention divided, Red Lantern almost caught one of the mages unawares, and he had to duck and roll to avoid becoming barbeque. Mei Li reached for the nearest mage and warrior, slapping them on the shoulder. "I'll deal with the dragon. Use these talismans, get in the directional corners, link the talismans! It'll create a box-shield around it."

They nodded toward her sharply, taking the talismans, and immediately followed her directions. Or tried. Red Lantern made it difficult for anyone to hold their ground.

Mei Li quickly backed off, buying herself some distance. She needed to see if she could make the dragon an ally or if she'd have to fend it off. It was red, so a young dragon. That wasn't entirely promising in and of itself. Still, there was something about this dragon that seemed oddly familiar. It took her a minute to place it, but the body shape and the curve of that wide wingspan reminded her of Shunlei. Was this perhaps an ancestor of his?

Tossing caution to the wind, she put both hands around her mouth and belted in Long-go, "Dragon! I require aid!"

That great head turned sharply downwards, eyeing her, and he dropped with two hard flaps of the wing, coming in closer to her. As soon as he did so, Mei Li's mouth went dry. She'd recognize that elegant, elongated bone structure, the high curve of his eyes, anywhere. It wasn't that he looked like Shunlei. He *was* Shunlei.

Shunlei the Red.

Mei Li's knees went weak and she almost dropped to the ground. Was she really five thousand years in the past?!

A burst of flame from Red Lantern scattered in all directions, like a whip seeking a target, and Mei Li dropped heavily to the ground to avoid it. She swore viciously as she threw her shield back up and around, strengthening it. Red Lantern was getting stronger. She wouldn't be able to protect herself at all in a minute, not at this rate. Her magic wasn't up to the task.

Red Lantern bellowed fire again, the sound so hot it sounded like a damned soul screaming at her. The heat of it flashed over her skin, and she flinched at the feeling. Although it had fortunately mostly missed, it was still hot enough to be painful, forcing mages and soldiers alike to leap clear. Mei Li had no room to maneuver, trapped as she was still on the ground. She ducked her head down and threw her full magical strength into the barrier.

Something heavy landed over her, the wind rushing and

throwing her hair around wildly, rustling her clothes. She smelled the warm scales, the sunlight still radiating from his skin, and peeked up to discover Shunlei had landed protectively over her, his wing thrown ahead to block the fire. A being of fire himself, the Red Lantern couldn't harm him, and its attack bounced harmlessly off.

Something in her unwound, and she grinned up at the feathers in front of her. Shunlei the Black was right. If she asked Shunlei the Red for help, he'd grant it.

"Fair mage, you know how to defeat this?"

"I do," she answered in Long-go. "We need talismans on all four corners and one above to seal him in place. If I give you a talisman, can you carry it above him and hover in place?"

"I can." Shunlei turned his head toward her for just a moment. "After, we must talk."

"Trust me, I want to talk more than you do." Mei Li scrambled to her feet and grabbed more talismans from her bag. She scraped hair out of her face with her free hand as she moved, using his wings for cover as she made quick preparations. "Here, take this one. On the count of three, I'm rolling free. You can lift into the air then." Switching languages, she yelled at the rest of the humans, "Dragon is an ally! Don't fire at him!"

Shunlei hunkered down, readying himself to leap into the air. "Three, two, one, go!"

Mei Li threw herself off to the side, giving him space. As soon as she was clear, she scrambled up and ran for the mages again, this time trying to stay low and keep situationally aware of Red Lantern.

The beast tried to run free now—not just attacking but charging different areas, testing the defense. The sight of a dragon had panicked it, as well it should. Its attacks would have no effect there. The humans blocked it with talismans, sword and spells, and finally they were able to get into the right positions.

Mei Li scrambled toward the northern direction, the only one left untaken by a mage, and lifted her talisman. She ran her eye over the rest of them as she got into place, found them ready and grimly watching Red Lantern like a hawk. "Link on three! One, two, three!"

It wasn't seamless—no magical linkup with relative strangers ever was—but there were at least three powerful mages in this group and it was enough to cover the gaps. The magic raced to each talisman like blue lightening, and once it hit all four directions, it shot upwards toward the talisman in Shunlei's grasp. The spell cemented with that and solidified into thick chains that glowed with blue fire.

"Release!" Mei Li snapped out the order.

Everyone let go of the talismans. The paper, unable to withstand the power of the magic, burned up immediately to a crisp. But the spell on the talismans glowed and stayed in place, locking the seal. Red Lantern tried to rage, to fight free, but the seal used every bit of magic it had to subdue its prisoner. The glowing lion faded slowly, shrinking in on itself, and finally it lost the animal form. Under her watchful eye, it resumed the form of a paper lantern once more, its raging fire no more than an ember.

A ragged cheer went up and the mage nearest to her reached out a hand to clap her on the back, a bright smile on his face. "Mage! You're a stranger to us, but welcome. I'm Hawes. Tell me your name and let me treat you to a feast tonight."

She smiled back at him, glad he had taken her orders so well. They'd have all been in trouble if anyone had tried to argue with her. "I'm Mei, from Demarest. I'm more scholar than mage, and sorry I couldn't be of more help. My magic isn't very strong."

"Don't apologize. You told us how to defeat it neatly," the female mage of the group denied. She came in closer, absently pulling on her singed hair and clothes with a faint grimace. "And just in time, too. We were not winning. But how did you know the dragon was friendly?"

"I recognized him." Mei moved through the humans and to Shunlei, who had landed nearby and was watching them cautiously. "Shunlei the Red, well met. Thank you for your help."

He lowered his head so that they were more on speaking level, sparing her from craning her neck upwards. "Well met, Lady Mei. I was surprised you called out to me, and in my own language. Most humans fear the dragons. They have good reason to. Not all of us are rational."

"No, they are not." Apparently. Mei Li silently bemoaned her luck. Of all the times, why did the time-traveling spell dump her *here*? Had everything she needed records for even been sealed yet? Somehow she doubted it. Shaking her head, she brought her attention back to the present conversation. "But I know of you. You're trying to get the dragons to recognize laws, to behave and be humanity's allies. I knew you'd help if I asked."

His tail thumped happily, a wide grin on his face. Which, with the five-inch-long incisors, was a bit alarming to the uninitiated. "You've heard of me? Truly? The humans know of my goals?"

"I do, at least. Others surely do, as word spreads quickly." It was so very strange, speaking to this younger Shunlei. His expressions were more open, more inherently innocent. He had none of the caution or the mantel of confidence of his older self. He was, what, perhaps eighty at this point? So incredibly young. When had this wide-eyed innocence and puppy energy faded?

The warrior who looked part dwarf, with that powerful build, approached slowly. He stopped at her shoulder, looking up at Shunlei with a strange expression on his face. "Lady Mei, you know this dragon?"

She belatedly realized she shouldn't have been talking to Shunlei in Long-go. It didn't tell anyone else much about him. "I do. Mostly by reputation. This is Shunlei the Red. He's trying to bring the dragons under control, civilize them."

The warrior's bushy eyebrows shot into his hairline, getting lost in his bangs. "Is he, now. Then well met, Shunlei the Red. If you can pull that off, you've got all our thanks. I'm Melchior of Horvath. Thanks for the aid. We were struggling with this one."

"I am glad to help," Shunlei answered with transparent sincerity.

"Come with us into town," Hawes invited. "You should celebrate this win with us."

More than a few looked at Hawes askance, clearly not on board with this plan. For whatever reason, no one voiced a rebuttal. Hawes was either well-respected, or they were playing this by ear, willing to play along and see how friendly the dragon supposedly was.

Shunlei's tail didn't thump again, but his entire body vibrated as if he wanted to roll around and jump for joy. Was this the first time a human had invited him to go anywhere but away? "I'd be glad to! Here, let me change forms. Less trouble that way."

Mei Li expected him to do that but everyone else bit off a surprised oath when he smoothly transitioned from dragon to human form. His skin wasn't the brilliant red of his dragon self—more a brassy shade, perhaps with a touch of amber. It was a sign he was only recently in Red stage. Mei Li mentally revised her estimate of his age down. He was likely closer to twenty, then. So incredibly young.

He straightened the basic white robes he wore, tucking his hands into his long sleeves, giving them a bright smile and polite bow. "It is an honor to fight with you."

"D-d-dragons can...." The female mage spluttered to a stop and just gapped at him.

Mei Li gave her an odd look. "You didn't know dragons can take human form?"

"I'm surprised you knew." Shunlei regarded her thoughtfully. "It's not something my people do often. Most consider a human form as beneath them, inferior. For that matter, I'm surprised you know Long-go."

And how did she cover that? "I was, ah, shipwrecked not long ago. A dragon aided me and took me in for a bit before taking me home. He was very chatty and kind."

"Ah. That would explain it. I'm glad I'm not the only dragon helping humans. You've brightened my week considerably, Lady Mei."

"I bet. Well, Hawes, where's a good place to sit and celebrate?"

"Not far from here is a decent sized town. Let's retreat there." Hawes regarded her and Shunlei thoughtfully and the wheels were quite obviously turning. "I think there's a great deal to talk about, too."

Mei Li couldn't argue there. She'd only read histories regarding the original group that helped the first Tomes seal some of the major dangers—and this was them. Melchior of Horvath. Mage Hawes. Mage Kiyo. Mage Nord. This wasn't the full group, not yet, but it was the initial core. It was heady and bewildering to meet them like this. Mei Li never once imagined she would and she was a tiny bit star-struck. These people were her predecessors, her professional ancestors, in a sense. She absolutely had to find a way to stick with them.

People gathered up dropped luggage and started walking. The town was at the bottom of the hill, within sight, obviously not far.

As they walked, the woman introduced herself. "I'm Kiyo of Floating Isles, by the way. It's nice to meet you, Lady Mei. The silent one following us is Nord. What brings you here?"

Mei Li turned and gave Nord a nod hello. He looked too thin, as if he regularly missed meals, a goatee obscuring his mouth. He inclined his head politely in return. Answering as honestly as possible, Mei responded, "I'm a traveling scholar. My goal is to help defeat anything that's tearing up the countryside."

"Oh! Then your goal is similar to ours. Does the prince of Horvath know of you? He's offered to fund us as we work."

"Ah, no, I wasn't introduced to him." Right, the record had mentioned that the princes of Horvath were always the ones to bankroll these expeditions. Bless them for it, too.

Hawes turned his head to say over his shoulder, "I'll send him a message tomorrow, telling him of you. If you're interested in joining with us, that is. We'd dearly love to have another mage."

At this point, they might be willing to take any helping hand. Only three mages and a warrior were not sufficient for the tasks they were tackling. Then again, she rather had made a good showing back there. Maybe that was sufficient to gain their tentative trust and interest. "I'd much rather fight with you. Groups work better for this kind of thing."

"Trust me, we know," Hawes said on a rolling laugh. "Learned that the hard way! Master Shunlei, you said you're trying to make friends with humanity. We saw how helpful having a dragon ally was today. Will you consider joining us too?"

The smile on Shunlei's face put the sun to shame. "I'd love to. Thank you for the invitation."

Nord looked a little alarmed at Hawes' casual invite, shooting his friend a warning look, but Mei Li knew for a fact they'd be lost without Shunlei. She quickly spoke up in support of this. "Most of the sealing spells I know require a full box, like the one we just used on Red Lantern. Having Shunlei to fly them overhead is essential to that."

"I'd dearly like the chance to build some goodwill with humanity," Shunlei added earnestly. "Not all of us are interested in rampaging. And I'm subduing the ones who are as I come across them."

Kiyo leaned forward to see around Mei Li to look at him. "Really? How?"

"I challenge them to combat," Shunlei answered forthrightly. "When they lose, they form a blood oath with me that they'll no longer harm humans or human property. It's a slow process, but I'm making progress."

Hawes shot him an intrigued look. "How many duels have you won?"

"Thirty-six at this point."

"And how many losses?" Melchior inquired dryly.

"As I said, thirty-six wins."

Melchior slapped a hand against his thigh and guffawed. "A dragon after my own heart! I support your endeavors, young red. I'll tell the prince of Horvath about you, too. Only fair you get paid with the rest of us."

"I appreciate it." Shunlei looked over them, considering. "What other dangers do we need to tackle? Does anyone know?"

"We basically go by rumors—" "Oh, there's a list." Kiyo and Mei Li answered at the same time. Then they paused and looked at each other.

"You know of such matters?" Kiyo asked her in sharp interest.

Mei Li cursed her careless mouth. The first Tomes didn't have exact dates for everything that had happened before he joined the group. And if she only had four people teamed up, then it was early days yet. She kept her answer vague enough to not stir suspicions later. "I know of a few, although we'll have to chase them down. I only know the approximate area for them."

Nord spoke for the first time. "That's still much better than what little information we have. Give us a list as we eat."

"Certainly." Mei Li made it her immediate goal to figure out exactly what day it was now without raising eyebrows.

She let the chatter flow over her for a moment, trying to buy a minute to think and piece everything she knew together. The initial sealing team was only five people strong. Red Lantern was just sealed for the first time, which happened approximately spring of 1236. The first Tomes didn't join them until 1238. Which meant Jingfei and Zaffi weren't even properly awake yet, and Odom was not due to fall as a deity until next year. Even Ghost General's Sword might not happen until later this year.

It was all well and good to go into the past to copy the missing records, but if the records didn't even *exist* yet, that was rather a problem. Mei Li looked around her, flabbergasted with fate. Five thousand years into the past. She was five thousand years into the past and stuck there for the foreseeable future—not to be punny.

Just how long would she stay here? Was she possibly not looking at days or even weeks in the past, but *years*? Mei Li felt faint with the thought. This was not at all what she'd envisioned when she'd first considered time travel.

"Lady Mei, is something wrong?" Shunlei asked her, a touch of worry coloring his tone.

She looked around to him and wondered, how in the world did she answer that? "I'm feeling a little overwhelmed, I think. The full scope of the task just sank in."

He gave her a small, supportive smile. "It's alright. You'll have help."

Remembering what his much older version said to her before she left, Mei Li couldn't help but take heart from him. "You'll help me."

"Of course."

Red or Black, he really hadn't changed much at his core. It gave her courage, having this man so solidly on her side. "I'm banking on that, Shunlei the Red. You have no idea how much."

1

Mei Li had expected many things when she used the time traveling spell. On par with her usual luck, her guess had been entirely wrong. She had not gone back to the time she hoped for—a handful of years into the past—so she could copy the missing Tomes records for sealing the demon Zaffi and the fallen deity Odom, both of whom threatened to break free.

Instead, she'd landed *five thousand years* into the past, before the events even happened. Much less before the records she needed were written.

Mei Li wanted a nap. She wasn't tired. She just didn't want to be awake right now.

What made her mad was that Future Shunlei hadn't *told* her any of this. A head's up would've been nice, right? Not that cryptic line about her not going to the time she aimed for. She meant an actual warning before her life went spiraling off in a random direction. Again. She mentally aimed a kick in the man's direction. They would *so* have words when she got back.

Most of those words would not be clean.

It kept mentally throwing her when she looked at him now. This younger version had deep, copper-red skin and flaming red hair, entirely different from the dark-skinned, raven-haired version of the future. Mei Li expected to get used to it in time. And in the meantime, deal with the headache the differences gave her. And if Shunlei the Red thought he could just meet up and then part from her, he was sadly mistaken. She was latching onto this man like a limpet.

Mei Li might be stuck in the past, but she refused to do it alone. She was holding Shunlei accountable for this mess.

Yes, yes, it was unfair to hold Younger Shunlei accountable for Future Shunlei's actions. So? That wasn't about to stop her.

It was a struggle to keep her head in the game and a reply on her tongue as she answered questions and asked her own of the group. They walked and talked, deciding to sit and eat so they could relax after a hard battle and converse more easily. She tried to draw out Nord twice, but he had slid right past 'hard to read' into 'elective mutism.'

According to the records, Red Lantern was defeated in eastern Horvath. Lorré, wherever that was. Mei Li hated ancient records because so much of them weren't recorded with future generations in mind. Lorré, for instance, did not exist in her time. She only knew it to be in Horvath because it referenced the mountain region nearby.

Future Shunlei had done a superb job in preparing clothes for her, at least. She blended right in. Kiyo wore something similar to Mei Li's sturdy boots and plain, dark-green traveling clothes. The skirts and wrap-tops of this time sported little to no embroidery. Kiyo's black and grey outfit showed the barest hint of silver thread picking out a pattern on her belt.

Kiyo was from the Floating Isles, which was interesting, as Mei Li knew her to have graduated from a university in Laborde. She looked similar to Mei Li—a little, at least. Her hair wasn't the black of Mei Li's people but brown (and singed on the edges still), and she had almond-shaped eyes and pale skin, with a hint of a sunburn on her nose and cheeks. She looked very much the odd duck out of the bunch, as Nord clearly hailed from Laborde. The light brown hair and brown eyes were a staple of that people, not to mention the western-style coat he wore over his black pants.

The inn Hawes took them to was lively, clean, and with good service. A family seemed to run it, the mother of the group checking people in and calling out orders to various children for bedding, baths, and food to be brought to different guests. Lanterns hung from the sturdy wood rafters spanning the room, keeping it well-lit, and the tables were rough-hewn but of sturdy quality. Straw lined the floor to help absorb spills, and at this time of night, it had a faintly sour smell to it.

Still, for its time period, this was a nice place indeed. Well-vented with the open glass windows, and a roaring fire in the main hearth to ward off the evening chill. It wasn't crowded when they first entered, but two groups came in behind them, and Mei Li knew that status quo wouldn't last long.

It was still sinking in that she was not only five thousand years in the past, but working with *the* original group who'd sealed so many magical problems. Her brain cramped under the realization of when and where she was. But if she had to land somewhere in time, even Mei Li had to admit this wasn't a bad place to be. This group was trustworthy, even if they weren't entirely sure of what they were doing yet, and look! She'd even run into Shunlei quickly. If nothing else, she could depend on his help. Future Shunlei had said so.

They all ordered drinks first, as everyone was parched from running around and shouting. Sensing that only Hawes was truly comfortable with Shunlei, Mei Li encouraged her dragon friend to sit next to her.

No one else around them seemed to realize they had a dragon in their midst, though a few people looked at Shunlei askance as they passed by. Seeing anyone in pure white was rare in this mix of farmers, traders, and day laborers.

His dark skin tone and flaming red hair gathered their own looks. But this world was used to all sorts of races mixing with humanity, and Mei Li could see them leap to their own conclusions after that once-over. A glance was all he got before they found a free table and went back to their own business. Odd, how things changed over time. In Mei Li's time, people would have recognized Shunlei as a young dragon because of his skin tone.

Hawes cleared his throat. A burly figure, his shoulders overflowed the dimensions of the chair, rather like a dwarf but far taller. Judging from the state of his beard and clothes, he'd been on the road for a long while and seemed just as glad to sit down for a few minutes. "Lady Mei, I think proper introductions are in order. We barely told you anything on the road. We're a group of people dedicated to fighting the stranger magical problems, demons, and what-have-you the world is now experiencing. We're under the patronage of the Prince of Horvath, who generously funds us. I understand they're trying to get the rulers of the other countries on board with this plan, but while they're in negotiations, it's our job to solve problems as we see them. You said before that you were also solving magical problems as you encountered them. Surely not alone?"

Oh dear. It would look strange to them, wouldn't it, a lone woman doing such dangerous work. And for good reason— it was a stupid thing to do. Mei Li frantically tried to come up with a plausible reason that was at least semi-truthful so she wouldn't get caught in a lie later. "I mentioned before that I was shipwrecked? My master and I were lost to each other two years ago. He was on one ship, I another, and I'm not sure where he's gone to. He's not where he should be, at least. I'm searching for him. And, well, solving problems along the way."

Hawes' concern didn't clear from his face, but he did nod in understanding. "You're a good apprentice to do so. You're magically trained, clearly?"

"Yes, I am. And I have experience in this sort of thing. I'm very pleased to help all of you."

Kiyo stirred. Her oval-shaped face grew thinner still as she pursed her mouth in doubt, looking Mei Li over. "I'd like to know more of your magic before we depend on it. And running around with us will surely hamper your search."

Mei Li expected that argument. She gave the woman a tight smile in return. "You're traveling all over the continent. I don't see how that hampers my search, as I have no good leads on where to look next for my master. And it's safer to travel in a party, is it not? We can sit down and properly discuss magic so we know what each other is capable of."

"I'm all for more magic," Melchior declared. He was as stout as Hawes, but shorter, and Mei Li would swear he had a dwarf in his ancestry. The red beard flowing halfway down his chest was only part of the reason for her assumption. "But I'm more intrigued by another heavy-hitter like myself. Shunlei the Red. You're really keen on joining a party like ours?"

Shunlei gave him a bright smile. "I'd be delighted to. I've long wished to work alongside humans, and this would be a beautiful opportunity to do so. Not to mention that it will further my goals. I wish to prove that dragons and humanity can be friends."

Feeling like she should back him up, Mei Li threw in, "And no one can deny that dragons are formidable fighters. I, for one, would love to have Shunlei in the party. His dragon fire can do things magical fire cannot."

Nord looked intrigued by this. To Kiyo he said softly, "A good point."

Kiyo's mouth puckered even more, but she didn't say anything in response.

In the end, it wasn't their call. Hawes gave Mei Li and Shunlei both a wide smile and pounded a victorious fist against the table. "If you're willing and able, I won't turn you down. Now, let's give you an idea of who you're working with. I'm a battle mage, so I'm not much good with the complex magics. Melchior"—he gave a nod to the shorter man at his side—"is my brother in arms and the only traditional fighter in this group. Or was before Shunlei joined us. Lady Kiyo and Nord are university trained in Wu Xing magic. They both volunteered to go with us and have been incredibly supportive. Lady Mei, you know Wu Xing magic, obviously?"

"Yes, that's what I'm mostly trained in. I'm more of a historian of magic, I should say, but I've a good foundation in Wu Xing. If we stumble across something truly complex, I will be out of my depth. But quick, ready-made spells, simple barricades and sealings, traps—all that I'm quite comfortable with."

"Good, good." Hawes paused as the first round of drinks and a plate of bread was set down, along with a bowl of butter and soft cheese. "Miss, an order of the special for the whole table, please."

The serving woman gave him a nod and headed back to the kitchen with the tray tucked under her arm.

Kiyo cleared her throat. "I didn't recognize the seal you used for Red Lantern. That's not a basic Wu Xing spell."

"Ah." Mei Li pinned a smile to her face even as she scrambled for words. Words that made sense. "No, that's a specialty of my master's. He taught me that one."

"I see. Do you know any healing magic? Only Nord knows anything about it."

"I do. Some of my knowledge is theorical, but I can heal most common ailments."

Nord watched her carefully and spoke in his soft voice. "I would like to compare notes with you later."

"Yes, of course. I'd like to know what everyone is comfortable with, for that matter. You know, before trouble hits us." Mei Li meant every word. Doing otherwise was suicidal.

Melchior drained his tankard in one gulp before raising it over his head and calling out, "Another! Alright, Lady Mei, you said you'd heard of other things wreaking havoc in the world. What things?"

Mei Li had not had much time to think of events (what year was she even in, precisely?!), so she answered carefully. "I've heard rumors of some. There's one that's truly worrying me. A minor deity—a water god—is trying to establish more dominance in the land. Gong is his name. I believe if he's not intervened with soon, he'll go power crazy and flood us out."

Nord hissed in a breath, goatee working into a deep frown. "Where?"

Mei Li almost said Tanguay without thinking about it before remembering at the last possible second that in ancient times, it was known as Thibault. "Thibault, I think. Near the northern bay."

Hawes nodded. "Makes sense, that's a lot of water to play with. But that means a northeastern trek that will take weeks. What else?"

"There's a white bone demoness on the loose," Kiyo reported flatly. "I received a message about it from my home last week. She's apparently moving south, searching for a holy man to eat."

Seeing Shunlei's confusion, Mei Li explained, "Bai Gu Jing is its true name, a skeletal monster that believes if it eats the flesh of a holy man, it'll have immortal life. They're tricky to catch, as they are very capable shapeshifters. They can look human when they put in the effort, so much so that they can pass a cursory inspection."

Hawes looked at her with interest. "You've heard of even that? Most people don't know of them. The creatures originated from the Floating Isles, far north of the main continent. You are very well-informed, Lady Mei."

Mei Li gave him a smile. To hear the man she regarded as

a hero praise her was...well. That was heady stuff. She tried not to let it actually go to her head. "I was very well taught. But in this, I think we have an advantage. Shunlei should be able to detect the white bone demoness well before we can. Shunlei, you should be able to smell her. She'll be wearing perfume to disguise it, so a human nose will be fooled, but she'll smell of the grave and decay. If you detect that scent, covered with perfume, follow it immediately."

He nodded instantly. "I'll do that. And the water deity? Which of these tasks should be our priority?"

That was an excellent question. Mei Li looked to Hawes for an answer. She didn't begin to think she was in charge of this group. It would be wise of her to show that from the outset.

Hawes made a low, guttural sound in the back of his throat as he ruminated on it. "Kiyo, any direction other than south for the white bone demoness? Any hint who she might be chasing?"

"Only that she's been sighted in two different temples in Thibault and seems to be heading south."

"So, she's hitting holy places. That's good to know. And that's two mentions of Thibault. What do you think of going north to cross the mountains, then heading east toward the sea? We can start with this water deity and then head south. We may or may not cross paths with the white bone demoness that way, but at least we'll be heading the right direction."

It was a sound plan, and Mei Li had no issue with it. She nodded, echoing the manner of everyone else at the table.

"Then we'll do that tomorrow. I'll step out now and inform the Prince we've acquired two new people in the party. Hopefully funds and supplies can catch up with us on the road that way." Hawes heaved himself to his feet and left with an intent air.

As Hawes left the table, Shunlei noted to Mei Li, "I adore

you humans. You're so quick to action."

That remark made absolutely no sense to her whatsoever. "Are dragons different?"

"Oh yes. We'd still be greeting each other if it were only dragons here. Never mind having a plan of action before dinner even arrived. My people are only quick to move during an emergency."

Interesting. That wasn't the case in modern times. Had dragon society changed to accommodate humans? Mei Li belatedly realized there were many questions she'd failed to ask Future Shunlei.

Knowing some of the stories, at least, Mei Li thought it prudent to ask, "Do you have anyone you need to alert before we leave this area?"

"I do, in fact. After dinner, if it's acceptable, I'll make a quick trip and be back by morning." To everyone at the table, he explained, "I found a pair of orphaned eggs three days ago. I've negotiated for a broodmother to take them in and raise them. She finally agreed this morning. I was in fact on my way back to fetch the eggs from their hiding place when I stumbled upon all of you."

Mei Li's mouth opened, the offer on the tip of her tongue to go with him to help juggle the eggs, then she thought better of it. She was not in a time where a human could waltz into a broodmother's nest and be welcome there. In fact, her presence might undo all the negotiations Shunlei had managed. "Should I carry a scenting stick so you can catch up with us on the road? You'll need to get some sleep tonight."

"That's very kind of you, Lady Mei. If you would. I'm not sure how travel arrangements will work on the road with all of you, actually." Lips pursed, he frowned sightlessly ahead. "I've no experience riding a horse. That is what you will mount, is it not?"

"It is," Melchior agreed, also frowning. "We don't have

time to teach you."

Likely not. Mei Li felt it prudent to offer, "You can ride with me."

"If I'm not an imposition, I'll do so."

Dinner arrived, interrupting them, and they set to eating. Mei Li was dying to ask questions, to really capitalize on the chance to know her heroes better. She'd idolized these people for most of her childhood. She was terribly afraid that if she didn't keep hold of her tongue, she'd start babbling. Mei Li had time to slowly get to know them better.

Probably too much time, truth be told.

Shunlei excused himself after dinner with a promise to catch up with them on the road. Mei Li caught her bag, intending to stand as well and find a shop, perhaps buy something for the road tomorrow.

"Lady Mei," Kiyo stated in a demanding fashion. "You said your master taught you magic. Is he a crafter of spells?"

Right. Apparently with the dragon no longer present, at least one person felt freed enough to demand answers. In this day and age, mages were known to make their own spells rather than rely upon those already designed by predecessors. It wasn't unusual for spells to vary wildly from person to person depending on their schooling, their nationality, and the whims of their teachers. "He is indeed. He also liked to learn from different histories and records, so my spellwork is a gestalt of different things."

Her thin brows creased together. "I see. That would explain it."

Melchior stirred, leaning forward on his elbows. "And how do you know the dragon's language?"

"It's called Long-go. When I was shipwrecked, I got stranded in a very remote area up past the Spine Ridge Mountains." When that got blank looks, she tried the older name for the area. "Barren Mountains."

"Oh," Kiyo said in recognition. Of course she would know

it, as her homeland was nearby. "There's nothing up there."

"Well, there is a single fishing village. They took me in but wouldn't let me leave. I finally stumbled across a dragon living in that area, and he kindly gave me shelter and flew me back to civilization." All true, if very misleading.

"So, you learned about dragons from him?"

"Some. My master taught me some as well." Mei Li's tongue was getting quite the workout. "It was my master who told me about Shunlei, in fact. I know it's a bit hard for you to believe a dragon wants to be humanity's friend, but he truly is sincere. And he's steadily making progress. I've heard many stories about him."

Hawes slapped the table with his hand. "I like his spunk. Any man willing to help in a pinch I consider a friend. If he's game to tame all of his race, I'll offer my aid. Better to have the dragons tamed anyway."

Right, Hawes was one of Shunlei's first friends by all accounts, a steadfast supporter of Shunlei's cause from the very beginning. She'd almost forgotten that in the heat of the moment. "I feel the same way."

Being a practical leader, Hawes next asked, "What provisions have you?"

"Not enough for a long trip," Mei Li answered readily. She'd managed only a peek inside the bag Future Shunlei had packed for her before engaging the time travel spell, but it was enough to tell her it was only meant to tide her over to the nearest town. "I've provisions for about two days. Really, if we're going to be traveling and battling as we go, I don't have enough ink or paper, either. And does anyone have twine?"

Nord raised his head and finally contributed to the conversation. "I do. A spool."

Kiyo's eyes were sharp on her, evaluating. "We've found it to be useful on several occasions."

"Yes, so have I." Despite Mei Li's help earlier, it was clear

Kiyo didn't trust her magic just yet. Mei Li would have an uphill battle with her. Which was a shame, as Kiyo was the only other woman in the group, and Mei Li would much rather be friends. "How about I step out, pick up a few things?"

Melchior stood. "I'll accompany you. I'm also short on food and water. All of our provisions are low. We'll need to acquire a horse for you as well."

Also a good point. "If you would, sir."

Melchior led the way out, his short and stocky frame barely clearing the width of the doorway. He moved like a boulder on legs—powerful, but not entirely agile. He still was somehow walking Mei Li's legs off, though. She had to stretch to keep up with him.

The town wasn't large, barely big enough to be considered a trading hub, and all three main roads connected directly to a major highway. It made things easy when it came to finding a stockyard, as everything was visible from the center of town, where they now stood.

Mei Li found it interesting to look about. The world was so very different now. Less technology, to start with. She didn't see the hint of a single waterwheel despite a river being nearby. More magical talismans seemed to be doing the job instead.

Abe had mentioned to her a few times that magic stunted the growth of technology until the trend switched to Evocation magic. Why bother inventing another way to do it when a magical talisman would do the job? He felt it impacted the world in a negative way. Mei Li, now that she saw the past, understood why. Using magic to solve every little problem did no one any favors.

Melchior struck out, keeping her on the inside, placing himself as a buffer between her and the road. It was a sweet gesture and warmed her up to the man.

"You'll need to be patient with Kiyo," he said, voice

rumbling like gravel rolling downhill. "She likes to think she's the smartest out of all of us. You showing her up like that will have rubbed her the wrong way."

"Oh, is that the problem? I wondered."

"It's good for her. Don't worry about it, things will work out on their own. They always do." Melchior shot her a look from the corner of his eye. "Your dragon, now, that might take more getting used to."

"I know it's a bit much to take in all at once," Mei Li responded, trying to be sympathetic. "I swear on anything you care to name he's a good man, though. The dragon that rescued me sung his praises."

"He's certainly the most rational dragon I've ever seen. I'm inclined to give him the benefit of the doubt just from how he's reacted today. But Kiyo's not going to be won over easily. Neither will Nord. Do you think he'll handle that well?"

Future Shunlei certainly would. But Younger Shunlei? No idea. "I hope he will."

"Hmm." Melchior abruptly changed subjects. "How good of a rider are you?"

"I can stay on and get the horse to go in the direction I want."

"So, not an expert."

Mei Li shrugged. "I've spent most of my life studying. When we did travel, it was sporadically. I can ride. I'm just probably not as good at it as you are."

"Then let's try and find you a nice, steady gelding. Something stout enough to carry double." He shot her another look from under his bushy eyebrows. "If you're sure on that."

"Absolutely sure." Probably.

Horvath, especially, was a hunter/gatherer culture with towns built to house its citizens in times of danger and during the cold, brutal winters. They sold many furs and animal hides, but little in the way of finer linens and cottons. Mei Li had precisely one other change of clothes in her bag, and considering how long she'd be on the road, she would need more than that. She shopped as best she could, adding pieces of different garments that could be cobbled together to form another outfit as needed. She also snagged a waterproof cloak, as she had the sneaking suspicion they would be riding through a lot of rain.

Shopping in ancient times was an educational experience in and of itself. It was one thing to know intellectually that magic, ink, and books had made significant advancements, and quite another to walk up to a bookmaker's shop and realize he only offered thin wood slates bound together with twine, or vellum to write on. And powdered ink instead of bottled liquid.

The paper, though. She wasn't sure what to do with the paper. Even what she had on her was something from modern times. Shunlei likely hadn't been able to find something made with the old, ancient methods. Mei Li knew how, technically, to make her own. But it would take a good week at the very least. And that was with spells. Surely they sold traditional paper *somewhere*. Even Horvath, which was the last one to the game, had picked up the process at this point in history.

The frustration of not immediately finding what she needed fed straight into her frustration over everything else. Mei Li was glad to be here, in many ways, as she could have landed in much worse times in history. But it didn't alter the fact that *this* wasn't where she wanted to be, either. People had been hurt before she'd left. Even though Shunlei had been up and moving, his hands were still recovering from the burns he'd acquired battling Jingfei. She didn't want to be stuck back here, five thousand years in the past, longer than she had to.

And yes, that was a totally irrational thought. Future Shunlei had explained that time travel didn't move at the same chronological speed. Even if she spent years in the past, only hours would move in the future. And yet, the urgency ate at her. To get everything done *now* and head immediately back. But she couldn't. And she couldn't force things to go any faster. It was entirely outside her control.

"Lady Mei?"

Jerked back into the present, she turned to the man standing at her side. Melchior watched her with caution, as did the shop keeper. Right. Shopping for paper. She was supposed to be shopping for paper. She looked again at the two tables, with all the wares displayed, and bit back on a frustrated sigh. "I'm afraid this isn't what I'm looking for, good sir. I need something thin and light-weight."

"Oh, like that fancy Laborde paper?" the shop keeper asked, cottoning on.

That sounded promising. "Yes, that's probably closer to what I need. Do you have that?"

"No, but my brother's a trader. He just came back with Laborde goods last week. Might have some left." He popped around his table and pointed down the road. "If you go three stores down, that'll be his."

"Thank you," Mei Li said and gave him a smile of relief. Maybe she didn't have to make her own paper after all. "May I buy two jars of your ink, that brush there, and do you have an ink stone? Excellent, I'll take that as well."

Melchior paid for it all, the master wrapped it up for her with twine, and she thanked him again before they moved off.

As they walked, Melchior shot her an odd, questioning look. "You don't have an ink stone?"

"I do...but I think it's cracked. I heard a very suspicious breaking sound when we were fighting Red Lantern earlier. I basically dropped my bag and dove in, after all."

"Ah. Is that why you were frowning so intently at the table?"

Had she been? She probably had, at that. "No, I was envisioning making my own paper. That would take a straight week to manage."

"We don't have that kind of time," Melchior objected.

"Believe me, I know. It wasn't a happy thought. Oh, now, here we go." Mei Li stopped at the trader's table, and a smile of relief crossed her face. He had a stack of paper bound with string, three books bound in rough leather, and even liquid ink in various hues. Not that she needed that. Finding a woman in an apron who seemed to be manning the store, she flagged her down and promptly bought all of the paper. The price made Melchior wince, but he paid out for it.

Satisfied, she stowed it all in her pack. Her now bulging pack. "Alright, horse and provisions. Do you have enough on you to pay for all of that?"

Melchior's smile was a bit strained. "I suggest some strenuous haggling."

Right.

2

Due to the crowded nature of the inn, Hawes asked Kiyo and Mei Li to share a room, which Mei Li was happy to do. She hoped to get on a more friendly footing with Kiyo, maybe subtly pump the woman and get more information. She really didn't know much about her except in what remained of the existing records.

With high hopes, she went into the room, her bag over her shoulder. To the woman at her heels, she asked politely, "Which bed would you—"

"Window," Kiyo responded curtly.

Um. Well, that didn't sound friendly. Mei Li must have upset her more than Melchior thought. She set her bag down on the other single bed in the room. Taking inventory of the contents in that bag was a high priority for her. She'd known from the size and weight that it couldn't possibly contain everything she needed, hence her shopping trip with Melchior earlier, but...well, everyone knows what they say about assumptions. Better to get a thorough idea of it for herself.

And frankly, Mei Li did *not* trust a man to pack for her. Even if that man was Shunlei.

Kiyo sat down her bag and then promptly yanked out what looked to be sleepwear. She didn't, however, remove any of her clothing.

Mei Li dared to ask another question. "Are you heading for the baths?"

"Yes." Without a single glance in her direction, Kiyo left, shutting the door firmly behind her.

Staring at the door, Mei Li arched an eyebrow at it. "I got the message. Yeesh. Isn't there some rule that the heroes have to be nice? I guess she isn't a hero yet, but still...."

Mei Li hoped that at some point they'd get on better terms. It might take a while. In the meantime, inventory. She opened the bag and pulled things out, stacking them in neat rows along the quilt. Two sets of clothes that she would bet her eye teeth would fit perfectly. A sleeping roll, but no pillow. That made her neck twinge just thinking about it. She had the basics for creating talismans, some money, and sure enough her ink stone was cracked right in half. Good thing she'd bought a new one with Melchior—

That thought twinged for some reason. The last time she'd gone shopping, it hadn't been with a man she barely knew. It had been with Shunlei. And the time before that Leah and Teoh. In a time that was her own, not this place she didn't really know.

Mei Li abruptly sat down, her butt on the floor, and stared sightlessly out the window. The realization of where and when she was washed over her, and this time, all the emotions hit with it. She felt overwhelmed. More than overwhelmed. Tears tried to leak out of her eyes, and she let them fall. When she'd made the decision to step into the past, she'd thought she understood the decision and its consequences.

A few weeks didn't begin to compare to ten years.

She wasn't ready for this. In no way was she prepared. Not mentally. Certainly not emotionally. Mei Li felt lost in a way she'd never experienced before, not even while shipwrecked in a village that served as her jail. What was she supposed to do, here? Just ride with them and help solve magical problems until she finally stumbled across the ones she actually needed?

That sounded simple, but it meant *ten years* of that. With a people and in a time not her own. Frankly, Mei Li found it a little horrifying.

Shunlei's words from the future floated back through her mind in his gentle, calm tone. *"Ask for me. I will help you. Be honest as much as you can about your goals, and I will work with you to achieve them."*

Wiping her eyes, Mei Li tried to get hold of herself. Aloud, she muttered, "I'm holding you to that, Shunlei."

Still, she needed a few more minutes to process. She could give herself that. Deities knew Mei Li would be on the move soon enough. So, for a few more minutes, she'd give herself time to absorb the drastic cleft point fate had just handed her.

Her mind drifted, thinking only random things that had no connection to each other. Mei Li had no idea how much time had passed when Kiyo stalked back in. Without acknowledging her, she put her dirty clothes into her pack, crawled into bed, and snuffed the lantern out, pitching the room into darkness. Mei Li was stuck on the floor, in the dark, with her bed still full of things.

Well. This was an auspicious beginning.

They got an early start in the morning. Mei Li's gelding was a gentle giant someone named Peanut—probably because of his palomino coloring—and he plodded along with everyone else without giving her a hint of trouble. Mei Li had a feeling they'd get along fine.

The sky was clear, not a cloud to be found, the weather perfect with a slight breeze to take the edge of heat off. It was a good day for riding, and she was determined to enjoy it while it lasted. It was spring, after all. It wouldn't last—the rains would hit them sooner rather than later.

Melchior rode alongside her and explained things as they rode. "The Prince of Horvath is very generous with his funds, but he can't always anticipate where we'll be. We move about as rumors and emergencies demand, and it sometimes causes cash flow problems. The towns we help will often assist as they can—by offering food and board most of the time. We do take on side projects, though, in order to earn a little cash."

"That makes a great deal of sense." Mei Li actually knew all of this but knew better than to give the game away. "Do you go year-round?"

"No, we stop in late fall and pick up again early spring. Impossible to travel in the winter months, after all, and we have families and homes to visit. Everyone needs to rest by that point."

Good for them, but poor for her. It meant Mei Li would have to find somewhere to stay every winter. Since she would apparently be stuck here for years. "How did this group get together?"

"It was Hawes, really, who got us started. He tackled three different problems in Horvath, got the Prince's attention. When asked if he'd assume responsibility for all magical problems in the world—at least as a stop-gap measure until our esteemed leaders figured out a better solution—Hawes immediately agreed. Then volunteered me to help him."

Hawes could hear this conversation, as he cast back over his shoulder, "I wouldn't dream of having all this fun without you!"

Melchior rolled his eyes. "I could stand to have less fun. You crazy man. Anyway, it was the two of us for a bit, but then we ran into Kiyo and Nord about two months in—we stopped to help, found that we worked well together, and Hawes invited them to join us. So really, this group hasn't been together long."

That also helped Mei Li grasp precisely where she was in the timeline. "I see. And there's no possibility of us working in the winter?"

"Only if absolutely necessary. We'll try to get things solved by fall so we're not slogging through snow."

Mei Li appreciated this attitude even though she knew it wouldn't work out that way. Not always, at least.

Kiyo dropped back to ride at her left side. "If we're to work with each other for a while, I wish to know more about you. You know Wu Xing, obviously, but anything else?"

"The basics of I Xing, but I've rarely used it."

"Hooo?" Hawes' bushy eyebrows rose. "You're more well-rounded then most mages if you know both, even if it is just the basics."

Kiyo sniffed in disapproval. "I don't care for I Xing. It's too simple. I know it's the foundation of most magical principles, but it's not handily applied to practical problems."

Mei Li gathered the impression that she'd just fallen a little further in Kiyo's estimations by admitting to this. Oh well. "Yes, well, as I said, I don't really use it. But it's good to know if you're trying to blend magics with another mage who does use it. Hence why I was taught it."

"I still—" Hawes started.

"Dragon," Nord announced calmly.

Mei Li lifted a hand to shield her eyes. Indeed, there was, coming straight for them. From the hue of red and the general shape, it looked to be Shunlei. He was far enough out that she readied a talisman just in case that assumption was wrong. But the dragon glided to the road and settled there, landing on three legs to accommodate the bag he carried, shaking his wings once before he shifted over to humanoid form in a smooth transition. It had to be Shunlei.

He walked toward them steadily, a large pack stuffed to the gills over one shoulder that he carted along without seeming to really notice the weight. As he came closer, the horses startled, their noses telling them a dragon was there, even if they couldn't see one. Shunlei stopped uncertainly and stared back at them, sharing the unease.

Mei Li blew out the scenting stick in the flag boot on her saddle. She patted her horse on the neck, soothing it, and called out, "It's alright, come on. You made good time."

"Thank you for your patience," Shunlei answered, still eyeing Hawes' stallion uneasily as he sidled past it. The horse stared right back, mostly in challenge. "The broodmother was glad to hear of your mission and offered her own thanks. I've roasted deer in my sack to share with you." He hesitated, looking up at Mei Li. "Is this something humans eat?"

"Yes, we eat venison quite often," she assured him. Strange that he was so lost on human eating habits. He really was inexperienced with humanity, wasn't he? "And I'm thankful for the food. We'll be hunting part of the time, I think, as we travel."

His expression cleared, and he smiled up at her. "Excellent. And I will help you hunt, of course. I've also collected two skins of pure water, a change of clothes, and some furs. I didn't know what else to bring."

"That's fine." Mei Li wanted to pinch his cheeks. Why was he so cute like this? "Here, tie that to the back of the saddle with my pack."

He did so promptly, then stared up uncertainly. "Ah... how do I mount...?"

Mei Li kicked a foot free of the stirrup and held out a hand. "Put a foot in there. Good, now take my arm and boost yourself up behind me. One, two, three."

It was awkward, Shunlei nearly toppling her in the process, but he got up. With him semi-settled, she re-seated herself and claimed the stirrup back. Shunlei didn't seem to know what to do with his hands, so she pulled one toward her hip. "Hold on there. Or you can let your hands relax on your own legs. But definitely hold on if we move faster than a walk."

He settled with an almost audible sound. "Thank you."

Hawes checked them over with a critical eye. "I think you'll do. Alright, let's move again. Shunlei, we may or may not make the next town. You alright sharing a tent with one of us?"

"Yes, of course, that's fine. On clear nights, I should probably sleep outside in dragon form, however." Humor in his voice, he tacked on, "Few would molest a campsite with a dragon curled around it."

Snorting, Hawes agreed, "True enough. Alright. We're still playing catch-up with Lady Mei about what all she knows and what she can do. Turns out she knows two different types of magics, so we're doubly blessed to have her."

"There are two different types of human magic?" Shunlei asked in interest.

Kiyo's head jerked back, aghast. "You don't know about human magic?"

"No, indeed, few humans have been willing to converse with me. I've mostly learned your language by hiding and eavesdropping. Lady Kiyo, if you wish to instruct me, I'll be most grateful to learn."

Kiyo launched into a rather elaborate explanation of magical theory. She did seem a little too pleased to have a captive audience, but Shunlei was very much the attentive student. He didn't just listen, but asked intelligent questions. Kiyo didn't cover in detail how to create spells or talismans—she was only discussing magic in generalities—but no one seemed to think Shunlei would be able to grasp it.

Mei Li had to bite the inside of her cheek to hold back a chuckle when the dragon quietly proved their assumption dead wrong. She wasn't in the slightest bit surprised. She knew how intelligent this man was, after all.

As they rode, the conversation turned from magical theory to the problems they'd tackled. It gave Mei Li an even better sense of timeline, and she became increasingly sure she was in the spring of 1236. Jingfei, the demoness they had so much trouble sealing in the future, wouldn't even awaken until 1246. Likewise, the volcano demon Zaffi wouldn't awaken until that year either. So, not only was she five thousand years in the past, she would have to wait ten years before she even got where she needed to be!

Mei Li was very much of two minds on that account. She knew the spell would bring her back into the future at roughly the same time she left it. All other accounts of time travelers said that while they might spend months or years in the past, only a few days would pass in the future. She might miss her friends and Shunlei from her own time, but no time at all would really pass for them. It gave her mixed feelings.

Was she relieved about that? Sad? There was a hollow ache in her chest, and it brought her hand up there several times, patting it as if she needed to reassure herself that her heart was still there. Mei Li didn't know how to feel at this. She'd left without saying goodbye to anyone—and yet it would be strange, from their perspective, if she had. But she felt the need to do so, even still. And she couldn't even talk to anyone about this now, or reveal too much of herself, for fear of disrupting the timeline.

It left her feeling very, very alone, even when surrounded by good people. It was not a comfortable sensation, and Mei Li could only hope it would pass with time. She had no other remedy to offer.

Being here as she was now, she finally understood Shunlei as she hadn't before. No wonder he'd so instantly latched onto her when Hui brought her to Dragon's Peak. No wonder he'd already been invested in her. He was reconnecting with a woman he'd known well and missed. Mei Li was already forming a connection with Shunlei the Red—she knew it would develop into a very strong bond eventually. The man was completely adorable, so of course it would, and part of her looked forward to that. The other part of her looked forward to regaining the future, because then she could respond to Shunlei the Black in the same way he had toward her.

Mei Li would have to watch her words, though. Their roles were rather reversed at the moment. She now knew more about Shunlei than she should, just as the future Shunlei had known too much about her. He'd confused her badly because of how he'd acted. Mei Li was determined not to do that to younger Shunlei.

In a practical sense, she needed to be alert for her personal safety as well. Just because she was from the future didn't mean she was safe in the past. Or immune from somehow altering it.

She'd have to be very, very careful moving forward.

Oooh, actually, she was in the right time to meet Shunlei's bride. She'd always been intensely curious about the woman. Shunlei had spoken of his wife with such fondness and pride, it would make anyone curious. Mei Li couldn't wait to meet her, whoever it was. And it should happen in the near future. Shunlei was about this age when he married.

Rats, but she really had to keep that behind her teeth. She couldn't even tease him about it.

Being a know-it-all did have its downsides.

They rode steadily, only breaking for lunch, and Mei Li's thighs cramped from the atypical physical activity. It was uncomfortable, but she had a feeling she'd get used to it. No other choice with all the riding in her future.

As the bright, sunny day slowly faded into sunset colors, Hawes called a halt on the road. They were surrounded by fields on their right and a sparse copse of trees on their left.

"I was afraid we wouldn't make a town, and looks like I was right," Hawes stated, scratching at his beard. "The map I've got isn't exactly accurate. Alright, let's find a likely spot and make camp for the night."

Shunlei pointed off into the woods. "If you'll go a little

further in, there's a small stream nearby. I can smell the water."

"Oh? Then lead the way."

Mei Li turned Peanut's head in the direction he indicated, and they plodded carefully between the evergreens until even the humans could hear the bubbling of a brook and smell flowing water. Without warning, they broke through the underbrush into a small clearing, the brook wrapping partway around the clearing before disappearing into the trees again.

Hawes looked around for a moment and nodded. "Yes, this is perfect. Good nose, Shunlei. Let's settle here for the night. Lady Mei, Shunlei, we've got the tasks broken down like so: Kiyo cooks, Nord takes care of the horses, Melchior and I set up tents. Melchior and I also take turns hunting, if we see something in the area. Lady Mei, are you comfortable helping Nord with the horses?"

"I am."

"Good. Shunlei, perhaps gather some firewood? And then help Kiyo."

"With pleasure." Shunlei beamed a bone-melting smile at the mage in question.

Even Kiyo's stiff attitude melted a few degrees under the force of that smile.

They dismounted and set to their tasks. Mei Li unsaddled the horses and helped rub them down while Nord set up feed bags and took them to the brook to drink. They had the horses hobbled and settled for the night before the three tents were fully up. Kiyo had plenty of firewood, and she chose to make vegetable skewers to go along with the venison Shunlei had brought them.

It was a comfortable, if silent, dinner. Everyone chose to eat rather than talk. Mei Li helped wash dishes afterward and was about to retire for a while to the tent she was sharing with Kiyo when something caught her attention. Shunlei lay sprawled along the edge of the clearing. He'd shifted over to dragon form already, wings stretched out, and was nudging at one with a disgruntled series of grumbles. It didn't take a genius to guess that his wings were bothering him.

Knowing how painful that was, she couldn't let it be. Mei Li hesitated for a split second before making a decision and going back into the woods. She found a suitable branch and broke it off, then took a knife and honed it down to something smoother, with a thin end. Only when she was satisfied that it had the right size and texture did she gather up her courage and go to where Shunlei lay.

Unlike the first time she'd done this, she wasn't family to Shunlei. He didn't have the same reasons to trust her. But the need was there, and she knew what she was doing. All she had to do was convince him. Easy, right?

Stopping in front of him, she let the handmade dowel hang at her side and cleared her throat. "Shunlei."

He turned his head and regarded her, blinking. "Yes?"

"I can help you preen, if you'd like." She lifted the dowel in illustration, a hopeful arch to her brows. "I know it's something dragons view as a more personal thing, but...I know how."

Head cocking, he repeated somewhat incredulously, "You know how. As in, you've been close enough to a dragon before to help them?"

"Yes." She left it at that because she could hardly say, *It was you, actually.*

Flabbergasted, he stared at her for a long moment before managing to find words again. "Well. I won't turn down experienced help. Thank you."

"Stretch out and relax," she encouraged as she stepped around to his tail.

Shunlei craned his neck to watch her go but obediently stretched out both wings. A mix of astonishment and mystification warred across his face as he watched her slide the dowel under and smoothly lift the coverts out of the way. Mei Li was not oblivious to the attention from the rest of the camp, either, but she strove to ignore it. Let them watch and learn as well.

The first look brought a hiss of horror from her lips. As bad as it had been the first time she'd seen Shunlei's matted down feathers, this was so much worse. The down was just greyish pink clumps that pulled painfully at the skin underneath. In a few spots the skin was bleeding. Unlike in her present, she could hardly scold him for the self-neglect. In this day and age, Shunlei had few he could trust to turn to.

"It's bad, isn't it?" he asked in a resigned tone.

"I've never seen down this...knotted." She chose the word with clear distaste. "I'll try to sort it out as gently as I can."

"I'm in your care," he answered with a crooked smile, revealing canines.

With fingers and dowel, she set to it, and she did have to pull a few places that earned a wince from him. Still, he uttered not a word of complaint as she righted twisted primary feathers and even plucked out a few broken ones. The state of his wings made her want to curse. It hurt her heart that he'd been in this state with no one to help him. Future Shunlei adored their preening sessions.

Shaking the thought off, she worked steadily along and noticed that while he occasionally flinched, he steadily sprawled out completely on his belly. He'd started off a little uneasy and cautious, as any dragon would be with a person he barely knew preening him. But as her hands worked through the knots, releasing those pin-pricks of pain, his body language slowly relaxed, sending him splayed across the grass in boneless pleasure. Preening sent him into a dreamy state most of the time, and it amused her each time, seeing him nearly comatose in pleasure. Preening for a dragon must be like a massage for a human. By the time she finished and his wings folded back in, Mei Li wasn't entirely convinced he was conscious.

Coming back around to his nose, she rubbed that one spot right below the ridge that always got him to thrum at her. His eyes opened a mere slit so he could look at her. Teasing gently, she asked, "Is that better?"

"Marry me," he sighed.

That got her laughing, head thrown back. "Oooh, marriage proposals. You must feel better. Don't let your wings get into that state again, alright? As long as you need it, I'm willing to preen you."

"Prepare yourself. I'll shamelessly take advantage of your generosity."

"I'm prepared," she responded, still laughing.

"If dragons only knew how nice that felt, they'd befriend humanity instantly," he said, still in that dreamy state.

"How about you fight them to a standstill, and I'll preen them? We'll conquer your race in an instant."

A wicked curve slanted his mouth up. "Let's do it."

Mei Li knew Shunlei's wife had done this very thing. Their tag-team duo of stick and carrot had worked so well they'd tamed most of the dragons during their marriage. Mei Li didn't see the harm in helping him until his bride-to-be showed up. Frankly, even though she knew he succeeded bringing the dragons around, the man could use all the help he could get.

3

They started out early the next morning. This time, Hawes did not lead from the front, switching out with Melchior and riding alongside Mei Li's right. He directed most of his conversation to the man riding behind her, expression open and curious.

"Tell me how it all started. Your taming of your race, I mean. No offense, but you seem a bit young for such an ambitious goal."

Shunlei snorted but didn't sound insulted by the observation. "Isn't it because I'm young? That's what two broodmothers have told me, anyway. That I'm too young to know any better, and that's why I'm willing to try it."

Hawes grinned at him. "Praise youth, then! But truly, what made you start?"

There was a long pause. For a moment, Mei Li wondered if he would answer, that's how long the pause stretched. She could see everyone else intently listening, even Kiyo, who steadfastly stared ahead.

"It was a culmination of things, really. I saw the industry of the world, always watching from the shadows. But I couldn't join in. I couldn't partake of the revolutions in technology or magic you've all created. I couldn't even easily stroll into a town and buy a book or a sweet cake. For years, I practiced switching to human form, speaking your languages, trying to mimic it all as closely as possible so I could be mistaken as one of you. This was easier before I turned Red," he added, with a wave toward himself. "My skin tone now tells people that I am not human."

"No, makes you look like an elemental," Hawes agreed, stroking his beard. "But go on."

"One day, some three years or so ago, I was in this form while traveling through a town. There was a grand festival in process, and I was enjoying myself immensely trying all the foods. Then I came to the center of it and realized what the festival was for—a dragon had been killed. He'd razed the fields of the area and taken off with so much of the people's flocks that they'd taken him down like a rabid animal.

"I stood there for the longest time, petrified, staring at his corpse. It horrified me in many ways. And it was that display that showed me the future. Unless my people changed their ways, unless we became friends instead of foe, that would be our fate. Slaughtered and displayed like trophies."

He sounded so heartbroken and upset that Mei Li wanted to turn and tell him: *It'll be alright. You'll fix this. What you're imagining now will never come to pass. You win this battle of attrition.* She had to bite the inside of her cheek to keep from blurting this out. She leaned into him, wanting to give comfort. Shunlei went taut against her—startled, perhaps? She almost thought better of the gesture before he settled into it.

It was, unexpectedly, Nord who spoke. He twisted in his saddle to look at Shunlei directly. "When the gods first created the world, they had a purpose for each race. We were meant to keep within balance of each other, to achieve overall harmony. Many now say the dragons were here to test the mettle of the other races. But I've studied the ancient records, and this is incorrect. Dragons were always meant to be mankind's ally. In fact, they were given domain over the skies to help safeguard those on the ground."

Shunlei sucked in a deep, startled breath. "Truly?! My people do not keep records aside from oral stories. I fear much has been lost because of it. I would love to hear more of this, Lord Nord."

"Of course. I'm equally fascinated by dragon physiology. As we ride, perhaps we can exchange information."

"I will be glad to do so."

Nord dropped back to ride at Mei Li's other side. They ended up spanning the width of the road in this configuration. Someone would have to move if they encountered anyone else on the road, but for now it was fine.

Mei Li was happy to just listen as the two men exchanged notes. Much of it she already knew due to her own studies. Still, as repetitive as it was, she was happy to hear Nord speaking more than three words at a time.

They rode in this manner for several hours, the group changing up around Mei Li's gelding as Kiyo got dragged into the conversation. Hawes moved ahead so he was still within earshot but allowing Kiyo to more easily converse with the others.

It was nearing noon when the first whiff of trouble passed their way. A logger with a full team of horses approached them with a troubled frown, his pace quicker than a walk as he hurried his team along. As he spied them, he waved one hand energetically, flagging them down.

Melchior stopped and addressed the man. "Ho, friend."

"Good sir," the logger said with an uneasy glance behind him, "I wouldn't suggest continuing down this road. Unless you're part of a guard or army?" His dark eyes roved over them uncertainly, hands tugging at the bushy hair trailing out from underneath his brown cap.

Hawes urged his stallion forward to answer. "We're a team of magical troubleshooters, organized under the Prince of Horvath. What trouble lays ahead, sir?"

"Prince of Horvath?" The logger muttered something not

quite audible under his breath but seemed to take this at face value. "Well, I'm not sure what's going on, but it's something strange, for sure. I'd say it was dragon fire, but the trees are still standing. See, there's a virgin wood ahead. If you follow this road straight up, till the fork, you'll see the tip of it. I've been logging around the edges of it, and intended to go straight in today, but it's strange today. Yesterday, it was green and flourishing, like an Elven forest of the stories. But today? It's like a cursed and haunted wood. All the leaves are gone, the bark of the trees looks blackened and cursed, and there's not an ounce of noise coming out of it. Not birdsong, insect, not even the rustle of wind through the branches. Too eerie for me. I'm not going in there."

"Huh. Does sound strange, I grant you." Hawes half-turned to face the rest. "Cursed?"

"Perhaps." Kiyo put a finger to her lips thoughtfully. "But why curse a virgin forest? Good sir, is there anything else in this area?"

"Just a logging town, a river that meets up with the road, and a few small settlements."

"Nothing of value or remark?"

"No, not that I can think of."

"Then this is all the stranger," Kiyo observed. "You said it didn't look like dragon fire to you?"

The logger nodded immediately. "I've seen dragon fire in a forest. Nothing standing afterward but ash. The trees are all still there. And it doesn't smell of smoke."

"Hmm. Hawes, I believe we need to take a look."

Hawes nodded in agreement. "Yes. Thank you, sir, we'll investigate it."

The logger looked doubtful. "Just...take a care."

"We will, thank you."

He urged his team in motion, no doubt eager to get home and away from the strange, cursed forest.

Hawes turned his horse to face the team as a whole.

"Well? Any thoughts on this? Or do you want to take a look first?"

"I'm all for taking a look first," Mei Li admitted. "That description wasn't enough to tell us what's going on."

"Agreed." Kiyo nodded firmly. Nord echoed the movement.

"Then let's go forward."

They did, but with considerably more caution than before. There was no chatter this time, the mood quiet and oppressed for the next hour. The logger's directions were accurate to a fault, but even without them they would have found the cursed forest in question easily. It was impossible to miss.

The line of trees on the side of the road was in stark contrast to the forest dead ahead of them. What was green and vibrant with life to their left showed spring in its fullness. The area ahead was...not. It wasn't dead so much as utterly still. The trees were massive, reaching far into the sky, their branches spreading in all directions and twining with each other. The ground underneath was entirely barren—not a single shrub, fern, or flower to be seen. Only piles of dead leaves that smelled of decay even from the road. It was as if the woods had shirked the blooms of spring and immediately shut down into the defenses of winter all at once.

Mei Li shuddered a little looking at it. "The more I stare at it, the more I'm waiting for something to pop out of the shadows. It truly does look haunted."

Melchior grunted agreement, eyes narrowed as he stared hard. "Is it magical, the cause?"

"No—" Mei Li started.

"Yes—" the three mages said at once.

"That clarifies matters," Shunlei drawled.

Kiyo gave Mei Li an irritated look. "There is magic there."

"There is, I see it, but I don't think the magic caused this. Not directly." Mei Li didn't know of this particular case that the team had solved. Not every problem had been recorded, after all. Just the ones that had to be re-sealed or had a time limit before they needed to be addressed again. That said, she did have a hint regarding this situation because of the location.

Unless she missed her guess, this was Nidffer Wood.

Nord gave her a steady regard, a study. "You see the blood magic. This is the cause."

"Yes, that's foul and easy to see," she said with a grimace of distaste. It was impossible to mistake—this inky, dark film that laid over every surface. "But that's not directly the cause of the forest looking like this. Hawes, is this Nidffer Wood?"

Hawes pulled out his ever-handy map from the top of his saddle-bags, unrolling it across his arched pommel, and took a moment to look it over with a deep hum. "Yes. I believe it is."

Mei Li nodded, not surprised. "This forest is sentient."

Head snapping around, Kiyo took a deeper look at the situation. Not satisfied with her eyes, she pulled out a jar from one of the many pouches on her belt and applied a thick smear on the top of each eyelid before putting it away and peering again. Nord joined her. Mei Li assumed it was some kind of enhancement cream and didn't question it.

"Ah," Nord uttered in a tone of enlightenment. "Yes, of course. That makes perfect sense with what we're seeing."

"The forest is not cursed, but rather in a defensive mode." Kiyo took a few steps forward, leaning over her pommel to stare at the forest from an even closer vantage point. "Much like a turtle that has withdrawn into its shell. I would say it has reacted like this in order to protect itself from the blood ritual magic being enacted within."

Melchior asked the obvious question. "So, if we just bull inside the forest, what are the odds we'll be recognized as the rescuers? Or will the forest fight our intrusion?"

"It might," Mei Li allowed, already resigned to a very

rough few days ahead. "And we of course have to be aware that whoever was stupid enough to set up shop inside a sentient forest will be quite paranoid about defending the area. There's likely booby-traps all over the place."

Groaning, Melchior stated rhetorically to the air, "I'm not going to like this. Not one little bit."

Shunlei lifted a hand, shifting around so he could speak over her shoulder. "I can go up and scout from the air."

That was an excellent idea, and Mei Li was all for it. "Yes, let's do that. Take me up with you."

"Oh." Shunlei sounded excited. "You want to fly with me?"

Tilting her head back, she tried to look at his face. Was it really that strange...no, of course it was. She might be the first ever to fly with a dragon in this age. "I rather need to. You won't be able to see everything, as you can't see magic."

His face fell a little. "Yes, of course."

"And flying's fun," she added to put the smile back on his face. "I won't miss the opportunity."

There was that happy smile again. It stretched from ear to ear and made him look like a giddy child. "Yes, yes, it is. For such a short flight as this, I'm confident I can hold you with one arm."

"If you drop me, I'll never let you live it down," she warned teasingly.

Hawes seemed alright with this plan and urged them on. "We'll settle over here, off the side of the road, and wait. Try not to make more than two passes, Shunlei. The first time overhead, whoever is inside will dismiss it as a dragon simply traveling. But more than that, you might tip our hand."

"I'll swing wide on the return trip," Shunlei promised.

Mei Li gave him a hand down, then swung free of the saddle herself before handing Melchior the reins. She did pause long enough to grab a blank talisman and write a quick and dirty spell that would enable her to see longer distances. She'd need it up in the air. Her eyes couldn't begin to compete with a dragon.

Shunlei had shifted into dragon form by the time she had this written out and waited patiently on her. She went confidently into the arm he extended, tucking the talisman into her bodice for now. She'd need both hands until they were in the air. His arm wrapped around her back, massive claw fitting under her thighs, and she put both arms around the base of his neck with confidence.

"Ready?" There was no mistaking the emotion in his voice. He was happy and pleased she wanted to fly with him.

"Ready. Let's go."

4

Mei Li was very, very glad of the firm hold Shunlei had on her. She'd never tell him so, but being in the air like this without a physical carrier around her unnerved her on some level. But she had faith he wouldn't drop her. His strength was carefully leashed so he didn't squish her, but there was no mistaking the iron grip of his claws.

"Alright?" he asked her in Long-go.

"Yes," she confirmed. Oh my, he was still very happy to have her up here. Mei Li tried to see the situation from his perspective. Was it the trust she showed in him? Or was this some goal of his finally met, that a human would agree to fly with him? It could be either, or both, or something else entirely. Either way, it amused her.

There was no time to talk about it, as the forest was fast approaching. Shunlei had flown around, coming in from a different direction to get his speed up. She had no idea where in the wood the blood mage had set up camp and hoped they could find it on the first flight in. Otherwise they'd have to set down, wait a few hours, and try again in order to avoid raising suspicion.

Retrieving one of her hands, she pulled out the talisman in a strong grip. Shunlei was not flying fast, but the wind still swirled around her, tugging at her hair and clothes. If she wasn't careful, the talisman would be ripped free of her fingers.

"I'm going as low as I dare," Shunlei informed her, dipping and slowing his pace a step.

"Don't go too low," Mei Li warned. "A blood mage is not something we want to tangle with in the air."

"Understood."

Mei Li held the talisman firmly over her eyes like a blindfold, and the world took on a sharper focus. It was distinct where she concentrated and fuzzy around the edges. She'd always imagined this was how an eagle's eyesight worked, but of course she could hardly ask for a comparison. She combed the ground as they flew, trying to see between the branches. It did help that the limbs were stripped bare. If there had been leaves still attached, this would have been an impossible task.

Something smelled up here. She caught whiffs of it as the wind flew and snatched around them. It also carried the hint of smoke, burned flesh, and that acrid aftertaste of dark magic. The blood mage was definitely doing rituals in here somewhere.

Not good.

Mei Li strained her eyes, but even with the talisman she couldn't seem to pinpoint the source. The branches overlapped each other too much, and it was quite possible the blood mage had a glamour over the site to keep it camouflaged. Nothing even looked suspicious when it was, in fact, quite suspicious.

"Anything?"

Mei didn't lower the talisman as she answered grimly, "No. I think he's got a glamour up. Have you flown most of the distance?"

"Yes. I'm going to bank and circle around to the left, see if I can spot a good place to make camp. I have a feeling we'll need it."

"Do that. I'll look as you go, just in case."

Shunlei banked a gentle curve and circled wide. Strain as she might, Mei Li still didn't see anything suspicious or even vaguely questionable. She frowned, vexed. The idea of blindly tromping through the woods sat ill with her. Well, maybe they could try a good seeking spell that could go through a blood mage's glamour. With all four mages working together, odds were they could overpower it.

Maybe.

"There, I think."

Mei Li turned her attention from the decrepit forest. "Where?"

"The spot near the river."

She almost asked for more clarification before she spotted it. Ah, there. It did look grassy and flat, a good place to make camp. Also, it was just far enough away to avoid getting them entangled with the Woods, but still close enough they could make forays into it. "Can you find that again on the ground?"

"I should be able to."

He sounded confident enough in the answer that Mei Li took his word for it. "Alright, bring us back down, then."

Shunlei slowed their descent in gradual degrees. Mei Li knew very well that he could and did routinely bank harder than this and set down with more of a thump. The care he exhibited with her now made her smile. Shunlei had apparently always been a gentleman.

They landed on the road with a jolt. Mei Li slid out of Shunlei's arm with a pat of thanks against his shoulder. "Thank you. Hawes!"

Hawes jogged toward them, expression hopeful. "Anything?"

"Nothing I could see," she answered, still frustrated. "I think he's got a glamour up. There's such little indication of anything wrong that I'm sure I overlooked the spot, but I couldn't pinpoint the area where he's set up. I did smell burning flesh, acrid magic, and a few other things that make me believe he's got a ritual altar set up in there."

Hawes let his head flop backward in a dramatic fashion. "This will be an absolute bear. Alright, Shunlei, you see anything?"

Shunlei transitioned smoothly into human shape and only answered once he was settled, shaking his sleeves out before folding his hands together. "No, I'm afraid not. But I did spot a good place near the river to make camp."

Grunting, Hawes agreed sourly, "Probably the best use of our time at the moment. We might as well settle in. This will likely take a few days. I hate to spend the time on this when we've got two other leads to follow, but..."

"We can't bypass this," Mei Li agreed. A sour, yawning pit opened up in her stomach at just the thought. "Blood mages are ruthless, and if he's doing ritual sacrifices in there, he's building his power up for something truly awful. We can't give him the time or freedom to unleash his plans."

"My thought exactly. Alright, let's set up camp and then come up with a plan."

Kiyo joined them, her pace unhurried. But then, the woman seemed intent to never seem unsettled by anything. "If your aerial reconnaissance failed, perhaps a seeking spell?"

She seemed smug that Mei Li had not succeeded. Biting back her temper, Mei Li said, "I think if all four of us combined forces, we might be able to break through whatever glamour is in place."

"Quite. Nord and I will make the necessary preparations."

It was hard, but Mei Li didn't smack her for that smugness. "I'll help with setting up camp, then."

Shunlei led them to the spot, and she was grateful he'd seen it. They'd never have guessed it existed from the road. It wasn't as wide a clearing as last night's camp—Shunlei would likely have to stay in human form here—but it had all the necessary components to make a good campsite. The trees lining the clearing gave shelter from the wind, the ground was mostly flat, and the water ran clear nearby.

Mei Li helped set up the tents, off-loading the horses of their burdens. Since it was more or less time for lunch, she started a fire as well. They could eat while Kiyo and Nord made the necessary talismans and artifacts for the seeking spell.

It felt very odd to be on the outside of magic. She'd grown up her entire life being in the middle of things. Even as an apprentice, she was there to watch and learn, assuming she wasn't assigned some task to aid Abe. It grated along her nerves unpleasantly. Mei Li kept reminding herself that Kiyo didn't trust her magic yet. She'd have to take this in steps.

Kiyo called her forward after the fire was started. "Light these two candles, then let's begin."

The four talismans were posted at the four corners of a large, shallow bowl. Various small knobs of wood floated along the top of the water, scattered around the bowl. Mei Li would not have chosen a basic seeking spell—they only told the general direction on where to go—but bit her tongue. It might be best to start out simple, anyway. Easier to power.

Kneeling to the right side, she put her hand over Kiyo's outstretched palm. Nord's came to settle on top. His long, pale fingers were uncomfortably cool. Did the man have no blood in him? Hawes finished the circle, lending his magical power to the proceedings.

"Begin," Kiyo ordered coolly.

Mei Li lent her magic to the spell, a steady thread of power humming and building between the three of them. The ink on the talismans glowed with increasing brightness, turning gold under the force of their combined magic, and the wooden floats in the water started to move.

They whirled and whirled and for a sinking moment, Mei Li didn't think even this basic spell would be able to bull through the glamour. The floats moved suddenly and with quick precision, heading directly to the north-eastern edge of the bowl and staying there, all bunched up together.

Mei Li pursed her lips as she studied them. Well, they had a direction, at least. No idea of distance, but at least a direction.

"Hawes," Kiyo stated authoritatively. "We have a direction. Northeast."

Hawes stared hard at the bowl. "So I see. Distance?"

"I can't tell with this spell. I chose the simplest one, as it had the best chance of working around the mage's glamour."

"Hmm. Makes it tricky to plan, though."

Mei Li bit her lip and thought about offering another tracking spell. Hers would take a bit more prep, though, and she wasn't sure if they had all the right elements to create the spell. No, better not. She had a feeling that even offering would put Kiyo's back even further out of joint.

"What if we bait it out?" Kiyo offered. "I can create a more elaborate talisman that will register as a human and carry a strong blood scent. If we send that in, the blood mage will react and come after it. It'll be too rich a prize to pass up out here. Then we can lure him to us and choose our own ground to fight."

Mei Li could think of several things to go wrong with this plan and protested instinctively. "Wait, you're assuming we can enter the woods without alerting him that we're there."

Kiyo's eyes snapped to her, and she ended the spell with an abrupt clap of her hands. "My method will work."

Shunlei and Melchior came to join them, drawn in by the argument.

Mei Li could tell Kiyo had her own opinion on this. It was an odd feeling, realizing she was not the expert—or at least, not the acknowledged expert in this group. She was the newest to join, the most untried of all of them, so no one would naturally defer to her. How did she phrase her words so she could get her point across without further putting

Kiyo's back up?

Sucking her bottom lip into her mouth, she thought on it for a moment, mentally phrasing the approach. "Lady Kiyo, my master faced a blood mage once—"

Kiyo immediately snapped, "So did my instructors."

Keeping her tone patient, Mei Li soldiered on. "—I, of course, do not know how they subdued them. I can only tell you how my master successfully did so. Perhaps if we—"

"I assure you this method works. We'll use it." Kiyo sniffed, looked at her sideways, then left in a huff, her skirts lashing out behind her like a cat's tail.

Mei Li stared after her in dismay. That...had not gone well. Mei Li didn't know if she'd said something wrong, or if Kiyo really was that threatened by having another female mage in the group.

Nord gave her a long, silent look before standing and quietly following Kiyo. That left her with Hawes, who was rubbing at the bridge of his nose, and Shunlei, who seemed puzzled by the discord. Melchior was studiously staying out of it, not even facing her direction.

Trying to make the situation clear, Mei Li turned to Hawes. "I'm not trying to start an argument."

"Yes, Lady Mei, I see that," Hawes assured her patiently. "But she doesn't take it well when someone questions her magic."

"I'm not even doing that. I believe the method she just outlined will work."

Hawes' head canted to the side, a movement Shunlei weirdly echoed.

"Then what is your issue with it?" Shunlei inquired.

"Lady Kiyo's method assumes we can all get into the correct position on time, that no one's injured or distracted in the process, and that the blood mage falls for the trick."

Shunlei's face drew down into a frown. "That's a lot of assumptions."

Glad he saw her point, Mei Li nodded vigorously. "And that's my issue. If everything goes perfectly to plan, then yes, her idea works. And will likely work well. But what if it doesn't? If even one thing goes wrong, we won't have the necessary magical force to overpower the mage. What then? He will break free and either turn on us or run." Seeing that Hawes was half-persuaded, she pleaded with him, "I'm not trying to overturn her. I just want a backup plan."

"Plans rarely survive the first contact with an enemy," Hawes stated slowly, each word paving the road forward. "I agree it isn't wise to bank everything on one move. But I don't want discord in this team, either. Lady Mei, this other method of yours, is it something that can be adapted on the fly?"

"Yes. It doesn't kill the mage, but it will entrap and hold him for forty-eight hours. More than long enough for us to find another method to destroy him utterly, if we need to."

"Is this something we can use against something other than the blood mage? Such as demons?"

"In theory, yes."

Hawes slapped a hand to his knee, satisfied. "Then create what Kiyo's asked you to do first. Make what you like second. I will tell her honestly that we've discussed this method and that you've prepared it just in case we come across something we need to pursue."

Relieved, Mei Li agreed without hesitation. "I will. Thank you."

With a deep sigh, Hawes reluctantly stood. "I'll go smooth some feathers."

As Hawes departed to the far side of the camp, Shunlei scooted in a little closer and asked softly, "I do not entirely understand what just happened. From what I see, Lady Kiyo is not older than you are. Why is she senior?"

Knowing how important seniority was to dragons, Mei Li tried to explain it so it made sense to him. "Part of it is that she joined the team first. And it's not so much that she's senior, it's more they're used to working with her. They know her better, and they're still feeling me out."

"Ah. As they are with me."

"Yes, in a way."

"Is that why she battles for a higher position than you?"

Mei Li almost corrected this as being a misinterpretation, but actually, Shunlei had hit the nail rather squarely on the head. "It might be part of it? That she sees me as competition. Some women always view another female as a rival. It makes no sense to me—never has. But I think Kiyo's the type."

For a moment, Shunlei's expression was that of Future Shunlei, the one wise and experienced, a little cynical. It was odd to see it on this younger face, odder still to hear what he said next. "Perhaps, perhaps not. But her rebuff of you is understandable. If the two of you were dragons, you would be the one chosen as an Elder. She would not."

Blinking, Mei Li ran this through her head twice but couldn't understand why he'd said that. "Why?"

"Confidence. You exude it in an open aura. She is constantly trying to prove herself even when it's not necessary. The difference is obvious to anyone observing."

"And Kiyo instinctively understands that, which is why she's constantly trying to show me up?" Mei Li couldn't offer a counter argument. He was quite likely right.

To Mei Li, Kiyo of Floating Isles was a mage of legend, one with incomparable skills and a lioness's courage. Everyone in the academic world knew not only her name, but her achievements. Not once did Mei Li ever suspect that in the beginning, before Kiyo became known as the Archmage of Floating Isles, she was a regular woman in her early twenties. Straight out of school, freshly thrust into the world, struggling to properly manage the road she'd chosen to walk. She wasn't the mage of legend yet. It would be wise for Mei Li to bear that in mind.

"Competition is good for people," Shunlei opined, tugging his sleeves to cover his hands, looking quite snooty as he did so.

It was so mock-serious that she snorted a laugh. "You say that, but I bet dragons deal with competition quite differently. Mr. Duelist."

"You really should consider challenging her. It would settle the matter of who's right."

"Right by might? You know that's rarely true. It'll just prove who's stronger." Mei Li thought about it, lips pursed. "And I'm not convinced I could beat her on a magical level. Magically speaking, she's probably stronger."

Shunlei regarded her doubtfully. "Truly?"

"You'll see," Mei Li sighed, shoulders slumping. "In the meantime, I guess I'll win her over by a battle of attrition."

5

Trapping a human was both simple and complex. The bait had to be believable to draw them in, after all. The goal was to create a magical figure—a young person who could move and 'flee' from any pursuers. Blood mages were always in need of fresh meat, as it were, and giving him a teenager nearby would be too irresistible. Or so was the hope.

Kiyo cut out a simple paper doll and then painstakingly drew the talisman on both sides. Mei Li tried to casually glance over now and again to look at her progress and not make it seem like she was studying every line drawn over the woman's shoulder.

What she was in charge of was the actual trap. Binding was the spell, and once engaged, it would lock the man in place. Mei Li made several trap talismans because, while these were very effective, they were also tricky to use. It was a matter of getting the right timing. Thrown in too quickly or too late, the spell didn't have the time to properly activate before the prey escaped. They needed at least five seconds.

Frankly, Mei Li didn't give this plan a high rate of success.

But she made ten of the traps just in case she was proven wrong. Since this was something that needed to be thrown, she used the heavier wood chips, shaped as narrow planks, for her talismans. Then she started in on her plan—the rope trap. This she had more faith in. Once targeted, the rope could be thrown, and it wouldn't be stopped or blocked until it wrapped its way thoroughly around its prey. Or it was utterly destroyed. Mei Li made a six-foot section, with the talismans woven into the rope. Then, thinking better of it, she started a second. It was a blood mage, after all.

Shunlei came to sit next to her. The night had fallen as they made preparations, and it was only by the round mage lights hanging overhead, and the nearby fire, that she had light to work by. Her hands flipped and twisted, pulling the fiber strands together—partially by will, partially by magic. It looked a little knotted and uneven, but she was hardly an expert at this.

Without a word, he extended a hand to her.

Eyeing him sideways, she carefully transferred all four strands over to him, and then watched in bemusement as he smoothly took over. He was much faster and more confident than she had been, catching the paper talismans in with the pattern without faltering.

"Now when did you learn how to do that?" she asked in curiosity.

"Oh, fairly early on," he answered with a quick, boyish grin at her. "All dragons do, really. Because we have to transport things, and there's no one willing to make harnesses for us. We have to make them ourselves."

She smacked her palm against her forehead. "Of course, I should have realized. And no one's really willing to sell you rope."

"Not usually. And I don't normally have human coin to use. Sometimes I'll go hunting—for ore, or game—before coming into a town, and use that to trade with. But there's not a universal coin, so trying to carry anything around with me is more aggravation than not."

Melchior came and sank onto his haunches, also observing, his head canted to the side, arms dangling over his knees. "Huh. You're quite good at that, Shunlei. We had that much twine?"

Lifting a hand, Mei Li pointed toward her nose. "I picked some more up when we went shopping yesterday. I always try to carry twine or rope on me. It comes in handy more often than not."

"Like now," Melchior observed, humor crinkling the corners of his eyes. "If you're making two, then are you sending one up with Shunlei?"

She blinked several times. "I hadn't thought to, but that's a good idea. Shunlei, if we tweak the rope spell correctly, then we can send it up with you. That way, you can just release it while over the blood mage. It's bound to catch him."

"I am amiable to this, but..." Shunlei paused, his fingers still entwined with the rope, and regarded her steadily. "I thought to stay on the ground with you."

He had? Why?

It was Melchior who objected. "But in human form, you have no effective way of fighting, correct? Wouldn't it be better to be in the air, in dragon form?"

Shunlei shook his head indulgently. "First of all, I cannot see much from the sky. The covering over the woods is too tightly interwoven. It allows me only peeks. I would be of little use."

Ah, good point. Mei Li hadn't been able to see anything with enhanced vision. Of course he hadn't been able to make out much more.

"Second, while it's true that I have neither claws nor tail in this form, I'm hardly defenseless," he corrected, blue eyes sparkling with amusement. "I can breathe fire in either form."

Mei Li was back to blinking again. This was not something she'd ever seen Future Shunlei do. "You can?"

His head turned toward her and he smiled openly now. "So, there are things about my kind you do not know, eh?"

"I'm hardly a dragon expert," she retorted with a toss

of the hand. "On the contrary. I just know more than the average person."

In a rhetorical tone, Melchior muttered, "That's a vast understatement. But alright, Shunlei, I see your point and agree. Is your dragon fire and strength diminished in any way?"

"Not really. My range is, as of course my dragon form is larger. But the strength of my fire is the same."

"I think having a dragon's fire on the ground would be hugely beneficial, in fact. Let's tell the others about this so there's no confusion tomorrow when we go in."

Melchior stood and went to the other side of the camp, where Kiyo, Hawes, and Nord were bent over their own projects. Mei Li could hear him hail the three and repeat in an abbreviated manner what Shunlei had just told him.

If Shunlei were on the ground, then didn't that mean he would also be in the line of fire? Melchior had an amulet of magical protection on him, a sturdy thing pinned to his chest. Mei Li had noted it in passing but not thought much more of it. Of course a man battling magic on a daily basis would have such basic spells of protection on him. Hawes, Kiyo, and Nord had their own protections, stronger and tied into their magical core. Melchior's amulet only warded against him being drained of his life force, and also had a general shielding spell that would deflect most attacks, much like chainmail would do. It was hardly enough against the higher magics, or the demonic attacks, but it was a good sight better than nothing. Mei Li's protections were wrapped around her body at all times, carved as they were into her belt.

But Shunlei didn't have even that.

She knew dragons were hardier than humans—unreasonably tough and able to withstand all manner of things that might slay a human outright. But this gnawed at her. She couldn't in good conscience let him go into the upcoming fight without offering him at least basic protection.

Mei Li didn't really have much to work with. Paper, ink, what was left of the twine, some cloth. The protection spell she had in mind wouldn't anchor well to any of that. It drew strength from the element it was inscribed into. If she made it from paper, it would only offer a paper's strength. If she made it from iron, then it was as good as iron armor. It's why most pendants were made from metals.

What could she possibly use to inscribe the spell on? It would have to be flexible, too, to transform with the rest of his clothes as he switched between forms. Was this something she could even feasibly do in this moment? Would Mei Li have to put this idea aside until they reached a proper town and she could buy materials to work with?

Her eyes caught on the pearl embedded in his forehead and a wild idea caught hold. Could she use that? The manner of the spell embedded in the pearl only vaguely made sense to her. She knew it acted as a storage space, and that it was universal among dragons, but was vague on the particulars.

Shunlei caught her intense stare and paused again, hands stilling in his lap. "Is there something wrong?"

"I have a wild idea, and I'm not sure how feasible it is," she answered slowly. "Shunlei, tell me about your pearl. I know it carries your clothes in a pocket-space built for that purpose, but nothing else."

"It's a gift from our broodmothers once we reach the age of eight. It's a matter of convenience, as we can choose to put whatever we want inside, but I generally use it for my human clothing and such. There's not much space inside, so it can't handle more than two outfits and a few accessories. What is this wild idea?"

"Everyone in this group has basic magical protections except for you," she explained, still staring hard at the pearl. The way the spell was worked into his skin, it actually tapped into the dragon 'magic' coursing within Shunlei. Dragons always maintained they didn't have magic, but in truth, their shape-shifting abilities and dragon fire were very magical in nature. It was more accurate to say they were very limited in their magic. And the pearl spell was part of the shape-shifting magic, hence why it was tied into Shunlei on a basic level.

"This bothers you?" Shunlei prompted her when she fell silent again.

"Huh? Oh, yes, quite a bit. I know dragons are tough," she explained with a quick smile at him before her eyes were drawn back up to the pearl. "But there's certain things you can't really protect yourself from. Like the upcoming fight, for instance. Blood mages can draw your life force directly from you, so quickly that it will rob you of all strength before you can get a proper hit in. I don't want you to fall prey to him because none of us thought to properly shield you."

Shunlei's voice came over her like a caress. "You think to protect me. I am awed and thankful for the kindness."

Mei Li's eyes dropped back down to his. He looked overwhelmed by her consideration. Had no one ever...no, of course they hadn't. Was it any wonder he always gravitated to her side? Mei Li was the first ever to try and befriend him. And now she was fulfilling another first by seeking to protect him. It touched him deeply, that was clear by the expression on his face. His eyes burned bright with the emotion.

"Of course," she said. "You're my friend, after all. And I have an idea on how to manage this. Will you let me tinker a bit with the spell on your pearl?"

"I trust you," he answered simply.

She really had the worst impulse to kiss his cheek for that. Why was he so absolutely adorable? "Thank you. Give me one moment. I think I need—" She twisted and grabbed pen and paper before kneeling so she could stare more directly at the pearl. "Yes, alright, keep working on the rope. Be prepared to put it down for a minute. I'm going to sketch out the design for a talisman first."

With a nod, Shunlei went back to the rope, his hands working faster now.

Mei Li stared hard at the pearl. With the right concentration, she could see how it was designed and functioned. The spell was basic, the only complication being how it was tied into him. She sketched it out first so she could stare at something without going cross-eyed. It might be basic, but it was also miniscule in order to fit within the confines of the pearl. Which, really, was as big as her pinky's nail.

Her hand flew over the page as she got it down, then she stared at the paper as her mind worked out the possibilities. If she tapped into that line there, the one that linked into his dragon fire, wouldn't that give her the power source she needed? And really, that would be one fine protection. There wasn't much in the world that could stand against dragon fire. Forget a shield. Her talisman would be offense, not defense, and use dragon fire to destroy any insidious magic that tried to hurt him.

Offense always was the best defense, according to Abe.

Grinning at the thought, she worked out a talisman, then stared at it a bit longer, tweaking things here and there. She tried to keep it basic, as she would have to write very, very finely in order to make this fit. Looking it over carefully once more, Mei Li tested each element of the design against the gestalt of it, but saw no weaknesses. In fact, she was rather proud of herself. This might be the most ingenious design she'd thought of yet. Someone further down the line might see this and think of a way to improve it—Mei Li had never looked at Future Shunlei's pearl design closely so couldn't say—but for now, this would do.

"Alright, put it down."

"One moment," Shunlei requested. "I'm almost finished. Annnnd there. I'll tie this off."

Distracted, she looked down at the rope and was pleased

that the latter half of it, at least, looked excellent. (Her half looked like a novice's attempt. Which couldn't be helped, as she was a novice.) "I'll have you braid ropes for me from now on."

Shunlei chuckled, a rolling sound that was deeper than expected. "I'm at your future service. You've thought of a way to do this?"

"I have. Please sit perfectly still and…" She tapped his knees with her hand, urging him to change how he sat so she could kneel between his spread legs. "I need to be very close to see what I'm doing."

"Ah. Yes, of course."

Mei Li kneeled directly in front of him, her chest nearly pressed against his. Seeing his blush, she teased, "I know I'm pretty, but don't fidget. And hold the design up for me."

Snorting, he held it up, but sassed back, "You're more than pretty, and you know it. Stop teasing us poor dragons. We've no defense against such blinding beauty."

"Ha, you smooth-talker. I bet you say that to all the ladies." Mei Li's tongue crept out the side of her mouth as she focused hard. The pen in her hand had an extremely fine tip, and she used it delicately as she imbued her magic straight through the tip. No ink for this design, just magic and direction.

In an effort to keep her own balance, she slid a hand onto the base of his head, her fingers tangling with the coarse red hair. Shunlei really needed someone to take his poor hair in hand. Clearly, he didn't care what it did as long as it wasn't a tangled nest around his head. Future Shunlei held a similar opinion, and age hadn't helped his hair texture any. But she put that aside as a thought for later. With glances at her design, she double-checked each line drawn. This wasn't a time or place for mistakes.

Shunlei was incredibly warm, even in this cool evening air. His breath touched her skin in a warm caress that felt nice. And was distracting. Mei Li was honestly a little chilled out here.

She had no awareness of anyone else but the two of them, so intensely she worked, and she jumped a little in surprise when Nord spoke.

His tone was incredulous as he asked in a reed-thin voice, "What are you doing?"

"Gods above," Kiyo said in the same tone, but closer, so she was clearly leaning in to get a good view of it. "To write in the spell using *dragon fire...*" She spluttered to a stop, speechless.

Mei Li sat back about three inches and stared at the overall design with a critical eye. "Anyone see any mistakes?"

"I'm not even sure I'm clear how you did that." Hawes leaned in as well, his head nearly even with hers. "And I specialize in shielding."

"I'm using I Xing principles here. Pure elemental magic, as it were."

Shunlei went taut under her hand. Mei Li knew he had to be uncomfortable sitting there with so many people staring at him, and soothed him with a stroke of her fingers along the nape of his neck. He settled again with an audible sigh of pleasure. Oh, liked that, did he? Mei Li stroked him a few more times, enjoying the rumble coming from his chest. He sounded like a cat.

"That is—" Kiyo started, then she paused and had to clear her throat before trying again. "That is fine from what I can tell. That is your design in his hand? I wish to study it at more length."

Mei Li silently asked Shunlei with her eyes if that was alright. He acquiesced with a dip of the head before silently handing it over. Feeling that she should move, Mei Li rocked back onto her heels before standing. "Well. You should be protected from blood mages from now on. At least from their life-stealing magic."

"Truly," Nord said, still faint. "I almost wish he'd be foolish enough to attack you."

Mei Li brightened at this idea. "Ooh, that would make the fight easier. But I don't want to put Shunlei directly in his path."

Shunlei's smile spoke of blood and trouble, much like Future Shunlei's did sometimes. "That's quite alright. I'll put myself in his path."

Mei Li didn't give yonder blood mage very good odds. "But what are we going to do with him once we catch him?"

"Oh, I don't think we'll catch him," Hawes disagreed with a shake of the head. "Most blood mages go down fighting. But if we do, we'll figure it out from there."

Mei Li would rather work that out now rather than spur of the moment, but she let it go with a shrug. They'd discuss it when they needed to, apparently.

6

Nidffer Wood looked like the skeletal version of itself. Mei Li had passed through here once, many years ago, and while that was thousands of years in the future, every record she'd read indicated the Wood didn't really change. It was a sentient primeval forest, after all. Most had better sense than to mess with it. And the Wood didn't think of 'change' or 'time' in the same sense as humanity, so of course it would stay as it always had.

Right now, it looked beyond disturbing. Mei Li felt as if she stood on the edge of an open crypt, the air of staid decay and rot wafting toward her with every breath.

Shunlei came to a stop right at her side, their sleeves brushing. He drew in a breath and then coughed, making a face with his nose scrunched up in protest. "Smells wrong."

"Doesn't it?" She made a similar face. "Like death."

Nord drifted up to join them. "I believe the blood mage set up here under the assumption that he could drain the Wood easily of its magic. Considering its state, I would say his attempt met with limited success."

Mei Li gave a nod of agreement. "Because the Wood is still alive. I'd say the Wood has been fighting him, in its own way."

"Entirely possible. I would think setting up shop here

would be more trouble than it's worth, really. The spells he must have done to keep the Wood from destroying his blood altar or killing him is…" Nord shook his head as he trailed off, utterly flabbergasted. "He might well have used more energy to subdue a section of the Wood than he will be able to recoup from."

Mei Li grimaced. True, the math didn't work out. "It does seem stupid, doesn't it?"

"Either way, it gives us an opportunity to end his practices before he destroys the Wood utterly." Nord sounded pleased by this. Also pissed that it was necessary, but there wasn't a legitimate magic user in the world who liked blood mages.

Looking behind her, Mei Li saw Hawes and Melchior double-checking armor, Kiyo putting the last touch of magical protections on both of them. Since last night, Kiyo's opinion of Mei Li's magic had visibly changed. She no longer viewed Mei Li with the same smug superiority or misgivings. She didn't trust Mei Li completely yet—that would take more time—but she was inclined to think Mei Li might in fact know something about magic after all.

Little victories. Mei Li would take them.

"I have belatedly realized that I do not know what a blood mage's objective here would be," Shunlei admitted slowly. "I gathered from the way you spoke of this person that their intentions were nefarious and they must be stopped immediately, but what is a blood mage's aims?"

An excellent question. Mei Li opened her mouth to respond, but Nord surprisingly beat her to it.

"Blood mages often have their own agendas, so I can't speak to this one's goals." Nord fussed with his sleeves, tying them back and to his elbows, clearing his forearms and getting ready to move. "But it's standard that they never use their magic for good. Their very method of extracting magic is through a person's blood, hence their name. They leave only corpses in their wake. It's a highly addictive process of magical empowerment, but to detrimental ends. They gain immediate boosts in power that is unparalleled, but it turns them mad."

"Think of them like mosquitoes," Mei Li couldn't help but throw in. "The only good mosquito is a dead mosquito."

Nord snorted, some humor dancing in his dark eyes as he looked at her. "You're not wrong. However, I put forward that mosquitoes are in fact more elevated. At least they only suck blood to survive. A blood mage has no such excuse."

Delighted he was going along with her poor joke, Mei Li graciously extended a hand, acknowledging his point. "Agreed. But the world will still be better with one less blood-sucking parasite."

"Naturally."

Mei Li tamped down a brilliant smile. She'd gotten Nord's trust too. Or at least, he was thawing enough around her to banter.

"Alright!" Hawes thumped up to them, his armor making each stride heavier than usual. "I think we're all ready? Yes? Good. Shunlei, you staying human or going dragon?"

"Human, I think." Shunlei stared dubiously ahead. "The gathering of the trees will make for very tight quarters in my dragon form."

Hawes' worry cleared, leaving relief in its wake. "That's fair enough. I'd rather have your strength on the ground anyway. Alright, let's split into pairs. Blood mage will probably go for the richest target first, or the one he deems most dangerous. That means our magicians. Shunlei and Lady Mei, you take right wing. Nord and I will take center. Lady Kiyo and Melchior left. Let's stay a good ten paces away from each other, not give him a bunched target. Alright?"

That sounded a good enough strategy to her since they only had a general direction to go off of. Mei Li nodded acceptance.

With a deep breath, they set off. No one was inclined to

chatter as they waded through the dead underbrush. With all the dry leaves on the ground, there was no way to move noiselessly and they didn't even try, just moved through it. Mei Li had her eyes peeled in all directions, her head constantly panning from left to right, not wanting to be caught unawares.

It was nerve-wracking in the extreme to walk into hostile territory like this. She had no way of communicating with the forest that they were here to help, and only a limited understanding of where the blood mage was. And their plan basically boiled down to 'Catch him!' Which, really, lacked the logistical strategies she was accustomed to.

She *liked* plans, curse it.

The deeper Mei Li went in, the more tense she became. The pressure knotted badly in her shoulders and neck, and she had no doubt she'd have a whopper of a headache tonight from the stress. Gritting her teeth, she foraged ahead regardless.

Shunlei made a sound in the back of his throat, like a dog that came across a wretched smell. "What is that?"

Sharply, she turned to him. "What? What are you sensing?"

"It's like a charnel house," he explained, rubbing at his offended nose. "One abandoned for several weeks, no less."

"That's the direction," she said grimly. "Sorry, Shunlei, we need to follow that scent."

Grimacing, he gave a nod.

Mei Li turned to the left and signaled the others. They quickly caught up and hovered in a circle, coming in close enough to speak confidentially.

"Shunlei smells something like a rotten charnel house ahead," Mei Li quickly relayed in a low tone.

Kiyo hissed in triumph. "That's what we're looking for. Where, Shunlei? Directly ahead?"

"No," he said a trifle uncertainly. Pointing in a more

easterly direction, he suggested, "More that direction. I don't think it's incredibly close yet. I didn't smell it at all until a waft from a breeze carried it to me."

"We'll follow your nose," Hawes encouraged. "This is in the same direction as Kiyo's reading last night, more or less."

In an uncommon move, Kiyo graciously admitted, "I could have caught him while he was moving about last night and not in his, well, lair for lack of an appropriate term. But the charnel house smell, that would be correct for a blood mage's altar. Even if he's not there, he'll be close."

"Re-orient," Hawes ordered. "Spread out again, and let's take this a bit more slowly. I don't want to just blunder in there."

Mei Li was perfectly in agreement with that. She walked steadily once more, a half-step behind Shunlei as he led the way. Within ten paces, she caught the same whiff he had. Within twenty, it became nose-hair curdling, the inside of her nose wanting to shrivel up in protest. It was like rotten meat, gangrene, decaying mold, and several other unpleasant things mixed altogether. With every step she took, it became that much worse, and it finally got to the point she had to consciously control her gag reflex.

Shunlei cast her a glance over his shoulder. "Can a human nose smell it now?"

"I certainly can," she said, breathing through her mouth as much as possible. "Gah, that's awful! And I sorely regret my decision to eat breakfast this morning."

"Me too," he admitted, taken for a moment by a dry heave. "How can anyone stand to live in this...potent filth?"

"Sadly, to him this probably smells like power. When you start using blood magic, it will warp your senses to the point that the human body doesn't react the way it should anymore."

"And people do this to themselves willingly?"

"People," Mei Li said sourly, "can be incredibly stupid."

Shunlei snorted. "That I've seen, but what draws a person to try blood magic to begin with?"

"Desperation, usually. I've seen two cases where the person was suffering from a serious ailment, something magic couldn't help with. They tried blood magic as a last resort. And there's always a few who think they're somehow above the law, that they won't be sucked under like everyone else. I don't think they realize that when you start using blood magic, it affects every single drop of blood in your own body. There's no escaping that or the consequences of it."

He opened his mouth to respond only to stop, head snapping around to see something from the other direction. "DOWN!"

Mei Li dropped without a second of hesitation. Shunlei did the same, nearly flattening himself to the crumbling leaves. Not a second later, something whistled overhead, not a half-foot above Mei Li. She swore, snatching up a talisman from her belt pouch and activating it to wield a quick defensive shield. "What was that?"

"I don't know, I just caught sight of something metal glinting." Shunlei ducked behind the square shield she now held in front of her. "Why didn't you have this up before?"

"Magic can be detected," Mei Li answered succinctly. "It would have been like a beacon before now. Do you see him?"

"No. And I can't smell him under all this rot. Was that a trap we sprung?"

"Quite possibly." Mei Li turned to see how the rest were faring, only to see they were crouched down as well. No injuries, though. They were hunkered down with shields up, all ready to move. Perhaps they'd also heeded Shunlei's warning and dropped down before they could be ensnared.

"Let's move," Shunlei urged. "If you stand still, you lose."

Wise counsel, and Mei Li took it. She matched paces with him, keeping the shield up in front of both of them. The stench grew progressively worse, the environment around them changing as well. The trees that had looked dormant before looked ghostly now, like wood that had been burned so quickly the shape remained but only ash was left behind. On a whim, she brushed her hand against a trunk as she passed, and it crumbled to dust under her fingers.

"He's leeched all life from this area," Mei Li muttered, sickened and frustrated. It would take possibly a century for the Woods to recover fully from this.

"Don't worry, he'll pay for it soon enough."

"That actually does cheer me." From the corner of her eye, she caught a flash of movement between the trees and turned automatically to put her shield between her and it—whatever it was. Shunlei moved with her, attuned. Or perhaps determined to protect her flank.

Something else flashed out at them, but this time it wasn't a simple trap sprung. It was blood-red, a flash of blood and power forming a large scythe that blistered toward them as quick as a lightning strike. Mei Li had no time to swear, or gasp, or anything before it struck her shield dead on. With an ominous crack, the white power of her own shield splintered, like fracturing glass. She grasped her arm with the other hand, twisting her torso sharply in order to throw the scythe upward, away from her and Shunlei. If it struck through her shield, she'd be dead in an instant.

That movement cost her dearly. She panted, arm aching under the force of the blow. The shield splintered entirely, the talisman crumpling into a smoking ball of paper in her hand. She dropped it, useless as it was now, and scrambled for another shield talisman from her pouch.

Shunlei stepped in front of her as she did this, and her haste—as well as the pain in her arm—made her a little clumsy. She did *not* want him to deal with a scythe like that head on. It had nearly seared through her shield as it was and—

This time she heard it as it was released—a vibrating

thrum, like an arrhythmic heartbeat, mixed in with the sound of the weapon whistling through the air. She threw her uninjured arm up, the talisman gripped tightly in her hand, but too late. Shunlei still stood in front of her.

His chest expanded before a hot gust of flame burst out of his mouth in a steady stream. The red and orange flames crackled and burned through the air, enveloping the scythe and disintegrating it in a split second.

Someone yelped in panic as the flames kept going, and Mei Li sensed more than saw a shield thrown up. The blood mage was over there—and he was shielding against dragon fire. Just how much magical power did he have at his disposal?

Probably too much. Curses.

Hawes and Nord skidded to a stop beside her. Without a word, Nord grabbed her hand, their talismans overlapping and effectively doubling the shield. It snapped up with a hum, forming a perfect white square in front of them.

"Did I see that right?" Hawes demanded of her. "Shunlei's fire can combat his magic?"

"At least the blood scythes he's throwing," Mei Li confirmed. "Dragon fire can burn them to a crisp."

"Shunlei, step back and behind the shield," Hawes commanded urgently. He had his own shield up on his arm, his free hand clutching an enchanted sword in a ready stance. "Duck out only to spit fire at him."

Mei Li glanced back for Kiyo and Melchior, but did not see any sign of them. Ah, of course, they were enacting Kiyo's plan. They were likely hoofing it around the area, trying to sneak up behind the blood mage while the others served as a distraction. Mei Li crossed mental fingers that it worked.

"Hawes, I want to deploy one of my ropes," she whispered, ducking in close to him to keep her voice from spreading beyond the four of them. "It probably won't work, but I want to keep him distracted and focused on us as much as possible."

Hawes nodded. "Do it."

"Have Nord do it," Shunlei said, still standing and staring intently forward. "Mei's arm is hurt."

True, it was throbbing something fierce. Mei Li had a bad feeling she'd seriously injured it by forcing that scythe up as she had. Nord gave her a look askance, and she grimaced at him. "I caught the first scythe directly onto my shield."

His mouth formed an 'ah' of understanding. "Then I'll do it. Hold onto my talisman for a moment."

"Of course." She did so, then tilted her right hip toward him so he could retrieve the coil of rope hanging off her belt.

Nord slid his hands over the length of it, imbuing it with his power and activating the spells woven into the very fiber of it. He'd grabbed the first one Mei Li had made, which was just as well. It was the more poorly worked of the two, so would be no real loss. He aimed the tip of it toward the area the attacks had been coming from, and with a whispered word, released it.

The rope flew forward, snaking through the air with commendable speed. It hit something—hard—the sound like a slap against stone. Then the rope frayed apart and flew off into every direction.

Mei Li had expected that to happen but still found it disheartening. That rope had taken her a good two hours to make, after all.

Without missing a beat, Shunlei blew out a steady stream of fire once more, and this time its heat blistered the very air. It was nice, in a way, as it cleansed part of the area where the blood mage had been slaughtering and butchering. But it was also disturbing because the rotten meat left behind now smelled like cooked bacon.

Mei Li had a feeling she'd not be able to have bacon for a while.

The blood mage threw out a succession of strikes, varied

in all directions. Some of them were the scythe again, but others were darts—quick, small, and deadly. Mei Li instinctively dodged them even as Nord swore and threw up another shield above their heads. He wasn't quite quick enough. One of the darts slipped through, searing him along the top of his shoulder.

A cry of pain came out from behind clenched teeth, but Nord held his position.

Mei Li had had a bad feeling the night before that they'd be injured today and had come prepared. But there was no time to stop and treat anyone, even with a basic bandage.

"Shunlei, I can't see much beyond this heap here." Hawes craned his head around to see past the shield. "Where is he?"

"I can't lay eyes on him either," Shunlei said unhappily. He shifted from foot to foot, as if his instincts urged him to move. "I'd take to the skies if I had the room to do it. I think—"

He cut himself off as magic clashed ahead, sending a wave of both magic and air gusting over them, nearly strong enough to send Mei Li off her haunches and straight to the ground.

"They've found him," Shunlei snarled, and before anyone could say a word to him, he burst into a sprint. He nearly left vacuumed air in his wake he moved so fast, the dirt churning under his heels.

Mei Li swore viciously, taking off after him. She wasn't athletic, and not nearly as fast as a dragon under any circumstance, so he was far ahead of her in seconds. Hawes and Nord out-stripped her too, although Nord not by much.

The tree trunks and the men in front of her blocked her view, but Mei Li caught snatches. Kiyo held talismans in either hand, a white rope dangling in between her outspread arms, but she was clearly struggling to find the right timing to dispatch it. Melchior was locked in a physical tussle with the blood mage. Whatever protections he had in place kept him from being immediately drained of life, but Mei Li didn't give good odds of that lasting much longer.

The blood mage was a gnarly looking man—he'd probably been tall and ruggedly attractive at some point, but he was deformed by power now, almost hunchback in appearance, head seemingly permanently tilted to the side.

Shunlei struck with all the force of a typhoon. He slid to a stop beside the blood mage and lashed out with both fists at once. The hit was a solid one, with all the considerable strength and power in a dragon's physique.

The blood mage, even with all his magic, had no counter for this physical attack. Without his shield up, he had nothing to protect him. His body lurched abruptly sideways, flipping through the air, arms splaying without finding any purchase. He landed with a hard thud, skidding on the dead leaves a good two feet.

Kiyo lost no time in executing her spell, and the rope flew forward to ensnare his feet. The trap was meant to keep him still and in one place—nothing more—but Kiyo wasn't done yet. Even as the spell unfurled, working, she immediately whipped out a second pair of talismans. "Everyone, clear!"

People dove out of the way to give her room to work with. Both talismans flew through the air, slapping themselves over the blood mage's hands and mouth, respectively. Mei Li panted as she stumbled to a stop, looking their prone prey over from head to toe.

The new talismans locked his magic. With him cut off from his magic and physically bound in place, the blood mage wasn't capable of doing anything more than glaring at them. It was a good glare, though. Top notch.

Hawes looked him over and grunted in satisfaction. "Well. This one caused us some trouble. Thankfully he's not as powerful as all of us combined. What do we do with him? Kill him here?"

"No," all three mages protested at once.

Hawes' brows shot up. "Why not? Blood mages have a bounty on their heads. He doesn't need a trial."

That was true even of the future. Mei Li squirmed, a little uncomfortable with killing anyone in cold blood. But this wasn't a case where it was a matter of bounty or laws. She could tell Shunlei was clearly confused at their objections as well. They really, really should have talked this over last night. "I think we should still report it to the authorities, though."

"We can do that after he's safely dead," Melchior pointed out. "And I don't want to haul him to the nearest city. That's a dangerous task in and of itself."

"He's full of dark, twisted magic at this point," Kiyo hastily explained. "If we just kill him, all that dark magic will spill out through his blood, likely damaging the Wood. We'll need to haul him to a temple to put him through the proper purification ceremonies—"

The ground under their feet rumbled, rolling in the most minute of ways under Mei Li's feet. Alarmed, she stumbled back several feet, looking about her frantically. Now what was going on?!

The ground near the blood mage broke apart from the roots of the trees. The dark roots, dirt still clinging to them in clods, broke free of the ground with a snap of effort. Wrapping around the blood mage, the many roots covered him from head to toe and then with a snap, dragged him sharply underground. The ground closed up after him within seconds, like a reverse avalanche. It left no sign afterward that anything had happened except the area was now clear of leaves.

Shunlei stared at the spot and cleared his throat. "Correct me if I'm mistaken. But did a sentient forest just eat a man?"

"Sure looks that way to me," Hawes agreed, a little horrified. "Uh...are we next?"

"The Wood is reclaiming the magical power the blood

mage stole from it," Kiyo said confidently.

Nord tacked on dubiously, "I think."

Mei Li had to agree it sounded plausible, but she wasn't entirely sure on that point, either. None of the records mentioned that the Wood could purify a blood mage. But it was a moot question at the moment. Clearly, the Wood thought it could and fully planned to do so.

"I'm not inclined to argue," Mei Li declared firmly. "Let's leave."

Everyone seemed to agree on that point and hastily beat a path back to their campsite. As they moved, Shunlei came in close to her, looking her over with worry. "You're cradling your arm against you. How badly is it hurt?"

"I'm hoping it's just badly bruised," she admitted. The way it throbbed and ached with every breath didn't give her high hopes in that regard.

Kiyo cast a glance over her shoulder even as she hurried along, skirts flapping. "I'll take a look when we're back at camp."

"Thank you," Mei Li managed, surprised at the offer.

"Wait." Hawes held up a hand, stalling them all in their tracks. "Huh."

All around them, the trees began unclenching from their defensive stance. Buds and leaves slowly unfurled. The dry leaves under their feet crumbled and were replaced with budding green grass, pushing up and forming something that looked suspiciously like a welcoming carpet. Water started flowing from somewhere nearby, and a few insects and birds lent their voices to the transformation.

Mei Li's head turned in every direction, taking in the abrupt changes, and a smile lit her face. Oh, it was lovely!

"It's thanking us." Shunlei turned to stare behind him, a smile on his face. "The Wood is thanking us."

"I much prefer thanks over being eaten," Hawes muttered. Relieved, he waved them into motion again. "We still need to get back to camp. We have injured people to attend to. Good work, everyone."

They'd thwarted an evil blood mage and made a sentient forest happy with them. Mei Li counted that as a good day. Even if she'd possibly broken her arm in the process.

7

Mei Li's arm was indeed broken. Not badly, just a hairline fracture, and it was quite understandable under the circumstances. Kiyo had lightly touched a tuning fork to her arm in two different places and the tone of the ring was dull, indicating a break in the bone, but it did sound. At least it wasn't snapped in two. That's what Mei Li held on to.

Nord drew a talisman directly onto her skin with a steady hand, speaking in his soft voice as he worked. "The impact against the shield was hard enough on your bones, but by forcing the blow upward as you did, you forced the arm to rotate, and that's what did the most damage. You'll find that your tendons and muscles are significantly bruised. Please do not use the arm at all for the next week."

That sounded problematic. Traveling for a week with a bum arm? Mei Li frowned down at it, already trying to figure out how to manage things like tying a belt on. She doubted Kiyo would be willing to help much in that regard.

Well. This would be fun.

As Nord carefully wrapped the arm, Kiyo sat behind him, dabbing ointment on the scorched shoulder. "All said, we actually fared rather well," Kiyo noted almost rhetorically. "This is a very mild set of injuries considering what we were up against. Blood mages are usually horrible to handle."

"I think we have Shunlei to thank for that." Hawes came in closer to sink onto his haunches, looking the dragon over.

Shunlei was not-quite-hovering, holding both bandages and the jar of ointment out as an assistant. He regarded Hawes with some amusement, the hint of it curling up the edges of his mouth. "This is the point I try to make with my fellow dragons. If only we could work in harmony with humanity, we could achieve amazing things."

Mei Li nodded firmly in support of this. She wanted so dearly to tell him that in the future, they'd have this—the harmony of trust and support. She had to bite her tongue before she blurted out too much.

Fortunately, Melchior said what she thought. "It's true, we really do complement each other. The blood mage would have been very difficult for any dragon alone to take on—the dragon would have been drained of life and magic quickly. But we would have still been battling that mage if not for your dragon fire suppressing and distracting him. I think that crossing paths with you might well alter the preconceptions we have of dragons. I've certainly changed my mind."

Shunlei beamed at him. "You have?"

"Of course! You've been a pleasure to work and travel with. I'm glad Lady Mei called out to you." Melchior tapped a finger to his chin, eyes narrowed thoughtfully. "You said you've been challenging dragons as you've come across them, subduing them and putting them under contract. How often do you find another dragon?"

"Two or three a month?" Shunlei's head canted as he thought about it. "But I'm not always in the right areas for it. For the most part, dragons like to stay in the mountains or in the forests. It gives us better perches, for one, and safer places to sleep and hunt. But occasionally I'll see another down here, in the more civilized areas, causing trouble."

Hawes and Melchior shared a look. It was probably supposed to come off as solemn, but instead they resembled two little boys plotting mischief.

"I'm game," Melchior informed his friend hopefully.

"Heavens, man, like I'm going to turn down the challenge," Hawes snorted. Turning back to Shunlei, he stated firmly, "We'll help you. We were inclined to help you before, as no one wants the dragons rampaging about, but now? Seeing how well we can cooperate? We'll definitely help you."

Shunlei immediately put bandages and ointment down and bounded over to hug both men. Hawes and Melchior spluttered under this hug attack but didn't refuse it, although the pat on Shunlei's shoulder looked a bit awkward on Melchior's part. Their height differences alone made it awkward. Mei Li watched with patent amusement, which she strove not to show by covering her mouth with her hand. "Thank you, a million times, thank you!"

"Well. Least we can do." Hawes disengaged, bemused at the hug, but not unhappy about it. "Alright, let's get these two sorted. I see a storm rolling in on the horizon, and I'd rather not be caught out in it. Or stuck in our tents. Never a fun thing, rolling up wet tents."

Shunlei and Melchior started breaking down the tents while Hawes headed for the horses, getting them saddled. Nord wrapped Mei Li's arm and then put it in a sling about her neck. She wasn't at all looking forward to riding and having her arm jostled about. The binding spell on the bandages would help stabilize it, but anything faster than a walk would not be comfortable. Nord, at least, seemed fine, even if his shoulder did irritate him.

They went about the tasks of breaking down camp and, despite two injured people, managed it well enough. Shunlei helped Mei Li up onto the horse and swung himself up behind her. Mei Li could manage the reins with one hand well enough, and truly, this arrangement worked better. Even if Shunlei were more comfortable riding now, she wouldn't want to ride with her injured arm pressed up against his back. No, thanks.

By the time they got back onto the road, the storm was more than just dark clouds in the sky. The air was humid, and a strong wind ruffled their clothes and hair. Shunlei took in a deep breath behind her, head tilted back to scent the air. "I estimate we have a few hours, perhaps as much as four, before we're hit."

"I trust your nose. Hawes!" Mei Li called ahead. "How close is the nearest town?"

"According to my very inaccurate map, about six hours!"

Mei Li made a face. "Hopefully that estimation is off in our favor. And not against."

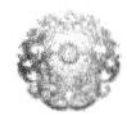

They didn't quite make it. The town was in sight when the heavens opened up and drenched them from head to toe. Even hurrying in didn't make much difference, and they showed up at the inn's door—the only inn, as far as Mei Li could tell—looking like drowned rats. The inn keeper clucked over them, gave them a fair price, and got his staff in motion with a clap of the hands to get everyone in and settled, horses included.

Mei Li wanted a bath and was determined to get it. She'd hail one of the female staff, if necessary, to help her back into clothes. With her dry clothes fetched and held carefully away from her sopping wet person, she headed back downstairs and into the back of the inn. In the process, she nearly bumped right into Kiyo, her own dry clothes and towels in her arms.

"Oh good," Kiyo stated, moving aside to give her room to enter. "This will make things easier. I intended to fetch you if you weren't down in the next minute."

Mei Li blinked at her. Come again? "You were."

"Absolutely. You'll need help in and out of the clothes. Maybe with your hair." Kiyo eyed her sideways as she slid the bathing room door shut. "Have you ever washed hair one-handed before?"

"No. I've, ah, never injured an arm before."

"It's quite the trick. Takes practice. I'd best do it."

She absolutely had not anticipated that Kiyo would willingly pitch in and help her. But Mei Li had no intention of arguing against it, either. "Thank you in advance."

"Clothes first." Kiyo came at her with a determined expression.

Having someone else unclothe her was strange, but Mei Li appreciated the help. She settled into the bath carefully. The wooden sides were taller than usual, and the tile floor a bit slippery from previous use. Snagging one of the smaller wooden buckets, she balanced a thick towel on it for padding before letting her injured arm rest on it. Mei Li didn't want to disturb the bandage or healing talismans wrapped around her arm, so she tried to keep it as dry as possible.

Kiyo was brisk and efficient as she shampooed Mei Li's hair. The massage against her scalp felt good, and Mei Li relaxed into it with a sigh. It had been years since anyone had washed her hair.

"Did you call out to him to make a point?"

Mei Li blinked. Ran that sentence through her head twice. Nope, still didn't make sense. "I'm sorry?"

"Shunlei. When you called to him for help with Red Lantern. Did you do that to make a point?"

"Just how conniving do you think I am?" Mei Li asked in bemusement. "No, I called to him because I needed aerial support to make the full seal. And I knew he'd help us."

"Because of the other dragon that rescued you." Kiyo said this with complete neutrality.

"Him, and my master. My master taught me the most about dragons."

"Hmm." Kiyo tipped Mei Li's head back so she could rinse, then grabbed the nearby hair oil to run it through the thick, black strands. "He's more polite than I expected."

Oh ho ho. Was Kiyo finally thawing toward Shunlei? She'd treated him with a sort of icy civility. Was that her version of caution? "Yes, his politeness caught me a bit by surprise too." On their first meeting, anyway.

"Do you think he'll stay with us long? Surely he has his own agenda."

"I think his agenda is taming the dragons and making better strides with humanity. I doubt he'll leave us anytime soon." Mei Li was sure of that, in fact. The records stated that Shunlei stayed with the first three groups of Tomes and their helpers until finally taking a break from it.

"So, you believe he'll stay with us."

"I do."

Kiyo hummed again, not arguing, and finally released her hair. "And what about you? How long will you stay?"

The question was likely meant to be casual, but Mei Li didn't hear it that way. It felt anything but. She was fairly itching with urgency, knowing Zaffi was close to breaking out of his seal in her present time, as well as a host of other problems she may or may not know how to defeat. She'd initially thought this trip would be quick—a week or two at most. Grab the records lost in the shipwreck and get back home before anyone knew she was gone.

The moment she'd appeared in this time and realized how far in the past she was, her mind had struggled to accept that she wouldn't be here for a few weeks. Zaffi hadn't even risen yet! It would be years before he did so. She still had that urgency burning in her to get things done, to wrap it up so she could go back home to her own time. It left her antsy in the worst ways. Being injured now didn't help.

Mei Li forced a steady stream of air out of her nose, forcing herself to calm. No use in rushing. Time wasn't moving forward in the future, after all. Not really. She had to keep reminding herself of that. "As long as I need to. I think

I'll be with you for quite some time. This isn't a situation I can easily walk away from."

That satisfied Kiyo, for some reason. She gracefully entered the bath and started soaping up her own hair.

"How did you come to join the party?" Mei Li asked. She knew the woman stayed for two decades, but none of the records mentioned a motivation.

Kiyo tilted her head for a moment to look at her before resuming scrubbing at her hair. "I think the family expectation for me was that after I graduated, I would quietly go home and use my training to help the family business. But I wanted to accomplish something. Do something completely on my own merits. Hawes knew one of my teachers, and when he came looking for help, I was introduced to him as a possible candidate. I fairly leapt at the chance."

Mei Li understood that feeling, in a sense. She liked being able to accomplish things. It seemed that, at heart, she and Kiyo were not so different after all. "And Nord?"

"Nord and I studied together. When Hawes accepted me, I asked if I could invite Nord as well. I was half-surprised he accepted, as he's rather a homebody most days. But I think he, too, wanted to really stretch his wings. And he enjoys the magical challenges."

"And it was only the two of you who accepted?"

"No, there was another. But he didn't last long, perhaps two weeks? Then he decided it was too much for him. He didn't like the uncertainty of it all, and how much we have to make up as we go along. He left. It's why Hawes latched onto you and Shunlei so quickly. If you have any skill and are willing, he'll draft you in."

Mei Li snorted. "I got that sense, yes."

Well, this was nice, having Kiyo act so friendly. Had she worked through matters enough to accept Mei Li? It looked that way. Mei Li heaved a secret breath of relief. She really didn't need antagonism on her own team. She was too alone in this world as it was.

Neither of them lingered long, as their stomachs were rumbling. They'd skipped lunch in the hopes of getting under shelter before the storm hit. When Kiyo got out, Mei Li did as well, out of necessity. Kiyo wasn't exactly nurturing while putting Mei Li back into clothes, but she did get the job done, and Mei Li appreciated it.

They exited, handing wet clothes over to the laundress on site for washing, then rejoined the men at the dining area. Mei Li settled on a cushion near Shunlei, her mouth watering from the tempting display of food on the table. Shunlei handed her a spoon instead of hashi and encouraged her by saying, "Anything you want to eat, tell me. I'll put it on the spoon for you."

He really was a sweetheart. The long span of time he lived had not changed that. "I will, thank you."

Shunlei's eyes flicked up to Mei Li's hair and lingered there. Kiyo had thrown it up for her into a messy knot with hair sticks holding it into place. It was a damp knot sitting on Mei Li's head and nothing more. "And after this, I will comb your hair out for you."

"Are you looking for a way to return the preening session?" she teased. She also found this offer amusing, as he'd apparently ignored his own hair. Even now it lay in damp tangles around his shoulders.

A light blush lit his cheeks. "Perhaps I am?"

"I will take the offer, thank you." Could she pinch his cheeks? Mei Li really wanted to pinch his cheeks.

Hawes cleared his throat. "If the two of you are done flirting?"

Shunlei spluttered, words tripping over themselves.

Staring him down, Mei Li drawled, "He's fun to tease. What is it, Hawes?"

"You fared alright on the ride here, but do you think you can continue to keep up? Should we arrange for you to stay here and heal, perhaps catch up later?"

"I'll help her," Shunlei volunteered immediately.

Mei Li shot him a smile. "I think I'll be fine. And truly, I'd rather stay with the group. There's no predicting which way you'll go. It will be difficult to try and catch up later."

Hawes nodded in satisfaction. "I expected that answer. Alright, we'll wait the storm out before continuing. I encourage you to rest while you can. We still have that bone demon and a trouble-making water deity to hunt down."

Mei Li had almost forgotten about those. It would mean a lot of riding in their near future. No wonder Hawes was checking in on her. Sighing, she looked down at her arm, back in its sling, and silently ordered it to heal faster. A week to heal was ridiculous.

She did not have time for a broken arm.

The main room of the inn was lively with people eating dinner, travelers escaping the rain, and a bored musician in the far corner plucking out one song after the next. Most of the instruments weren't ones she recognized, nor the melody for that matter. It was pleasant on the ear, though. Quick and lively.

They found an out of the way area near the fire, and Shunlei carefully unwound her hair from its messy bun. With comb in hand, he started at the bottom and gently worked his way through the damp strands.

"Thanks for this," Mei Li told him without turning her head. "Kiyo's helping me but her methods are...brisk. I was a little afraid of what she'd do to my scalp."

He chuckled in a low tone. "Quite understandable. And I'm pleased to return the favor. Does your arm hurt?"

"Not badly. The talismans Nord put on it help manage the pain. It's mostly difficult on my neck, which is taking the weight of the arm."

"Ahh. I've never broken a limb before. But I can see how that would be the case."

"It's the first time I've broken an arm too." Mei Li made a face down at her sling. "I can't recommend the experience."

"I've no desire to do it. I'll trust your word."

Silence for a moment, comfortable and easy, as Shunlei rhythmically stroked the comb through her hair. He only paused now and again to undo a tangle, his fingers gentle. With the warmth of the fire, and the sweet smell of cedar all around her, Mei Li felt her eyes droop. The atmosphere would lull her into a sleep soon.

"How long do you expect to stay with this group?" Shunlei asked her without segue.

"It's funny, but Kiyo asked me that earlier. I think I'll stay with them for some time. There's a great deal I need to learn, and being with them is the best way to do it. You?"

"You're the first humans to welcome me into their midst," Shunlei answered with transparent honesty. "I've no desire to leave any time soon. Do you think Hawes and Melchior really meant it when they said they'd help me tame the dragons?"

"I think they did. They're very keen on you succeeding. And really, you will succeed. It's best all-around if they help you."

Shunlei's hands stilled in her hair. "There's no doubt in your mind? You're that confident?"

Tilting her head, she shot him a warm smile over her shoulder. Oh, if only she could tell him. That this wasn't faith, but knowledge. "You'll succeed. There's not a trace of doubt in my mind."

The expression on his face was incredulity, and hope, and the faintest tinge of a blush on his cheeks. He seemed speechless by her attitude. Incredibly touched by it, too. Mei Li might not be able to tell him everything, but she saw no harm in encouraging him or displaying complete confidence in him. He really had taken on an incredible task. The very least she could do was support him.

Mei Li belatedly added, "I'll help you too, of course. I don't think I've said that so far. But of course I'll help you too."

His eyes were bright, too bright, and he had to clear his throat before he could bring himself to speak. "Thank you. I look forward to your help."

"You catch 'em, I'll preen 'em," she offered, trying to get him to laugh.

It succeeded. Shunlei choked on a laugh even as he resumed combing her hair. "You know, I think that'll work? After experiencing your preening, *I'd* certainly change my mind about being allies with humans."

"Right? Easier to tame dragons than fight them into submission. Can you imagine a world where dragons and humans were friends? Think of all that could be accomplished, of how much more peaceful the world will be."

They spoke of what if's and could be's as he combed her hair. Mei Li dropped hints, subtly, but drew him the overall picture, unable to resist. Even after her hair was combed and dried, they lingered near the fire and spoke of the future.

8

The next week was tedious and tiring. They spent all day in the saddle, stopping at random places at night as they made their way steadily east. Sometimes it meant camping outside, sometimes they could find an inn. Never had Mei Li so missed having an entire flight of dragons willing to fly her about. Air travel was just so much more convenient than being stuck on horseback. And her cramping thighs didn't like all this saddle time.

Kiyo continued to help her in and out of clothes. Shunlei took over doing her hair and refused to budge on this point. They were both patient as they aided her, and Mei Li appreciated it beyond words. Still, she was very grateful when her arm finally healed and the bandages came off.

The geography was such that it was easier to go north and then east rather than to try to cross over the Summer Winds Mountain range. By going north for a day or so, they could then cross over the bridge at Crimson Lake, a much faster and easier trek than going up and down a mountain. Considering the last time she'd been on that bridge, the idea didn't thrill her, but Mei Li kept reminding herself that the bridge was alright in this era. In fact, it wasn't even the same bridge—the Lost Souls Bridge of the future was the sixth incarnation of the bridge now in place.

Still, the reaction she felt on spying the glistening waters of Crimson Lake was a very mixed feeling. The last time she'd been here, they'd all been fighting to rescue the people trapped in Lost Souls Bridge. It had been difficult, nerve-wracking, and dangerous in all the wrong ways. The memory of it sent a cold shiver racing up and down her spine. Being here made her wonder how everyone was doing. Had Shunlei, Bai, and Gen's burns healed enough to use yet? How was Leah's thigh and hip? Mei Li had no way of tracking how much time had passed in the future, but her guess was only a few hours. She hated not knowing, though. That ate at her.

It also felt surreal to be here, in a place where she had worked alongside all of them, and have it look so similar but different. The similarities especially threw her mentally as if she were caught in a strange dream. At least, up until she reached the shores and realized she could easily see the other side. No fog here, or warning signs. Or even torii. The radical difference helped for some reason.

Mei Li thumped a palm over her heart and settled her unease as the horses' hooves clattered over the wooden bridge.

Hawes was at her right stirrup, and he lifted a hand to shield his eyes as he spoke. "Looks like we'll have a bit of daylight left once we've crossed. An hour or two. Still, I think we should stop for the night. There's a nice inn on the other side. My back could use a real mattress to sleep on for a night."

"Mine too," Mei Li agreed, heartfelt. "And baths."

"Please baths," Kiyo pleaded from behind.

"Then it's settled, we'll stay." Hawes squinted and leaned forward. "Shunlei, am I seeing a dragon up ahead?"

Shunlei studied the sky for a moment. "You are. And he's not just passing overhead. With the way he's circling, he's about to dive. Or land. Hawes, I think I'd best intervene."

"Go!" Hawes encouraged, worried now.

Shunlei didn't even wait for her to draw the horse to a stop. He just slid smartly off, darting ahead and then sprinting further down the bridge. In mid-step, he transformed and, with a powerful beat of his wings, lifted into the sky.

Watching him go, Mei Li bit her bottom lip, the unease back in her chest. She had no doubt he would win, but would he be injured in the process? Would the townsmen understand that he was the one protecting them? Or just attack both dragons equally?

Hawes apparently had the same thoughts. "Let's hurry and catch up," he urged.

Mei Li put heels to flanks and got her horse running, grimly hoping to cross the distance before something went very wrong. Even as she rode, her eyes stayed trained on the sky. The dragon they saw was diving, sleek and true, not seeming to care that Shunlei was quickly closing in on his location.

Shunlei didn't even pause or speak, just rammed right into the other dragon. The collision echoed, the sound as sharp as a boulder striking the basin floor.

"Gods, how hard did he hit him?" Melchior spluttered, his voice barely audible over the pounding of hooves.

Mei Li lost sight as the two dragons crashed sharply to the ground. She wanted to urge the horse to go faster, but in truth her gelding was already hoofing it as fast as he could. It seemed to take eons before she finally reached the end of the bridge.

The town on the other side seemed to be fine—no damaged buildings or fire that she could see. But she also didn't see any dragons. Mei Li hurried through the streets, and it wasn't until she'd reached the far end that she finally saw Shunlei.

Both dragons were in a farmer's field, the livestock having sensibly fled. Shunlei was perched on the other's back, and he had a firm grip on the back of the yellow dragon's head.

Still, the yellow one struggled, his claws digging up the earth all around, snarling.

"Get off, you brute!" Yellow snapped at Shunlei in Long-go. "What business is it of yours if I snatch a sheep?!"

"You'll yield to me," Shunlei commanded, still holding firm. "You'll yield and obey the laws I lay on you. I won't let go until you do."

"I'm not obeying some idiot I don't even know!"

Mei Li pulled to a sharp stop and sighed in relief. No injuries she could see. Shunlei had this in hand.

Hawes pulled up next to her and demanded in a low tone, "What are they saying?"

"Shunlei's demanding the yellow yield. Yellow is refusing, says he doesn't even know Shunlei, he's not obeying him."

"What can we do to help?"

"Go buy meat," she directed after a moment's thought. "Yellow's hungry, he planned to snatch a sheep. If his belly is full, he might be more cooperative."

"I'll do that," Melchior volunteered, turning around and heading back into town.

Mei Li slid off her gelding—Peanut blew out a thankful breath—and she fetched her dowel from the saddlebags. Then she approached from the front, giving both dragons a clear view of her approach.

Yellow stopped thrashing and eyed her suspiciously.

"His name is Shunlei," Mei Li informed him in Long-go. "I'm Mei."

Yellow's eyes nearly popped out of his head. "Wha—you know Long-go!"

"I do. I also know how to preen a dragon." Mei Li lifted the dowel in illustration. "How about if you promise to behave and talk sensibly with Shunlei, we'll feed you dinner and I'll preen you. Your wings seem to be in a state."

Yellow hesitated strongly. This was a very personal thing she was offering. Mei Li understood that and stepped lightly to Shunlei's wing, carefully showing the other that she did indeed know what she was doing. And that Shunlei trusted her enough to do it. Shunlei thrummed at her, a happy note, and she thrummed back with a smile on her face.

Yellow's eyes lingered longingly on the dowel, and he licked his lips. "No tricks?"

Mei Li smiled at him. Ah, so young. "My word on it."

"I'm Enlai," Yellow finally stated. "I'll listen and not attack. You've got my word."

Shunlei immediately released him. Enlai stood and shook his body out, rustling wings and laying them against his body, watching them all warily.

"Stretch out," Mei Li encouraged. "My friend went to buy some meat for all of us. I'll preen your wings while you and Shunlei talk."

Enlai settled on his belly, stretching out a wing and watching her cautiously. But when she didn't do anything strange, his head turned again to regard Shunlei. "Well. What's your stake in this? I've heard your name before. People are saying you're fighting dragons to a standstill, making them swear they won't hurt hum—oooooh that's good." Enlai's head dropped as he nearly purred. "Gods above, I didn't think a human would be good at this. Why is she so good at this?"

"A dragon taught her how," Shunlei answered, amused. He settled on his belly, looking for all the world relaxed in some farmer's pasture with a half-destroyed fence laying in mangled remains nearby.

Mei Li's ears perked as she heard Hawes send Kiyo and Nord off to find them an inn for the night, but their leader stayed planted nearby, watching this play out. He had no idea what they were saying, as Shunlei and Enlai continued to speak in Long-go. But he stood so he could watch Mei Li's face, and she gave him reassuring nods now and again so he knew the talk was progressing well.

Shunlei outlined exactly what he wanted, in an easy, no-nonsense tone. "First, you are humanity's ally. Act accordingly."

"What does that mean?" Enlai lost focus before the question was fully out, tilting his wing so Mei Li could reach a particularly troublesome spot.

Clearing his throat, Shunlei gently brought Enlai's attention back to him. "First, you protect them if there is danger nearby. Second, you do not hunt them. Third, you do not hunt on their lands unless you have permission."

"Is that all?"

"You'll find that most situations fall in line with one of those. Our goal is to be humanity's friend. If we prove to be a danger to them, they will hunt us. And while we are formidable, we are not without our weaknesses. We are also very outnumbered. In time, I think we'll be hunted to extinction unless something changes."

"You really—oh, yes, right there. You really think so?"

"I know it. I've seen this already in action. We must change, and change quickly, or there is no hope for dragonkind."

Enlai tried to ask further questions, but he seemed to be distracted by Mei Li's hands as she worked out the knots in his down and pruned out broken feathers. In fact, it quickly became clear this method was underhanded—Enlai was too engrossed in the preening to pay proper attention to Shunlei. It was like negotiating with a person while they were getting a massage with warm oils.

Melchior returned with the meat, and Enlai ate it so quickly Mei Li wasn't convinced he'd properly chewed. Or even tasted it much on the way down. He did look a little thin—was he too young to know how to hunt and survive properly? Was that what drove him from the mountains and down here into human settlements?

Right behind Melchior were two men, both nervous about having dragons so near their town, but Melchior apparently had spoken with both of them. He waved them in closer and brought them to stand near Shunlei.

"This is Shunlei," Melchior introduced with a smile. "As I said before, he's a friend of ours and really, a friend of humanity. Shunlei, this is Mayor Deming and the sheriff, Guiren. They saw and heard the crash."

Shunlei dipped his head toward both men. He switched from Long-go but spoke slowly, probably for Enlai's sake, who wouldn't be as comfortable with the human language. "My apologies for startling you. I wanted to intercept this young one. This is Enlai. We are discussing the terms for him to not attack human settlements. Enlai?"

Enlai at this point was little better than a puddle of drool as he lay flat on his belly. He tilted his head up and blinked sleepily. "Hmm?"

"Mei, stop preening for a moment," Shunlei requested, biting down a laugh with visible effort. "I need him to focus."

"Noooo, don't stop her," Enlai whined at him in Long-go. "Do you know how long it's been since I was preened? My broodmother last did it, that's how long!"

Mei Li stopped and patted his side. "I'll finish after you four talk."

Enlai turned to give her a pitiful look. Really, only dogs could match his puppy eyes. "You promise? You won't leave me like this, will you?"

"I promise," she soothed. "Now, focus."

"Enlai, there are benefits to being friends with humanity." Shunlei said this with such authority that he sounded like his future self for a moment. "Take right now, for example. Not only have you made a human friend who will preen you, but you have a chance to barter with these fine gentlemen." Switching from Long-go again, he addressed the men, "Mayor, Sherriff, would you not like to have a dragon's help here? Consider: very few dangers can combat dragon fire. If you have a dragon ally in this area, he can help you combat any number of demons, rogue magicians, and the like."

Sherriff Guiren looked at Enlai with new consideration. "That would be handy, I do admit. We don't have any magicians in town who can fight these things off when they come in."

"And Mayor, would you not like to have protection against *other* dragons from damaging the fields?" Shunlei continued with a nod to the damage nearby. "Do not worry, I will set that to rights shortly. If a dragon has claimed this territory as his own, other dragons will avoid it. We dragons can also perform cool burns to keep roads clear and help till the land during spring planting season. I myself have performed all of these tasks many times."

Enlai looked at Shunlei in a new light. "You did? What did you get out of it?"

"They fed me."

Mayor Deming watched Shunlei with a shrewd expression on his round face. "Have you? You seem to think Master Enlai will be willing to do the same."

"Young dragons do not always know what is best for them. Hunger will drive them to make rash decisions. Now that he knows what is offered, what is possible, I think you'll find he'll make very different choices. If, naturally, he is extended the offer." Shunlei eyed the mayor back and pointedly waited.

Mayor and Sherriff exchanged glances but really, the math was easy to do. Mayor Deming nodded and faced Enlai squarely. "For your protection, we'll feed you once a day and provide a safe place for you to sleep. For any additional work you do, you'll get payment directly from the person who employs you."

Enlai's tail thumped the ground in excitement. His words were a touch hesitant—he was clearly phrasing things in his head before he spoke—but the enthusiasm was unmistakable. "Preen me too?"

"Once a month, a dragon needs to be preened," Mei Li

threw in. "It's not difficult and takes about an hour to do. I'll be happy to show people how to do it."

"Preening once a month and a meal a day, plus a house of your own," Mayor Deming amended. "Um, the cabin isn't very big, though?"

"Dragons can turn into human form," Shunlei explained patiently. "It will do fine."

"Oh." The mayor seemed nonplussed by this information and not quite sure what to do with it. With a shake of his head, he re-focused. "Do you agree, Master Enlai?"

Enlai almost agreed, it was on the tip of his tongue, then he looked uncertainly at Shunlei. Switching back to Long-go he said, "But...if I can't hunt in the area, once isn't enough."

"Enlai," Shunlei said with exasperation. "Crimson Lake is *right there*. You can fish as much as you like. Without having to worry about someone spotting you, or trying to shoot you out of the air, you'll have plenty of time to gather your own food."

The yellow tail thumped the ground again in excitement. "Oh, true, true. I accept, then!" Switching back from Long-go, he carefully enunciated, "Thank you, thank you, I'll make sure no danger. No danger come here. House all mine?"

"There's a cabin near the lake that's been abandoned since a widow's passing," Mayor Deming said. "It belongs to the town now. I'll let you have it. Report to me each evening about your patrols of the area."

"Sure, sure."

Mei Li felt a little flat-footed about how easily Shunlei brokered the deal. She'd expected more resistance. Just what had Melchior told them before these two men had even shown up? "Sheriff, come around and let me show you how to preen. That way you can teach others."

"Yes, of course." Sheriff Guiren paused halfway there and eyed Enlai uncertainly. "That's alright with you?"

"Please, please," Enlai encouraged before nosing at the

wing Mei Li hadn't worked on yet and switching back to Long-go. "I've got itchy spots on this one. I'm turning Red soon, you know, and I'll start molting. Hideous process, I'm itchy for weeks. Ahhhh Mei, I love your hands. I can marry you, you know."

Mei laughed outright. "What is it about you dragons? I preen you, I get proposals."

Enlai knew immediately what she meant. "You too, Shunlei?"

"Her hands are magical," Shunlei answered, not at all embarrassed.

Flopping back onto the ground, Enlai returned to being the epitome of pleasure. "That they are."

For one reason or another, they ended up lingering in the town the next day. A storm was approaching—they could see it sweeping down from the mountains, and could hear the thunder and lightning. They may or may not have been able to ride ahead of it. In the end, they chose not to gamble and agreed to stay another day.

Most of the morning, Mei Li went about with Shunlei and Enlai and introduced Enlai to the town. For those brave enough, she brought them closer and showed them how to preen by working on Shunlei's wings. She explained about dragon colors as she did so, what they signified. It was odd, for humanity to know so little about dragons. Even this basic information was news to them and something to be surprised over.

Shunlei, in turn, showed both the townsmen and Enlai how having a dragon nearby was helpful. He took Enlai to the lake at one point and encouraged the fishermen there to lend them a net. Then he had Enlai carry it out over the water, scooping up fish along the way, and fly it back. The fishermen clapped like it was a show and were perfectly willing to split the spoils with a hungry young dragon.

By the time they left, Enlai was more situated and far happier about the deal he'd agreed to. The townspeople seemed to be cautiously optimistic. Mei Li felt better about leaving him there, too.

They set out the next morning, still doggedly going east. The road was wet and muddy, the horses' hooves kicking up mud splatter on their shoes and clothes. Mei Li sighed down at the splatter and then resolutely ignored it. There wasn't anything to be done about it. At least it was no longer muggy with humidity. It was pleasant again, the sky almost clear aside from a random puffy white cloud making its way across the horizon.

"At the pace we're going," Kiyo observed in an analytical fashion, "I believe we'll reach the Tri-Rivers in about four days."

Hawes turned in the saddle so he could respond. "I believe you're right. I keep hoping to run across some sort of news about the white bone demoness. We might as well tackle the water deity since we have a better idea of his location. Then hopefully we'll pick up the Bai Gu Jing's scent."

"My thought as well," Kiyo agreed.

That seemed to be the sum of the conversation as silence descended again. Mei Li rode along, the sun on her face, and realized the frantic urgency that had brought her here had lessened. She no longer felt she had to get things done *right now*. Had her brain finally understood this was a job that required pacing? Something about settling in Enlai, of spending a day in a place she knew, and seeing it in such a different light, had shown that there were things she could do here. Aside from the major events that had brought her back into the past to begin with, she could still aid Shunlei's goals. No matter how she struggled or focused, she wouldn't be leaving this era anytime soon.

And really, Mei Li was alright with that. Mostly alright. Intellectually, at least, she understood the world wasn't crumbling because she hadn't found all the answers yet. She had time. In fact, she might well sit down and record all of this when back in her own time. It would be a better record than what they currently had. Or should she start on it now? Leaving such records here in the past wouldn't be such a bad thing, right? In that sense, it was exciting. She had a chance to observe history unfold, to be part of it. How many people could experience things as she was now? Mei Li was determined to enjoy it.

Mei Li estimated that it would be another two years before the First Tomes became part of the group. She mulled that over as they rode. Two years of magical incidents that this group solved with no record beyond what they orally passed along to the First Tomes. No, she really did need to start writing things down. Or convince someone else to start writing things down until he arrived. Maybe that should be her immediate goal to work on. Mei Li liked having a dedicated task to focus her.

Oooh, or maybe her goal should be to organize the party so when she finally did meet the First Tomes, it would be all set up and organized and ready for him to assume the mantle. They needed to be in the habit of recording things, and while that was the duty of the Tomes, it was helped by the people who worked with him. Not to mention they needed to have a designated place to store those records. Just carting them about wouldn't do. Yes. That was a better plan. Mei Li felt utterly satisfied with herself and gave her own shoulder a pat. Good job, self.

Right. Now, how best to go about this?

Fortunately, she had plenty of time to think because they weren't going to arrive anywhere quickly.

By the time they reached the Tri-River, they were all grateful for the town spread out along its banks. No one had heard anything about the Bai Gu Jing, but at least they could sleep in an inn for the night.

Two more days of riding brought them to the northern part of Laborde, into the rather sizeable city of Iyhando. It sprawled along the flat plains of Laborde, surrounded on all sides by many, many grape vines and orchards. The scent of ripe fruit filled her nose even as they passed people harvesting. Mei Li knew this area was fertile ground for growing fruit, and some of the best wine came out of Laborde, but she hadn't realized the tradition of growing and cultivating wine went *this* far back.

The city itself had defensive walls, with more than a few magical talismans carved into the bricks making up the wall. Mei Li didn't see a brick wall that often, but it did make sense. This far from the mountains, stone wouldn't be the easiest commodity to come by. Making bricks would be far easier.

Both guards standing at the gate took in people, only stopping them long enough to get a name and reason for visiting before passing them through. Hawes dismounted to speak with the guard, creaking audibly as he did so. Then again, after two straight days in the saddle, they were all creaking.

"I'm Hawes, under the Prince of Horvath's orders to seek out and handle any magical dangers," he introduced himself with a hand to his heart. "With me are my companions. Have you word of trouble in this area?"

The guard—he looked early thirties and weary from standing—perked up visibly. "Master Hawes, I've a message for you. A messenger came through here and left word that a courier from the Prince of Horvath is waiting for you at the Sneaky Mouse and has both news and funds for you. I gather he's been hunting for you for a while."

"I bet he has." Hawes blew out a breath of relief. "For that matter, I've been wondering where he was, as we were supposed to cross paths a day ago. Tell me, sir, are there any troubles here? Anything of a magical nature?"

The guard's attention became razor sharp in its intensity. "Is there a reason why you ask, sir?"

"Indeed so. We're on the trail of a Bai Gu Jing that we believe might be heading toward Laborde. Have you see—"

The guard interrupted him with relief. "Yes, yes, we have. It struck here some days ago. Our fair Lady of the Fields left explicit instructions to send any mage directly to her. I'd go straight to Vine Manor and present yourself today. She's very anxious to confer with you. She spoke with all the guards herself to make sure we understood that."

Hawes blew out a breath. "My thanks, sir, you've saved us some trouble. Stop in at the Sneaky Mouse tonight and I'll buy you a round."

The guard's grin was quick and infectious. "I won't turn down that offer, sir. In fact, let me escort you to Vine Manor. It's a bit convoluted to find if you're not familiar with the city."

"And that I'm not."

"A moment, please." He stuck his head inside the guard room built into the massive city wall, spoke with someone, then came back to them. "I'm Earnest. Come with me, please."

"Of course, lead the way."

Mei Li personally would rather have a chance to clean up some, feel a little less like a drooping bat, but apparently they weren't going to get that chance until later. They followed their guide faithfully, and she more or less tuned out the conversation out of fatigue. Even the city passed by without her direct notice, as she didn't have the energy to really examine it much. It seemed nice, though. Clean and well-kept.

They reached the manor house in short order. Mei Li braced herself in the saddle as Shunlei slid off. Then she carefully dismounted, just waiting for a leg to fold underneath her. Fortunately, they chose to bear her weight instead. A groomsman in tan livery came and took the horse for her, which Mei Li appreciated, and she gave Peanut a pat on the shoulder before she moved off.

"Lord Hawes, we're grateful to see you and your party," a somewhat stuffily dressed man said, eyeing them all with a quizzical brow. His tan livery was a notch above everyone else's, made of very fine linen and not a crease to be seen. The majordomo of the house, if Mei Li was to hazard a guess. "Our fair lady has been quite distraught for some time. If you would follow me. I've sent a runner to alert her as to your presence. I'll bring refreshments out directly so you may rest as you await her. I have no doubt she'll see you directly."

"Thank you," Hawes managed even as he was politely hustled into the house.

Mei Li had not seen a house like this before. Sandstone, with red clay tiles on the roof that arched over the sides. There wasn't a trace of carpet anywhere to be seen as they traversed over terracotta tiles. The hallways were wide, the walls very thick, and the architecture was almost like a fortress in some ways. But she had a feeling the thickness of the walls had more to do with keeping the heat at bay. It was already warm in spring. What must it be like in full summer?

The majordomo led them into a sitting area with its padded white benches lining the windows, furniture made from birch, and some rather interesting murals painted directly onto the walls. Mei Li had no desire to sit again just yet. Her aching bottom protested the idea vehemently. She chose to study the murals instead.

Refreshments had no chance to arrive before the lady of the house practically flew in. Mei Li turned sharply when she heard her, and then blinked. Both guard and majordomo had referred to her as their 'fair lady,' but she assumed that to be something of an honorific. If it was, it was an accurate one. The Lady of the Fields was incredibly fair, with the lightest blonde hair Mei Li had ever seen, skin like cream, and a cute upturned nose. If she were older than thirty, Mei Li would eat her very dusty boots.

She came to a whirling stop just inside the door, looking around the room and at the somewhat startled people in it, her hands grasping nervously in front of her white skirts. "Lord Hawes?"

"Yes." Hawes approached with a smile and gave her a quick bow. "I'm Hawes."

"Thank you so much for coming," she said in a soft, lilting voice that conveyed both relief and distress. "I'm Ilona Harvest, Lady of the Fields. I've a most urgent matter to convey to you and wish to call upon your expertise, if I may."

"That is what we are here for," he assured her. "Let me introduce to you the rest of our party, and then we will hear every detail from you. This is my friend and fellow warrior, Melchior. Our mages, Lady Kiyo, Lord Nord, and Lady Mei. And last but not least, our friend and ally, the dragon, Shunlei the Red."

Lady Ilona seemed heartened at hearing there were three magicians, but her smile stumbled when she heard 'dragon.' She stared outright at Shunlei for two full seconds before recovering. "Forgive me, but I'd never heard that a dragon could attain any other form."

"Just our true form and this one," Shunlei explained patiently with a wave at himself. "It's not something most of my kind does very often. But I find it more convenient when visiting human lands."

"In fact, Shunlei joined us some weeks ago," Hawes informed her, perhaps trying to assure her. "We'd have been in a fine mess if he hadn't. He's an invaluable addition to our party. Whatever trouble you have, Lady Ilona, know we're all determined to settle it. Please, tell us what it is."

"Do sit," she encouraged, leading the way and taking a chair herself. "I'm not sure if you've heard of any of the trouble we've had recently. People call it the Bai Gu Jing."

"We've heard of it," Kiyo assured her darkly. "In fact, we've been searching for it, but no one's heard more than that it was in Thibault, was moving south, and seems to be attacking priests. Do you know more?"

Lady Ilona's eyes turned far too bright. "Unfortunately, I do. Edmond—Priest Edmond, that is, he's a very dear friend to my family. He has been my mentor since birth. He was attacked this past week by the Bai Gu Jing and is in a terrible way. He suffers as if he were fighting off a dreadful illness, and nothing we've attempted has helped him."

Mei Li's mind raced. "When exactly was this attack?"

"Five days ago."

"Then there's still a chance." Seeing she had everyone's undivided attention, Mei Li explained succinctly, "A bite from the Bai Gu Jing is poisonous, like from a venomous snake. He'll slowly die if it's not drawn out properly and the wound cauterized. Usually death happens within seven to ten days. If it's been five days, there's still a chance of saving him."

Lady Ilona's eyes were huge in her face. "You know this for certainty?"

"Yes. Where is he?"

Lady Ilona lost no time in getting out of her seat. "Follow me. I've had him moved to my wing so I could keep an eye on him."

As Mei Li moved, she spoke over her shoulder, "I'll need my satchel of supplies. I'll go fetch it."

"No, follow her," Melchior told Mei Li. "I'll fetch it."

Mei Li shot him a quick smile of thanks. "Shunlei, your dragon fire will come in handy for this, too."

"Of course."

Kiyo headed the opposite way in the hallway. "I'll get my own supplies and meet you there."

Mei Li rushed in Lady Ilona's footsteps. Exhaustion dogged her, and she had to bribe her body and mind with promises of rest as soon as this was over. After this, Mei Li really wanted a hot bath and to sleep for about sixteen hours.

They traversed three long hallways before reaching the room. Lady Ilona opened it without even a knock, just barged in and strode directly to the bedside of her friend.

Mei Li paused in the doorway just long enough to get an idea of the situation. This must be a former nanny's room—well appointed, but plain. The priest looked to be in his late sixties, his white hair damp with sweat and sticking to darkly tanned skin. He was sweating profusely, even with only a simple nightgown and a light sheet over him, his skin underscored with a greyish tinge. The right arm was heavily bandaged, the bandage discolored with a yellow-green stain against the white.

Well, she knew where to start. Mei Li went to the wounded side, reaching for the injured hand. She held it up as she undid the bandage and started unwrapping it.

"Edmond. Edmond, can you hear me?"

Dark eyes opened slowly and traveled to Lady Ilona's face. "Ilona."

Lady Ilona nodded, tears more evident now. "I need you to hold on for a bit longer. This lady who's unwrapping your bandage, she is Lady Mei, a mage. She says she knows how to handle your wound."

His eyes turned to hers next. Edmond was still lucid and tracking, all good signs. Mei Li gave him a smile. "You, sir, have been infected. A Bai Gu Jing is terribly venomous, and that's what's trying to kill you right now. I say try because I won't let it.

"Now, what I'm going to do is paint two talismans directly onto your arm. One of them will draw all of the venom directly to the wound site. The second will drain it. We're going to do that for about an hour or so, until I'm satisfied it's all out. Then my friend there, that's Shunlei, he's going to cauterize the wound with dragon fire. That should kill anything left remaining, and you'll be able to heal after this. How does that sound?"

"Unpleasant," Edmond told her bluntly, a smile trying to creep up. "But necessary. Thank you."

"Don't thank me yet. Lady Ilona, I need a basin, or a bucket, something to drain his arm into. It has to be metal. This venom will melt right through anything else."

She nodded several times, head bobbing. "I'll find you one. What else?"

"Water. It's important to keep him hydrated during all of this. And get your kitchens to make him some light broth, something easy for him to swallow. He'll need nutrients after this to regain his strength. He can try for real food tomorrow."

"I'll see to it immediately." Lady Ilona left the bed and dashed back out.

Kiyo had to slip sideways before Lady Ilona ran her over, and then she marched into the room. "Here, I brought yours and mine."

"Thank you. I'm low on ink, so I might need to borrow yours."

"What are we doing, exactly?"

"Bai Gu Jing is water based," Mei Li informed her. "There's an I Xing method of healing that's perfect for this. We'll use earth and fire to draw out the venom and drain it from his body, and Shunlei's fire to force the wound closed. The bite is vicious enough it won't close on its own."

"And if I didn't have a dragon on hand?"

"A focused fire talisman for two minutes should manage the job." Mei Li shrugged, not sure what else to tell her. The one other time she'd seen this situation, they'd had a dragon nearby willing to help.

Edmond turned to look at Shunlei in astonishment. "You're a dragon?"

"I am," Shunlei answered gently. "Just in my other form at the moment. Don't worry, I can still breathe fire in this form."

Kiyo had no patience for that side branch in the

conversation. "Priest Edmond, is there anyone else we need to treat?"

"No, I was the only one bitten."

"Fortunate," Kiyo observed. "Doing two of you at once might be a bit challenging. Mei, shouldn't you draw that right-side up?"

"I'd run out of room if I tried, his arm isn't that big," Mei Li responded, trying to be patient. The week of helping her dress had broken down another wall with Kiyo, and the woman was much more frank about just blurting things out now. Not that there was much holding her back before. "And I want the talisman to go in the same direction as his veins. It will flow better that way."

"As long as you're not drawing it willy-nilly."

Seriously, this woman.

Lady Ilona came back with a metal basin that had definitely seen some use clutched in her hands. She immediately handed it over to Kiyo, who took it and placed it under Edmond's arm.

"Kiyo,"—Mei pointed to the talisman that was wrapped around the wound, ready to drain it—"if you'll activate that one? I'll do the other."

"On three," she agreed, palm hovering. "One, two, three."

They activated both at the same moment. Mei Li expected it, but when Edmond started writhing on the bed, she found it difficult to keep his arm over the basin. He was weak, yes, but the pain made him strong, and he was clenching his teeth, straining as the venom was forcibly drawn from his body.

Mei Li dug her own weight in. She could feel Kiyo do the same but it wasn't enough, and she couldn't risk the venom hitting either her skin or the bedding. It would burn through the one and infect her. "Shunlei—"

He was there in a second, wrapping around her and clamping onto Edmond's wrist and upper arm. With no discernable strain, he held the arm steady over the basin. "Here?"

"Bless you, yes," she panted. Shunlei's chest pressed up against her back, arms caging her in, but she didn't mind that at all. It felt comforting to have that strength right next to her. He smelled nice, too. Mei Li always associated Shunlei with safety and kindness, and even though she probably shouldn't, she let him support her.

He took her weight without even a noise of complaint, which brought a half-smile to her face. Relaxing, she let him do the hard work for a moment. It was just so tiring to work magic when she already felt dead on her feet. Even Kiyo leaned back, trusting him to hold Edmond steady, though they both kept a keen eye on the wound. It had started out puffy and filled with pus, angry red lines radiating out from it and going up and down his arm. Those lines intensified as the talismans worked, the lines of the talismans turning darker with each second. They were drawing heavily on earth in order to force the body to expel the invader.

Edmond continued to writhe, teeth clenched in pain and straining, Lady Ilona clutching at his good shoulder. She wasn't even trying to dry her tears as she watched him. "Please tell me it's working!"

"Working well," Kiyo assured her, bending over Shunlei's arm to get a closer look. "The red lines are steadily retreating. That means most of the venom is now only in the right arm instead of his body. We're starting to drain, too. Aish!"

The first hissing spat of fluid hit the basin, sizzling on the bottom. Mei Li clapped her hands together, glad. This was exactly how it had gone on her last case. "Oh good, that's a good sign. Kiyo, do you have a good warding spell at hand? I'm out."

"I've got three, why?"

"We'll need to ward the basin after we're done, get it out into an open place. Let Shunlei completely burn it to a crisp.

That's the most effective way to handle the remains."

It seemed to take forever, but eventually it all drained. The wound in the arm sagged, looking bloody and open but no longer aflame. Shunlei very carefully cauterized it, but Edmond was so wrung out he barely said a word.

Mei Li applied a healing balm from her satchel before laying the arm carefully back down on the bed. "Let it air dry and relax tonight. I'll leave the balm here on the bed. You can apply as much as you like. How are you, Edmond?"

He gave her an exhausted smile, eyes barely open. "I feel done in. But so much better than before. Thank you, Lady Mei. Thank all of you."

"I'll check back in on you in the morning," Mei Li promised him. "Drink at least two glasses of water and a bowl of soup tonight, then you can rest."

"Thank you, I shall."

Mei Li was more than ready to follow her own advice. Bath, dinner, bed—it didn't have to precisely go in that order. But she was more than ready to rest.

10

Mei Li awoke the next morning feeling groggy and absolutely loath to move. Lady Ilona had been so frantically grateful the night before that she'd offered to lodge them during their stay, and the entire team had taken her up on it. The bed was sinfully comfortable. Mei Li couldn't imagine moving. Truly, out of respect to the bed and the fine craftsmen who made it, she really should linger to fully appreciate their work.

Mei Li promptly fell back asleep.

When she awoke again, it was much later, the sun slanting in from the windows and heating up her feet to an uncomfortable degree. It had to be mid-morning, at least. The thought of sleeping more sounded quite tempting, but her stomach rumbled petulantly, unhappy with her neglect. Sighing, she threw the covers back and climbed out.

Someone had kindly taken the outfit she'd been wearing yesterday and cleaned it, so she had at least one clean dress to wear. Mei Li took advantage of the ensuite bathroom to wash her hair. She felt much more alive with scrubbed skin and clean clothes on.

She wandered downstairs in search of breakfast and other people.

The majordomo of the house—she had never gotten

the man's name—directed her to an outdoor patio where she found people lingering over lunch. She'd have felt embarrassed about having slept so much, but her body clearly needed it.

"Lady Mei," Lady Ilona greeted with a bright smile. She waved her closer to the round table with its selection of fruits, breads, cheeses, and sliced meats laid out. "Please join us. You slept well?"

"A little too well, thank you." Glancing about, she saw Melchior and Hawes steadily eating, but no sign of Kiyo and Nord. Shunlei spread out over the courtyard in dragon form, eyes sleepy as he sunbathed. It was interesting to see him relax so openly like this in a place he barely knew.

As she took a seat at the table, Mei Li asked, "How is my patient this morning?"

"So much better." Lady Ilona's relief was clear in her radiant smile. "He ate something for breakfast this morning and actually stayed up and read for a while before taking a nap. I'm so grateful to all of you and glad you came when you did."

Mei Li cast her a quick smile as she filled her plate with food. "So am I. Although I also wish we'd been able to get here sooner. For his sake, at least. Not to mention we need to somehow pick up the trail of the Bai Gu Jing."

Hawes lifted his head, swallowing a mouthful. "Lady Kiyo and Nord are on that now. They're doing some complicated seeking spell to track the thing down."

"Are they using Priest Edmond's blood to target with?" That was how Mei Li would do it, at least. With the attack so fresh, odds were some of Edmond's blood was still in the creature. If they could use that as the base of the seeking spell, they'd have a chance to narrow where the Bai Gu Jing was going. It was temporary at best—the blood would fade as the demoness digested it completely—but it would give them a direction at least.

"They are," Hawes confirmed. "They were quite excited about the possibility, as much as Nord is excited about anything."

"Then we'll have a direction soon." Mei Li settled and asked quickly before taking a bite, "When do we leave?"

"The sooner the better, really. We can't give this thing any more headway. Our gracious hostess has given orders for supplies to be packed for us. I also met with the messenger last night and received more funds from the Prince of Horvath."

Melchior sighed, melancholy. "It's a shame to leave so quickly. It's beautiful here. But we really can't give that thing any more headway than it already has."

So, in other words, they were relaxing while they had the chance. Mei Li took that to heart and ate quickly, fully expecting Kiyo and Nord to come back with an answer soon. Seeking spells didn't take much time to set up or implement.

Mei Li chaffed at not being able to fly ahead with Shunlei. She'd gotten entirely too used to doing that with Future Shunlei. But even if she'd had a proper carrier to use, a Bai Gu Jing wasn't something she wanted to tackle on her own. Even with the two of them, it wasn't really advisable. Bai Gu Jings were notoriously slippery and it was always, always suggested to hunt them in a party.

Lady Ilona scooted in closer, dropping her voice to a more confidential tone while Hawes and Melchior began their own conversation. "Lady Mei, I spoke at length with Shunlei this morning. He's a very dear, gentle soul."

Mei Li's mouth being full, she nodded agreement, pleased that Lady Ilona saw this.

"He claims most dragons steal food for lack of a better option. Sometimes, they're either hunted or forced out of the good areas where food is plentiful. He said that before you reached Laborde, he was able to broker a deal with a young dragon and the town near Crimson Lake. I think he passed along the story to me in hopes that I might do likewise. Do you think this advisable?"

"Yes, I do." Mei Li was glad the woman asked for a second opinion and was equally pleased with the chance to back Shunlei up. "There will be a few dragons who are just rotten to the core and impossible to deal with—but the same thing can be said of men. Most of the dragons I've met have been kind. Helpful. If you offer them a safe place to stay, steady work, and food, you'll be amazed at all they'll be willing to do. I've seen dragons help patrol roads, fight dangerous things in their territory, and even fly things back and forth on behalf of another. Wouldn't you like to have such a guardian for your town?"

"It does sound idealistic. I have never met a dragon though."

"I think Shunlei can take care of that. If we meet another dragon in our travels—and I have no doubt we will—then we'll discuss with them the possibility of coming here."

That satisfied her. "Then do so. Shunlei's aid last night is part of the reason why my dear friend is alive and well this morning. And I saw how much you depend upon him. Whenever you asked him for help, he readily gave it. I want that aid and protection for my own people."

"It's wise. And I'm sure he told you that if a dragon claims this territory as their own, they'll keep other dragons at bay?"

"He did. However..." Ilona's brows screwed up in a quizzical fashion. "It does beg the question: How do baby dragons come about if they're that territorial?"

"Ah. They do pair up," Mei Li assured her, amused at the question. "Most of their pairings are for life, in fact. Babies come rarely—about two or three in their lifetimes. Sometimes accidental pairings will result in offspring, but there's always a broodmother somewhere willing to raise them in that case. I believe Shunlei was raised by a broodmother."

"How fascinating. I do wish I had more time to speak

with all of you. I hope you understand you're always welcome here. I want you to stop here if you're ever in this area again."

Mei Li answered on all their behalves with a smile. "We will, thank you."

She heard them before they appeared around the corner, their footsteps quick and heavy as they moved in a quick gallop. Kiyo almost spun out of control as she rounded the corner, catching herself on one of the stone support columns to the porch. "Found her! She's on the shore of the East Sea and heading south."

Nord, slightly more in control of his breath, panted out, "We're about two days behind her, I think. If we leave now, we might be able to catch up in four or five days."

Hawes didn't even have to think about it. "We leave in the next hour. Lady Ilona, you've been an amazing host. We're sad to leave you so quickly."

"I'm just as sad to see you go, but I do understand. Let me make sure my staff has everything together for you." Lady Ilona rose immediately and entered the mansion with a steady swish of skirts, calling out to people as she moved.

Mei Li really wished she'd had a chance to do laundry first. Her saddle-bag was full of dirty clothes. She'd find a stream somewhere when they stopped next, wash at least one thing, and let it air dry overnight. It was the only way. Right now, they had no time to spare, and it was very likely they'd be riding until after the sun set. There would be nothing leisurely about this pursuit.

The next few minutes found everyone throwing things into saddlebags and lashing down bags in organized chaos. Lady Ilona packed food, water, oats for the horses, and even pressed a money pouch on Hawes that she refused to take back. Even after he explained their funding, she was adamant in helping to support their cause.

Mei Li stole five minutes to go check on Edmund and make sure he had enough of the balm for his burn—frankly, nothing but magically-enhanced medicine would work on a dragon's burn. He was far more lucid and healthier than last night and sent her off with profuse thanks.

Then they were back in the saddle with final farewells. They rode as quickly through the city as they dared, careful among all the foot traffic, but as soon as they reached the outside gate, they fell into a ground-eating canter—something the horses could maintain for a while. They'd switch between canter and walking every hour, pacing the horses and themselves. It would be exhausting but effective.

The horses' hooves pounded on the hard-packed dirt of the road, thunderous and loud, leaving no room for conversation. It was warming to a slightly unpleasant degree, and the scant clouds offered no relief. Orchards on either side were picturesque but monotonous after a while. Mei Li found her mind drifting as they rode, her attention wandering to something else entirely. Shunlei once again wrapped his arms around her as he rode behind, and Mei Li was reminded of the conversation she'd had with Lady Ilona. It was true, Shunlei was always right there when she needed him. Mei Li hadn't questioned that before. To her, this was natural. From the day she'd met Shunlei, he had always been right there at her side, offering whatever she needed. Supporting her. It had felt natural to come back in time, meeting Shunlei's younger self, and still have that friendship and support.

But now that she thought of it, really considered it from another angle, it wasn't natural at all. Because Shunlei didn't have that shared history with her yet. He'd barely known her a month. So why was he acting so?

And yes, yes, that question should have occurred to her before, but going back in time five thousand years was *distracting.*

Some of it could be put down to Mei Li's reaction to him. She had been wholly welcoming from the beginning, displaying utmost confidence in him. For Shunlei the Red, that must be rare to receive from a human. He'd like her for that alone. But it didn't explain everything. It barely explained anything.

Mei Li suddenly had questions. But how did she ask any of them?

Because really, how did she ask this without giving away her own position or sounding like a crazy person?

The puzzle remained on her mind as they rode, begging for an answer. Mei Li detested things she couldn't divine on her own. Pure aggravation, that's all it was.

The hours wore on, as did her energy, and by the time the sun set over the horizon, she was willing to give her eye teeth to be able to dismount. Hawes spotted an area near the bank of the Tri-River as it wound its way down to the ocean. The location looked well-used by travelers, but vacant now. They swung into it and dismounted with tired grunts. Peanut blew out a weary breath, glad his insane rider had finally stopped for the night. Mei Li gave him a pat on the neck and promised him some oats.

"Tents?" Melchior asked the group in general. "No tents? It seems clear enough now."

Shunlei voiced disagreement from behind her. "A storm's blowing in. It'll likely hit early in the morning. I can smell it."

Now that he said that, Mei Li could feel the thick humidity in the air. "Oh dear. I wanted to wash a few clothes since we're near the river, let them hang over night."

"I can steam them dry," Shunlei offered. "My own clothes could do with a wash."

"I wish we'd thought of this last night," Kiyo grumbled, already pulling at the saddlebags on her horse. "I think we're all short on clean clothes. Gentlemen, if you'll set up tents, we'll wash what clothes we can. Shunlei, do steam them dry for us. That's the most sensible approach."

No one had any problem with the plan, and they all set

about it. This was a rare night when no one had to think about cooking dinner, as they had plenty of ready-made food prepared for them. Mei Li grabbed clothes and soap, carefully stepping down to the riverbank's edge. There was a rocky patch that looked good to her. She didn't want to work along the dirt-packed section—that would just make the wet clothes turn muddy.

Shunlei walked ahead of her, helping to carry clothes and giving her a hand to balance her over the uneven surfaces. He stayed in place and offered Kiyo a hand too, which the other mage took—at first with surprise, then a subdued smile. Apparently, no matter the age, Shunlei had always been a gentleman.

There wasn't much light, and the single lantern they'd brought with them was carefully perched between Kiyo and Mei Li. Shunlei tackled his own clothes alongside them, borrowing the bar of soap and getting the material sudsy before handing it back.

Not much was said between them as they scrubbed and rinsed, scrubbed and rinsed. Shunlei took over the duty of drying and then carefully folded things and stacked them on a flat rock. It went by surprisingly quickly with three adults focused on the chore.

Mei Li kept fidgeting, wishing Kiyo would finish and go away, give her a chance to ask Shunlei some questions. She lingered a bit longer on the last shirt, pretending to be working out a stain.

A moment later, Kiyo stood and gave the sock to Shunlei. "I'll take these folded clothes back. Mei, bring back a pail of clean water if you would."

"Sure," she answered easily. Yes! She finally had a private bubble. Mei Li tracked Kiyo's progress back to camp with her ears and made sure she was well out of earshot before turning and handing the shirt to Shunlei. "That's the last of it for me. Thank you. This was so much easier with your help."

He flashed a grin. "You're welcome."

In the dim lighting, his skin looked darker, and she could almost believe for a moment it was Shunlei the Black she faced. But it wasn't—his expressions were too unguarded. Only now, when she had the ability to compare, did Mei Li realize how much of Future Shunlei's mannerisms were locked down around her. But then, it made sense, too. He'd known from their first meeting just who she was—had known far more than Mei Li could even now guess. How many times had he been forced to bite his tongue before he revealed everything to her?

Mei Li, now being in that precise predicament, was utterly sympathetic.

Shunlei blew carefully along the shirt, his breath in a steady stream just on the verge of open flame. He paused to cast her a glance. "You might as well ask."

"That obvious, eh?" Mei Li pursed her lips and thought, trying to phrase this right. "Something Lady Ilona said to me brought a question to mind that I don't know how to answer. She made the comment that you were always at my side and supportive. She was awed, I think, by the trust we have between us. I didn't really question that trust until my conversation with her. I know very well why I trust you— after all, I knew about you before I even met you." Which was true, if misleading. "But you know very little of me."

He blew out a steady stream of air again, perhaps buying a moment to think. Then he folded the shirt in his hands, staring down at it as if it held the answers to the universe. "I was young when I made the goal of befriending humanity. Too young to really understand how much work that would involve. I stubbornly set about it anyway, but I've spent five years now slowly battling dragonkind into submission, and I really didn't have much result to show for it. I'd never spoken to a human for more than a few minutes at a time. I'd not formed a friendship with one. It was incredibly frustrating and I was beginning to lose heart until you called out to me. You ask me why I trust you."

Shunlei turned to her, his voice deepening, turning rough along the edges. "Are you blind, Mei? Do you not see the situation for what it is? Every day, you give me another reason to trust you. You've shielded me with your own magic and body. You've given me a defense against magic itself. You look at me and see a friend. *Of course* I trust you."

"Oh. Well. Put like that..." She trailed off lamely.

His eyes were penetrating even as he grinned at her, the smile encouraging her to join the in-joke. "Your trust in me makes even less sense. You were going off a rumor."

"A correct rumor," she pointed out.

"Isn't that the greatest oxymoron in the universe? A correct rumor?"

"I must say, I have to agree. But nevertheless, here we are." Mei Li did feel better having put this out in the open with him. So, he trusted her because she trusted him, in essence. Really, she should have suspected that. That's generally how trust operated.

Shunlei shrugged in agreement and extended a hand toward her. "Let's eat and sleep early. We're going to be up at the crack of dawn."

"A full day long pursuit," Mei Li sighed mournfully, accepting that warm hand. "I don't want to."

"None of us want to," Shunlei assured her sourly. "I'm even less inclined to stay on horseback than you are. I'd fly ahead if it was safe to do so."

"You might need to anyway, at least as a scout. Just so we don't accidentally head off in the wrong direction."

"You're assuming I'd be able to spot this thing from the air."

Mei Li grimaced. "True. Well, hopefully we catch up sooner rather than later."

Shunlei touched his mouth with light fingertips and then

tossed them toward heaven. "From your lips to the gods' ears."

11

Grueling was the word for the second day on the road. Mei Li clung to her saddle grimly and focused solely on keeping up with the group, nothing more. Shunlei was in the same state. After three weeks of riding, his body had adjusted to it, but even then the demanding pace they set was too much. It made their days of riding before look like a casual jaunt in comparison. He almost fell out of the saddle that night, his thighs cramping. Mei Li caught him, then Melchior stepped in, helping him stretch his legs so he could use them without hobbling.

If the second day on the road was bad, the third was worse, just because they were all tired and sore. Not to mention snappish and out of sorts. It was hard to keep an even temper when all anyone wanted was to be horizontal and comatose for eighteen hours. Still, they stuck with it, not stopping until the sun had set.

By the fourth day, Mei Li just prayed they were going the right direction. Kiyo had done a seeking spell again last night, trying to divine a more accurate bearing, but to no avail. Priest Edmond's blood had faded out. They were riding south, blindly, and hoping for the best. At the moment, it was all they could do.

The southern highway met up with the East Sea and

followed it down. The sea wind was crisp and salty as it flowed over them, seagulls squawking noisily above their heads. It felt oddly cool for being so late in the spring, but then oceans were naturally cooler than inland. Mei Li was grateful to have Shunlei's warmth pressed up against her back, as she would eventually have started shivering without it.

The road narrowed at one point, crammed as it was between the ocean and the rolling foothills, leaving only a narrow pass. They had to reshuffle and go in one at a time and they stayed in that formation even as the road widened back out.

Peanut blew out a breath as they dropped back down to a walk. Mei Li stroked his neck, soothing him. "I promise carrots and apples and all the oats when we stop in the next town, my friend. Thank you for being so patient."

The horse flicked an ear at her, showing he was listening. He really was a good-tempered gelding.

"Lady Mei."

"Hmm?" Mei Li turned her head a little toward Shunlei, partially to hear him better. The crashing of the waves against the shore was thunderous in this section, the sound echoing back from the hills.

"You said you were on a journey to find your master when you came across us."

"I did, yes."

"How did you lose contact with him?"

Mei Li phrased this carefully in her head before answering. "Well, there was a bit of a disaster in my town. We took separate ships when leaving, with plans to meet up in a particular place. But my ship didn't make it—we were shipwrecked. I was the only survivor. It took me two years to get back, and by that point, no one knew where he had gone."

"Oh." Shunlei ruminated on this for a moment. "It's just that I haven't seen you ask for him anywhere we've been."

Mei Li silently kicked herself. Shunlei was observant—

she *had* to remember that. "So far, we've crossed through areas I've already searched." Five thousand years into the future, anyway.

"Ahhh. That makes sense. Where have you not searched?"

"The far south and the far north-east."

"I see. When we reach those areas, I will help you search."

Such a sweet, gentle soul, this man. "Thank you."

"Can you—" Shunlei cut himself off, stiffening.

She looked around hastily, trying to see what had caught his attention, but it was just the road stretching out ahead of them. Well, no, farther along were signs of civilization as rooftops peeked into view over the rise. "What?"

"You said that a Bai Gu Jing would have a very distinctive smell," he said slowly, before inhaling deeply. "For just a moment, I caught a waft of something that smelled of the grave, entwined with a strong, flowery perfume."

"That's it." Raising her voice, Mei Li called out strongly to the head of the group. "HAWES!"

Hawes immediately stopped and stood in his stirrups, looking back at her. "Trouble?"

"Shunlei smelled it!" Mei Li navigated Peanut forward so she was more central to the group. Everyone moved around to hear better.

Shunlei was still breathing in deeply, grunting with dissatisfaction. "I can't pick it up again, though. It was just for a moment."

"Bai Gu Jing?" Melchior inquired hopefully.

"Yes." Shunlei growled low in his throat. "The scent wasn't strong, and only for a moment. I'd say she passed through here rather than stopped. We're going the right direction. That's all I can say for sure."

Hawes made a noise that was a mixture of relief and grimness. "That's all we need to know for now. Let's keep going. Shunlei, switch and ride with me. I want you to guide us forward."

"Yes, of course."

Mei Li locked her elbow, something he could hang onto as he slid down. He gave her a quick smile before maneuvering over and hefting himself up behind Hawes. All the practice of mounting and dismounting made the motion more fluid now than the awkward clambering he'd done initially.

They continued riding. Mei Li kept a sharp eye on Shunlei this time and saw him lift his head and scent the air several times, like a bloodhound trying to find the trail. As they got closer to the town, he reached around Hawes and pointed, saying something, his hand illustrating. With them moving at a canter now, Mei Li had no prayer of hearing him, but he must have picked up on the scent.

Finally! Some noticeable progress.

Mei Li had no idea which town was ahead of them—in her current timeline, nothing stood here—but it was something of a commercial hub, with ships coming in and out of port. Tracking the Bai Gu Jing in an urban area would make it that much harder on all of them, not only in tracking her down, but in fighting.

Shunlei's finger came up again, this time to the right, and her head swiveled to see where he pointed. A large shrine sat on the rise above the town, set a little apart from the populace. Mei Li's lips spread from her teeth in a feral smile. Of course the Bai Gu Jing would head there, hoping for some priestly meat.

But that also meant they would have the space they needed to fight her properly. Assuming they could catch her outside of the two-story building and in the walled-off grounds of the shrine. Mei Li wasn't counting on it. Frankly, her luck never ran that good.

They reached the base of the hill on which the shrine sat. There was a stepping stone at the path, and they all dismounted there, tying the horses to the hitching posts. Peanut immediately put his head down into the watering trough. Mei Li spared him a pat even as she reached for her kit, pulling out talismans and putting extra ink, paper, and the rope-trap she had made for this very purpose into her belt pouch for easy access.

"Welcome, travelers," a female voice intoned formally from the base of the stairs. Mei Li craned her neck around Peanut to see the speaker. She was a petite woman, thin in body and face, a cowl draped over her head in such a way that it hid her hair completely. A pleasant smile rested on her face as she asked, "Are you seeking peace?"

"We're seeking a Bai Gu Jing on your grounds," Hawes answered bluntly.

The priestess gave a startled intake of air. "There's a white bone demoness here?!"

"We've been tracking it for weeks. We believe it's here— or at least its scent is quite strong here. I'm Hawes."

"Giselle of Ocean Shrine. Please, come with me. We can confer with the head priestess."

"After you." Hawes made to follow but passed the word quietly back, "I'll talk with the head priestess, you fan out and find that thing."

Mei Li nodded and forced her aching legs up the multitude of steps to the shrine gates. After this, she would demand a hot bath and the chance to sleep on a real mattress tonight. But that was a fantasy for later.

Upon reaching the tall, dark wood gates, they did split up. Mei Li went right, following the gravel path that led between old, twisted peach trees in full bloom and the pond lovingly tended in the center of the small courtyard. She heard Shunlei follow, so she turned to ask him in a low tone, "Do you smell her?"

"Yes, but it's confusing." He paused, brows furrowed together in frustration as his head panned the area. "Her scent is literally everywhere. It's like she paced this area several times."

"Looking for an opening to get a priest alone, maybe?"

"Perhaps. I'm not sure. I just know I can't get a fix on her. She was here very recently, though, that I'm sure of. And I didn't smell her leaving this area, at least not from the main entrance."

"That's something."

There weren't many people out here in the courtyard, just a few either meditating on the long rock benches or crossing to another destination. The shrine itself had two stories, an open wrap-around porch for each, with the doors open on all sides to let the ocean breeze through. Mei Li had a decent view inside, but obviously couldn't see everything from where she stood. Since everyone else had already headed for the back, she chose to head into the main level.

Mei Li got all of three steps inside when screams erupted from the back. Swearing, she immediately raced around the altar, the cushions lining the walls, and the curious people popping up from their prayers, pushing her way through as necessary. Shunlei, faster than she, beat her outside by a sizeable margin.

The back garden was no longer the pristinely kept landscape it once was. In the twenty seconds it had taken her to get out there, destruction had reigned. Kiyo and Nord were already unleashing spells, talismans held up in front of them by their first two fingers, Melchior on the other side, hemming in the quarry. Mei Li took two seconds to catch her bearings.

The Bai Gu Jing stood between them, lips curled back in a feral fashion, her mouth stretched too wide to belong to a human. She wore the clothes of a matron in mourning—the easiest clothes to wear with the veil to cover her face, mask her features. They were excellent shape shifters, but when aroused by prey, their mimicry fell apart. This one had been smart enough to take precautions when in a target-rich environment.

She was hungry, and her true form showed through in little flashes, discernible to one looking for the signs. The black on black highlighted the bones starting to show through the façade of her skin. It was a macabre appearance, with half of her face and part of her hand more bone than flesh.

Shunlei didn't hesitate. He spat out a fireball, and for a moment, it looked as if he'd catch the Bai Gu Jing off-guard. But she spied the attack from the corner of her eye, twisting and flailing in a graceful move like a dancer pirouetting. Only the wide sleeve of her arm and the black veil were scorched. She flung both coat and hat off, preventing herself from being burned, then turned and spun again to avoid Nord's attack of earth.

Mei Li readied her rope, looking for a good chance to throw it, snag her prey. But with Shunlei in front of her, her team on either side, she couldn't find the right opening without risking snagging one of them instead. The garden was not so large that they could easily fight without being right on top of each other. It was likely the reason why Shunlei stayed human instead of shifting to his deadlier form.

"Dragoooooon~" the Bai Gu Jing crooned in a hiss, eyes nearly green with greed. She launched herself at Shunlei.

Alarmed, Mei Li shouted, "DON'T LET HER BITE YOU!"

Whether or not Shunlei meant to heed her was a moot point as the Bai Gu Jing crashed into him. Shunlei rocked backward, lost his balance against the uneven surface of the pond's edge, and went down with the Bai Gu Jing on top of him.

He grabbed her chin, shoving her head up and away, preventing her from biting any part of him. The other hand tried to cage her against his own torso, but she was already struggling to get free. Her kind was notoriously strong, so much so that she was a match in physical strength for even a dragon.

Mei Li snatched her bag around to the front, frantically rooting through it for spells. Even as she searched for the right talisman, she requested sharply, "Holding spells!"

"On it." Kiyo leapt into the fray, slapping a talisman onto the Bai Gu Jing's legs and locking them together with a sharp click of the ankles and knees.

Melchior was there in the next second, grabbing the Bai Gu Jing's other arm, keeping her from raking her claws against Shunlei again. She'd already scored him once, and the wounds bled brightly.

It felt like an eternity instead of seconds, but Mei Li found the talisman she needed. She'd prepped four of the things in preparation for this very moment, so why they decided to hide in her pouch, she didn't know, just cursed. Darting in between everyone, she slammed the talisman onto the back of the struggling demon. "From the earth you've come, to the grave you'll return!"

The Bai Gu Jing howled like the lost soul it was, writhing in all their grips, desperate to get away now. But as much as she was hurt, she shouldn't have the strength to howl. She should have just gone *poof.*

Cursing, Mei Li realized that in her exhaustion, she didn't have the usual reservoirs of magic. Between everything she had done in the past three months, she had overextended herself. She was currently no match for the Bai Gu Jing. "Nord!"

Nord, bless him, immediately leapt in as well and slammed his hand over the talisman, pouring his magical power into it and re-activating it all over again. This time, it worked as it should have. The Bai Gu Jing's howl turned into dust motes, lingering on the wind as she abruptly became nothing but ash and memory.

They stood there for a second, shaking with adrenaline in the aftermath. Then Mei Li fell to her knees, pulling the ruined shirt aside to look carefully at Shunlei's injury. The claws hadn't gone in particularly deep, but she'd scored three across his upper torso and along the top of his shoulder. It looked so incredibly painful. Her own chest clenched in sympathy, and she hissed in a breath. Mei Li hated that he had gotten hurt. Both Future and Past Shunlei somehow always took the brunt of the battle. "Shunlei, how bad is it?"

"Burns," he admitted between clenched teeth.

"They've got blessed water inside." Kiyo was already gathering up her skirts, dashing that direction.

Hawes came puffing out, carrying white cloth. "I saw what was going on up above. I've got some makeshift bandages."

Mei Li accepted them and pressed them against the wound. "I need to get him inside."

Melchior was the one to reach down and lift him up onto his feet. Shunlei wobbled a little, a grimace of pain on his face. He hadn't landed easily, and having a demon slam him into the rocks couldn't have been pleasant either.

"Don't bring him in just yet." Kiyo darted back with two vials of water in either hand. "Let's wash those out here, not inside. Easier to clean up."

Good point.

As Kiyo carefully rinsed out the wounds, an elderly priestess came out, her mouth round with horror as she took in her wrecked garden and the blood splattering the area. Her voice creaked and squeaked with age. "Oh my. Oh my oh my. Is everyone alr—no, clearly everyone is not alright. Is the white bone demoness gone, at least?"

"Yes, she's defeated," Hawes reported to her. "I'm sorry for the mess we made."

"No, no, I'm horrified it was even on our sacred grounds to begin with. Don't mind this. Rather, let's get this young man inside and attended to. You are welcome to stay here as you mend."

"Thank you, Priestess, we're grateful for the hospitality."

"You need to have a cleansing out here," Mei Li threw in,

even as she helped Kiyo wash out the wound. "A concentrated gathering of a Bai Gu Jing's essence will spawn another one."

"I'll attend to it myself. Inside, first. Let's attend to the living before the dead."

Mei Li had a feeling she was going to like this woman.

12

Shunlei was good-natured about getting patched up. Between a priestess's blessing of healing, and Kiyo's healing spells, he was assured to be on the mend and well able to resume normal activities by the next day. They were all anxious to keep a close eye on the wound, however, as it could easily get inflamed. And an inflamed wound with dark energy lingering in it was A Bad Thing.

The rooms they were given to rest in were traditionally set aside for travelers. Mei Li insisted on having the room next to Shunlei's so she could hear him in the night if he needed her. Hawes volunteered to keep an eye on Shunlei while they were in the baths. Mei Li was glad to see that friendship cementing and encouraged him even as she gathered up clothes for her own bath.

After soaking for a solid hour in hot water, getting the traces of the Bai Gu Jing off her skin, she felt human again. Mei Li put dirty clothes back in her room, and a passing priestess told her where to find the dining room, where everyone else was already mid-meal. Mei Li found a spot open next to Shunlei and joined him.

The spread looked scrumptious and still warm, steam rising gently from several platters. Mei Li might be late to dinner but not by much. She loaded a plate up, ears perked as she caught up with the current thread of the conversation.

Hawes, sitting across from her, was responding to something Kiyo, on the other side of Mei Li, had said. "—certainly advisable from my standpoint. We're all exhausted."

"What are we talking about?" Mei Li inquired, relaxing back into her seat.

"I suggested staying here for a few days." Kiyo lifted her cup, what looked to be a white wine, and nodded toward Hawes. "Our illustrious leader agrees with me so far."

Hawes flashed her a smile even as he spread butter onto a roll. "As I said, we're all exhausted. Traveling here took a toll on us, and none of us have been able to rest for more than a day in over a month."

"Two," Melchior corrected at his side. The man looked as if he'd nod off into his plate soon, his head bobbing, although he ate with gusto.

Turning his head, Hawes stared at him, expression falling. "Has it really been two months?"

"If you're talking about the original members. Closer to one for Mei Li and Shunlei."

Hawes shook his head, still dismayed. "No wonder we're all at the end of our tethers. Alright, I say we stay here for three days at least. Possibly four. We'll rest up, re-supply—"

"Your fellow magicians definitely need time to create more talismans. We're all dangerously low," Kiyo warned him. "You'd best make that five days."

"Five, then. Those talismans are a bit too complicated for my simple magic. I won't be much help there, but I'll do what I can. Maybe leave the simpler talismans for me—those I can usually manage." Hawes turned his head, panning the table so he could meet each magician's eyes. "All of you?"

"It's why I was so slow to react to Shunlei's distress," Mei Li muttered sourly into her plate. "I had talisman papers cut and ready, but few with them inked. I'm disorganized at this point, I think we all are. Low on ink, will be low on paper soon, and my magical energy is low enough to be sputtering."

"Like a candle in a typhoon," Nord threw in rather poetically. And accurately.

"Then five days. Lady Mei." Hawes handed her a chilled pitcher, which she took with both hands to avoid dropping it. "I know we're very far south now, but I feel we need to reverse directions and attend to that water deity. You said it's in Thibault. You're sure of that direction?"

"I am," she answered carefully. "It will be somewhere near the coast, I believe, as it will stay near the water."

"That's still a lot of territory to cover." Melchior gave a sour grunt. "Like with the Bai Gu Jing, we only have a vague direction to go off of."

"I don't think any of us have another chase in us right now." Hawes let out a long sigh, his exhaustion showing in the lines of his face and the slump of his shoulders. "Alright. We'll send forward some inquiries, see if anyone has something to report. But we need to rest. Five days it is."

Shunlei seemed very excited about this, for some reason. "Will you disperse some funds to the rest of us so we can go shopping?"

Hawes blinked at him, then seemed to shake himself. "I knew I was forgetting something. We tore out of Lady Ilona's house so quickly, I never got a chance to hand out purses. I'll do that first thing in the morning. Or swing by my room after dinner and I'll hand them out then."

Mei Li looked askance at the dragon sitting beside her. Was there something he wanted to buy in particular? Or was he just excited to finally have human currency, and be able to go through a human town? The latter was more likely. "Are you up to shopping?"

Shunlei flashed her a quick smile. "The wound is more irritating than anything."

Well, considering he battled fellow dragons on a regular basis, perhaps this really was only a flesh wound to him. And she couldn't discount a dragon's hardier constitution. "Good. I'm relieved to hear it."

"The Prince of Horvath does want us to take a moment and write an account of what's happening," Melchior threw in. "He likes to stay abreast of the situation as much as possible. In between creating your talismans, try to find time to write brief reports of what we've encountered."

This opened a conversational door for Mei Li's own campaign. Although she'd have to start out small to avoid sounding like a lunatic. "I can certainly write up things. And really, I think someone should be keeping a copy of what we report." Seeing that she had their attention, Mei Li added in a practical manner, "Think about it. How many people know how to defeat a Bai Gu Jing? Or can recognize trouble in a sentient forest? Or know how to combat a blood mage?"

Hawes pursed his lips, thinking this over.

Kiyo didn't need that second. "Not many, and I see your point, Mei. Really, if we could scatter records of our deeds around the world, in places people can go and read them, they'd have a ready resource. An instruction manual, of sorts. If we equip them with proper knowledge, they have a better chance of combating the trouble themselves. Our makeshift gathering of volunteers isn't sustainable."

Not in its current form, anyway. Mei Li had to bite her tongue before she said that aloud. Her mouth was not to be trusted some days, and this was definitely one of them.

Mei Li couldn't see Nord from here—he sat in line with her and Shunlei—but his tone conveyed that he liked this idea. "I would say all the major temples should receive copies of our reports. That's where people turn to first when trouble falls—either for help or shelter. If they're forearmed, all the better."

Mei Li mentally cheered this line of thinking. "It might be difficult for us to do that on a regular basis. Traveling as we are. But maybe an appointed record keeper could help us?"

"We send to a person in charge of this, let them handle the logistics of getting updated reports everywhere else?" Hawes nodded several times, his enthusiasm for the idea growing with each nod. "Yes. Yes, I can see how that would work better. I'll request for such in my next letter to the prince. It's a very viable idea."

Phew, alright. Seed planted. Mei Li didn't want to harm the timeline of the past, but she didn't see how planting the idea of the first Tomes would cause trouble. Shunlei's wife had been the one to drive that forward, to make sure the Tomes existed. Mei Li still wasn't sure when the woman would come into the picture. But creating a basis for the idea could only help her whenever she did join.

This much was fine.

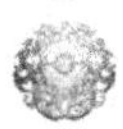

Priestess Giselle opened a room specifically for them so the three magicians could spread out and work. As they had their own mages in training here, there was not only space dedicated for such but supplies readily at hand. She generously donated several items.

Mei Li spent the morning going through shops, buying ingredients, then retreated back to the room. They divvied the basic talismans between them—holding spells, fire starting, traps, and so forth. Mei Li took on traps and fire starting, as they seemed to burn through those (pun not intended).

She took a break mid-afternoon and strolled through the recently cleansed back garden. As she walked, she stretched her arms over her head, rolling her neck around on her shoulders. It was nice to not be in a saddle today, although it would have been a good travel day, with the fair weather.

In the few weeks she'd been in this time, she'd not had much of a chance to really think on it. But several things were falling into place, giving her an entirely new perspective. Shunlei recognizing her instantly in the future—of course that made sense now. But the things that had bothered her before—like how he knew her tastes in food and clothing, or could anticipate what she would want to do next—all made much more sense now. She would travel with him for ten years. Be a friend and constant companion with him. Of course he'd know all of that about her.

What surprised her more was that even after five thousand years, he still remembered it all. And they said a Tomes' mind was sharp. Shunlei's might well put theirs to shame.

It also made more sense to her now why he had been so angry she had been lost in the first place. So quick to take her in as family. To him, she was family.

But it did beg the question—how much did she tell him? Mei Li must have told him something, if he knew she'd meet him again in the future. How much could she even tell him without risking messing up the past entirely?

And while Mei Li didn't have to think about this now, she really should consider how she'd gracefully extract herself later. The spell was set to keep her here until she learned how to defeat Odom and Zaffi. Ten years was a long while. The group would certainly ask questions and possibly look for her if Mei Li just suddenly disappeared after the battle. It was something she needed to carefully consider.

She might be able to split from them with the excuse that she needed to hunt down her missing master. But would that excuse still hold water after ten years? Ten years of them gallivanting around the countryside, no less. Hmm, likely not.

Oh dear. She really would have to come up with a good plan. Otherwise this wouldn't go down well at all. Stupid spell. Really, why did it land her *here* of all times? Couldn't it have done it closer to Odom's appearance? Wouldn't that have made more sense? It was causing Mei Li needless complications.

"Mei."

Turning at this hail, she spied Shunlei coming toward her. He looked better this morning, not as pale and tight with pain as he had been after the attack. His hair, for once, was neatly brushed as well and fell in a smooth curtain down to mid-torso.

"Are those new boots?" she asked, intrigued.

"They are. I stumbled across an excellent cobbler. He can custom-make any shoe to fit your foot within half a day. I'll introduce you to him. I think we're all in need of new boots."

It was all the traveling doing hers in. Even with Mei Li's being relatively new. "Yes, please."

"Excellent!" he said with an engaging smile. "But here, I bought something for you."

Mei Li looked at the bundle in his hand, wrapped in simple white cloth and twine. She accepted it with bemusement. "Thank you?"

"Open it," he encouraged her.

That was not polite in her culture—you weren't supposed to open gifts in front of the giver—but apparently dragons had different rules regarding that. She obligingly undid the twine and the cloth fell away to reveal a neck pillow. It was made of sturdy cotton, soft to the touch, and dyed in such a way that it looked like puffy white clouds on a blue sky. "Oh! Oh, it's cute. And feels very soft."

Shunlei looked pleased that she liked it. "I know you sometimes wake up with a crick in your neck. Pillowing your head on the bags isn't truly comfortable. I saw this and thought you'd benefit from it."

It was an incredibly thoughtful gift. "I'll use it well. Thank you. I hope you bought one for yourself?"

"I did," he admitted gleefully, like a young child who'd successfully raided the pantry for sweets. "Two, in fact. I couldn't decide between them. There's all sorts of blankets and such in the same store. In fact, they sold a traveling set that included a down padding, like a thin mattress. It looked very portable still, and with the summer months coming up, perhaps lighter blankets might be best?"

"To combat the heat with," Mei Li agreed thoughtfully. It was true, with them camping outdoors half the time, this was a consideration. They needed to sleep as well as they possibly could and stay rested. Her current collection of blankets she slept with were thick and warm and not something suitable for summer months. "I think I want to visit that shop. You truly found all the best places while you were out, didn't you?"

Shunlei shrugged, still with that happy sparkle hovering about him. "I love shopping in towns like this. I never know what you humans will come up with next."

"I'm definitely shopping now," Mei Li said with conviction. "In fact, let me go into town with you today so I can order those shoes. No need to force the man to make them on the spot for me when I'll be here for several days yet anyway. I'll put my pillow away and join you at the front door."

"It's fine, I can follow you out. Perhaps we should mention the stores to the others?"

"Yes, let's do that as we go." Mei Li walked around the pond, heading for the back door. Come to think of it, the mages would all be quite busy, but Shunlei had little to occupy his time. "Aside from shopping, how will you spend your time?"

"I thought I'd fly up and down the coast for a bit," he informed her, a trifle wistfully. "There's bound to be a few dragons in this area, as the sea makes for good hunting grounds."

That was a very good point. "You'll try to convert them over, too?"

"I hope to. It shouldn't be difficult. I've heard no tale of trouble from dragons in this area which means there's either none about—I'll be surprised if that's the case—or that they've struck a good balance in the area with the humans. If they're already peace-minded, it shouldn't be hard." Shunlei made a warding gesture with one hand. "I feel like I just jinxed myself."

"Don't do that," she agreed with a laugh. "You've got enough of an uphill battle as it is."

Giving her a rueful look, he agreed wryly, "Don't I know it."

Gaining the building, Mei Li popped her head into the workroom to tell everyone what they were doing, then put her new present away in her room. Shunlei offered his arm as they reached the main gate, and she gratefully took it, sliding her hand into his elbow.

"Thank you. The stairs are a little slick and worn, aren't they?" Mei Li kept a careful eye on them even as she stepped lightly down. There was a definite wear in the center, and the rainfall last night hadn't helped matters.

"My heel skittered out once on my way down. I don't want you to take a tumble."

"What a coincidence, neither do I." She spared him a saucy grin, pleased when he snickered. It was the nice part of being in Shunlei's company. They had the same sense of humor. "Phew, alright, we're at the bottom. Shoes first?"

Shunlei nodded acceptance and led them right along the road. "I've discovered in the time I've spent with all of you that dragons and humans are vastly different in many ways. So I'm not sure how to ask this without offending you."

She wasn't at all surprised at his hesitancy. This Shunlei was still learning about humanity, after all. She encouraged him with a nod and an inquiring noise in the back of her throat.

"Kiyo mentioned that you only had three changes of clothes, and this concerned her?"

For Shunlei, who only had two, it probably did seem a strange worry. But then, he spent a lot of time in dragon form, so it wasn't like the clothes he had saw much use. "Ah, yes. It would. Most humans have several changes of clothes, you see. Kiyo's just as worried about you. I think she feels that because you are a dragon there's a different set of customs involved somehow, but she keeps poking me about perhaps taking you shopping."

Shunlei glanced down at the clothes he wore. "They are a trifle worn. I've seen more use of them in the past few weeks than in the years I've owned them. Perhaps we should both shop."

"Yes, I think so. As for me, after I was shipwrecked, I didn't have anything that survived with me except what I was wearing. I've been steadily trying to amass my belongings ever since." Which was mostly the truth.

Shunlei indicated the shop ahead. "Then let's start with new boots."

"An excellent place to start."

The shoemaker was just short of being churlish, but the man knew his business. Mei Li had to give him that. He had her foot measured in seconds, wrote quick notes on her sizes, then shooed her off to the other side of the store. Mei Li went to pick out leathers and dyes with his wife, chose something sensible but flexible enough that she wouldn't feel like a hobbled horse, and received a promise in return that they'd be done in three days.

Exiting from there, she pulled Shunlei to the shop next door, which had several men's coats hanging in the window. "How about something not white?" she suggested even as she pulled him through the front door.

Shunlei grimaced agreement, willingly leaving his hand in hers. "I bought the white on a whim, as I liked the look of it. But it does get stained easily. Too easily on trips such as these."

"Yes, it's a real problem. And there's not many colors that will work well with your skin and hair—but I think blue, green, or black will do rather well. Green especially."

The store's interior was slightly dimmer, certainly cooler, and well-organized. Mei Li had to adjust her assumption of it being a clothing store for men almost immediately. The store was neatly divided into three groups: women's to the left, men's to the right, and children's in the back. They didn't have a wide selection of clothing but a little bit of everything, excluding shoes. No doubt because of their shoe cobbler neighbor.

Mei Li went straight for the hunter green coat, a lighter version than the one Shunlei currently had, and something that would be more appropriate for the summer weather they were sliding into. Turning, she held it up against his chest, eyeing him judiciously. "Yes, this looks excellent on you. What do you think of the color?"

"It's very keen," he approved. "I'm not sure if it will fit?"

"Try it on," she encouraged.

He slipped off the white wrap robe he wore, handing it over to her, and accepted the green to try on. It was a near-perfect fit, only a little long in the sleeves. "I think it fits well enough?"

"I can roll the sleeves up a little, hem them to the right length." Shunlei gave a pleased nod. "It fits fine everywhere else. This, then. What goes with it?"

"I think those black pants would."

It took a few minutes, but they assembled two more outfits for him. The shop owner, an aged and stooped grandmother, came and took everything from them to the counter so she could start wrapping things. Mei Li went to the women's section and did her own browsing, although nothing quite fit. As usual. Why did she have to be that much taller than the average woman?

Shunlei eyed the skirt she held up against herself with a frown. "That's a good two inches too short."

"I'm a little on the tall side," Mei Li explained on a

resigned sigh. "This is usually the frustration I have when I shop. And also why I haven't filled out my wardrobe yet."

The grandmother overheard her and lifted her head to call out in a creaking voice, "If you'll go directly across the street, dearie, that's my daughter's shop. She'll custom-make what you'll like. She's a fair price."

"Oh? I'll see her next, then." Really, getting something tailored to her was the only sane option Mei Li had.

"I'll pay for mine, and then we'll go speak with her."

"Alright." Mei Li lingered near the display case for women's combs, hair sticks, and tooled belts. One comb in particular caught her eye, and she stared at it wistfully. It was a fine one, but she didn't have the means right now to indulge in such an impulse buy. A comb she could live without. Clothes she could not.

Well, she *could*. But it would invite a whole new set of problems she'd rather avoid.

Shunlei caught her wistful stare and cleared his throat. "If there's something you like, buy it."

With a shake of the head, she explained, "Clothes and boots take precedence. Thank you, Mistress. Shunlei, I'll meet you over there."

"As you will."

She left him behind and darted across the busy street, finding the store in question. A younger version of the grandmother sat in front of a table, her hand steadily putting stitches into dark cloth. It was the high brow that gave the relationship away. She looked up with a polite smile. "Welcome."

"Your mother sent me to you," Mei Li informed her. "I need tailored clothes."

"Yes, of course, do you know your measurements?"

"I do, but feel free to measure me again."

"I'd rather do that," the woman admitted, putting her sewing down and fetching a white tape before bustling around the table. She had to slip sideways to avoid knocking over a stack of cloth bolts. Half of her shop was a selection of cloth, the other a workspace for three women all sitting at their own tables and steadily sewing on various projects. "What would you like to order?"

"Two full outfits, but I'm not sure if you have time to finish them before I leave. It will be four days."

"Four days is plenty of time," she assured, hands busy as she manipulated Mei Li's limbs to measure them. "I hope you're not going south, though."

Mei Li's attention sharpened on her. She saw Shunlei duck through the door and paused a moment so he could hear her inquiry as well. "Why do you say that? Is trouble brewing down south?"

"That's what my brother said." The woman cast her a glance from under her dark lashes, pushing a stray tendril of hair out of her oval face. "He went to fetch us cloth and supplies, as he normally does, out of Bader this past month. Half the suppliers he normally sees at the market weren't there. Probably avoiding the roads. He said everyone's hunting for someone who stole a sword." She shrugged, as if that shouldn't have been a big deal.

And it wouldn't be. Unless... "Did he say where the sword was stolen from?"

"Mmm, I think he said it was some kind of war trophy, that it came out of a mausoleum or something."

Ghost General's Sword, then. It must be. A little earlier than she'd been expecting it, but the area and timing was right for it. She was torn, though. That meant they were half-way in between two problems. Which way was better for them to go? North, since they were already relatively nearby? Or south, putting them on the opposite side of the continent from the water deity?

The logistics cramped her brain. She shot Shunlei an uncertain look, biting at her bottom lip. He'd clearly picked up on the implications and shared the same uncertainty. But he gave her a nod, as if promising they'd bring it up with everyone later.

It wasn't a problem she could solve right now, at any rate. Or even this week. So, she put it aside for now and focused on the more immediate problem. "Thank you for the warning."

"I tell everyone as I can." Straightening, the shop owner looked her over with pursed lips. "Well. What style and color are we aiming for?"

"This will take a minute," Shunlei predicted rhetorically.

Mei Li threw her head back in a laugh. "Oh, it'll take more than a minute."

13

Mei Li and Shunlei reported what they'd heard at the market, and Melchior did some investigation while everyone else prepped more talismans and shopped for necessities. He came back with the report that the sword seemed to have been cursed, confirming Mei Li's suspicions.

It was Ghost General's Sword, alright, but maybe it hadn't had time to corrupt the thief yet. They hadn't heard anything about someone on a killing rampage, at least. And since Mei Li knew for a fact that a water deity was on the rampage up north, they chose to follow the more concrete lead.

Their mini-vacation did them all good. Mei Li was very sad when it ended. Part of her—the part that was a child—wanted to whine and throw a fit and beg for just one more day.

Being a responsible adult was sometimes no fun at all.

Mei Li had everything organized on the bed to re-pack but was currently struggling with it a bit. She'd packed most of it last night, leaving essentials out for this morning, but her sleep clothes and new pillow absolutely refused to fit. Which wouldn't do at all. So, she'd resorted to taking everything out again and writing a talisman into the bottom of the bag to widen its dimensions. Pocket space, that's what Abe called it, and it only worked to a small degree. She couldn't jam anything in there. But it gave her just enough wiggle room to fit the rest.

With her wrestling of the bag, Mei Li had a bad feeling she was now running late. A feeling confirmed not a minute later when Shunlei knocked on her door and stuck his head in. "Mei? Having trouble?"

"I had to repack everything," she explained, jamming the last bit in and latching the top down. "Ten minutes."

He regarded her with his head cocked. "Hold that thought." Then he was gone again.

Mei Li had no idea what she was supposed to be holding. With the bag now packed, she pulled on socks, then shoes. Her hair was still in loose locks around her, and she growled in aggravation when she realized she'd packed her comb in the rush.

Maybe she could just chop all of her hair off. Oooh, tempting thought. A shaved head would be much easier to take care of.

Shunlei was back before she could hunt down scissors. In his hand was a lovely pair of combs, both of them a beautiful white jade with the carving of dragons along the edge. She stared at them with no comprehension for the longest moment because those could not possibly be *here*.

Those were the exact combs Future Shunlei had given her to wear the first night she'd met him. The ones she'd felt hesitant to use because they were so exquisite and expensive. She'd known he'd not bought them for her that night, that they'd been something he already had on hand. But...to have bought them now and somehow kept them for five thousand years—it boggled her mind. It truly did.

And it was such a Shunlei thing to do. She suddenly missed Future Shunlei very much. Unable to check the impulse, she closed in for a hug. She simply had to embrace this lovely man who had cherished her so much that he'd not only remembered her in the future, but kept her possessions close until he'd met her again.

There was a smile in his voice and a rasp to his tone as Shunlei spoke against the top of her head. "You like them. I'm glad I went back for them."

Mei Li would rather be hung, drawn, and quartered before she admitted that she hadn't seen these at all. She'd been staring at a different set of combs entirely. Regardless, she much preferred the ones in his hands. "You are the dearest man, and I do not deserve you."

Shunlei hugged her back, thrumming his own pleasure. The thrum spoke of affection, one used for closer-than-friends. A hint of smugness might have lurked in the thrum, it was hard to tell, but it vibrated her in a pleasant way.

Future Shunlei did this too—bought things for her without any rhyme or reason. It was always a sweet gesture, of course, but Mei Li had never been able to put a finger on the reason behind it. Was this a dragon thing? Rone had never done this. Maybe it was just a Shunlei thing?

Whatever the reason, he was once again pleased he'd acquired something she obviously liked. His smile went up a notch. "Here, turn, I'll do your hair for you."

Since her face was probably doing interesting things, it was wise to put her back to him for a while. So she did, sitting on the edge of the bed so he could easily reach her hair. He combed first, starting at the bottom and rhythmically working his way through the soft tangles, sorting out the strands. Then he portioned out the top part, creating a bun, deftly using the combs to keep it up and together.

Even as his hands moved, Mei Li puzzled over all of this. Was it the conversation they had that night near the river that prompted this? When she asked why he trusted her? He'd started doing things like this for her after that. Well, no, he'd done her hair when she was injured, too. So maybe not.

Men were confusing. Especially dragons.

A knock on the door and then Hawes' voice. "You two

ready to go?"

"Almost," Shunlei answered. "My bags are ready and in my room."

"Lady Mei?" Hawes checked next.

"Once he's done with my hair, I'm ready. Is everyone else already out?"

"Yes, although we're not mounted yet."

So, everyone was running a bit behind, eh? Mei Li somehow wasn't surprised.

With no real time to spare, Shunlei finished up. Then they scurried after Hawes into the stable yard. He said proper thank yous and goodbyes to the priestesses as everyone else mounted up. Mei Li said her own goodbyes with regret, as this really had been a lovely place to stay and rest.

The open road north greeted them like a friend. Not a good friend. More like the bad friend you could never seem to get rid of completely. For reasons.

Or maybe Mei Li was projecting. That was entirely possible.

They rode at a fast walk, something the horses could maintain for a while. Even as they rode north toward Gong, the water deity, Mei Li wondered how to get them back south again. The rumor she'd heard in the market about Ghost General's Sword bugged her. She knew the sword was powerful, able to tempt its wielder into doing unspeakable things, but this was also the first time it had been stolen. She wasn't sure how quickly after that its effects began to be felt. The records told her very little about its origins. She knew where they had finally trapped and sealed it—in a particular temple in the southern edge of the Summer Wind Mountains. But when? It was something of a question mark. This year, yes. She knew that for fact.

But the first Tomes hadn't joined until two years from now and had only recorded it as a secondhand account. No one had given him a precise day. In truth, it was hard to keep the days and calendar straight when riding like this. The time and scenery all blurred together after a while. Even Mei Li struggled a bit, through the haze of exhaustion, to mark the days properly in her mind.

It was just as well the spell that sent her here would re-engage on its own when necessary. If it was up to her to return by a certain day and time, there would be trouble.

They diverged mid-afternoon onto a different highway. It hugged the coastline tighter than the other one did and eventually descended right on the edge of land. With their goal of Thibault, this was the most direct road northward. With the winding nature of the road still hugging the coastline, it wasn't easy to converse with each other. Especially with the wind kicking up, snatching at words. So, they chose not to, just rode, steadily eating up ground. Mei Li was especially glad now that Shunlei had pulled the hair back from her face in such a secure bun. She would have been eating hair otherwise.

As the sun set, they found a sizeable enough town that offered an inn and stayed there for the night. They had a hearty breakfast in the morning, stocked up on their fresh water, and left for the open road once more. Road all day, stopped for the night at a different inn, soap, rinse, repeat.

Mei Li's bum and thighs were slowly conforming to the shape of the saddle. She would swear to this. But as heartily sick as they were of riding, they grimly stuck with it as they made their way north, crossing the Tri-Rivers again and veering east, away from Iyhando. She would have been excited about finally being in the right country, but, well. It was never sunshine and daisies when reaching trouble. That was never truer than now.

It wouldn't stop raining.

She wore an oiled water-proof cloak that still dripped water over her nose, she felt like her boots were sloshing despite not walking in the mud, and the road—aish. The road was nothing *but* mud. They'd taken to riding along the grassy banks as at least the horses had some purchase there. It was insane, and it only worsened as they trekked through Thibault toward the northern coast. Mei Li couldn't imagine how much worse it would be once they were really in the center of the storm. They were still on the outskirts now.

"Hawes!" Kiyo had to practically shout to be heard over the steady pound of the rain. "I think we need to stop and get dry!"

Hawes turned in the saddle to look back at her. "We've got another three hours of daylight, at least!"

Shaking her head, Kiyo corrected, "We need that time to plan and think! None of us know how to handle the water deity!"

Hawes did a double take, then looked around her toward Mei Li. Mei Li did the most elaborate shrug of "I've got nothing" she had ever managed in her life. This was one of those instances where the records of the past were absolutely useless. She knew the group had tackled Gong—and won the battle—but had no clue how they'd managed it. It was a one-paragraph summary in the records and nothing more. Likely because they didn't see the need to go into detail. When would they ever have to deal with it again?

They hadn't sealed it. That's as much as Mei Li could confidently say.

Their illustrious leader didn't like this answer. Disgruntled, he nodded, resigned and accepting, and turned back around.

Of course it wasn't that easy. They still had to travel for another hour or so until they found an inn. It was packed, too, with traders and merchants all looking for a chance to be dry. Mei Li kept her ears open as she slogged her way through the large, open main room and she heard more than a few conversations where people complained it had been like this ever since they crossed Thibault's borders. One man had said this had been ongoing for weeks now, without the sun shining at all in that time. Mei Li believed it, as they'd been riding in it for at least a week as well.

"You'll need to share two rooms. They're all I have left."

Mei Li was pulled back to the inn keeper, an elderly gentleman that manned the counter with a tired air.

"That's fine," Hawes assured him. "Baths, meals, and stable come with that?"

"They do indeed. Laundry as well. We're a bit full up—been using the back rooms to hang clothes in—but we'll do what we can to get you dry. Before you go out in that." He jerked a thumb toward the outdoors.

Hawes' expression was the epitome of sardonic. "We appreciate that, sir, thank you. Ladies, if you'll take this room? We're across the hall from you."

Mei Li followed Kiyo upstairs with her bags slung over one shoulder. It was a nice enough room—two beds, a rug in the middle to soften the wood floors, the curtains pulled aside on the window to show the grey, stormy day outside. Mei Li took the far-right bed, setting bags down and immediately pulling out something dry to wear. She couldn't wait to get out of these wet clothes. She felt chilled down to her soul in them.

"Let's get a fire going," Kiyo suggested, already bending over the small hearth in the corner to do just that. "Our boots will never dry out otherwise."

"Good thought. Although I'm not sure what the point is, as we'll be riding out in the mess again tomorrow."

Kiyo made a noise of disgust. "I know. But at least we'll be dry tonight. I, for one, am going downstairs barefoot."

"I plan to wear socks, but I agree." At least her hair was mostly dry, due to the protection of the cloak. She wouldn't have wet hair dripping down her back the rest of the evening.

They changed, bundled up laundry, and took it down with them. A maid relieved them of the burden at the foot of the stairs. Mei Li spied their group already at a table in the far corner and made her way there. Shunlei pulled out a chair for her, and she took it with a quick, grateful smile.

"We've food coming," Melchior informed them as they sat down. "Nord's been explaining some of the trouble with this hunt. Talismans are useless?"

"Talismans will be difficult," Nord corrected him patiently. He had both hands folded on top of the table, but one lifted to gesture as he spoke. "Because they are paper and ink, exposing them to rain would only make the ink run, the paper crumple, and the spell will misfire."

Mei Li canted her head toward him. "I've seen that happen once. Not pretty. I really suggest we think of something to use aside from talismans. Leather talismans might be best in this case. Either that, or find a way to protect them from rainfall to use them. With Gong determined to drown us all with rain, that storm isn't going to let up anytime soon."

"How is what I've been stuck on." Kiyo settled with an audible sigh that spoke of irritation. "I kept thinking about it as we rode north, but no obvious solution comes to mind. I do believe we need to force this battle to be on land as much as possible. Water and fire-based spells are not a good choice."

Hawes grimaced agreement. "Not with a water deity. Shunlei, can he douse even dragon fire?"

Shunlei spread both hands, indicating ignorance. "I've never battled a deity before. And are we so sure that battling it will be wise?"

"I believe," Mei Li translated dryly, "that he's politely asking, 'Who here is crazy enough to think they can beat a deity?'"

Melchior gave a snort. "I wasn't going to ask that."

"I'm not even sure if we have enough power to seal it." Kiyo glanced between the mages at the table. "Even borrowing judiciously from natural earth power, I don't see that working out well for us. I'm open to other ideas. Flashes of genius are also accepted.”

Dead silence.

Mei Li knew for a fact that they did manage this somehow. She could kick whoever it was who wrote the report in the first place. Right now, she could hardly give them an airy reassurance without anything concrete to back it up.

“Maybe food will revive us enough that we’ll think of something.” Hawes did not look convinced of this, however.

Well. They’d figure it out. Eventually.

14

They figured it out. Maybe. Heavily leaning on the maybe side.

The plan was this: use bricks with talismans painted onto the bricks themselves, wrap them in oil cloth to protect the spell design, then use them to form a barricade around the water deity. Shunlei would act as a decoy to bring it far enough inland to weaken the deity. As long as it was in pure water, they had no chance. But standing, with only puddled rainwater, gave them something of an edge. A minuscule edge, but they'd take any advantage they could.

They'd use the ring of bricks to form a temporary barrier and then take the time to properly form something more lasting.

Kiyo and Nord seemed to think this was plausible, but they weren't sure how high the odds of success were. It was hard for them to calculate at this point, as they had no idea how powerful the deity was. No surprise, as neither had faced one before. This was a little outside Mei Li's comfort level, truth be told. Their design took magic to a whole new type of innovation. This was her weak point in magic. Give her a problem that was similar to something else she already knew and/or had done, she was fine and could adapt. Give her a problem completely outside of her book learning and experience, and she was woefully out of her depth.

The Tomes had never truly been mages. They were guardians. Record-keepers. Instructors to the next generation. But genius mages? Not one. Well, maybe the First Tomes had been. By all accounts, they'd been quite handy and well-schooled in the art of magic.

They spent the morning creating the bricks based on Nord's design. Then a few backup traps to help supplement in case the bricks were not sufficient. With those created, they packed up around noon and headed out again. At this point, no one wanted to be out in the rain, but they were very invested in seeing the end of this so they could experience the warmth of the sun again.

Of course, they didn't reach the coast that night, so another stop was necessary. Nord secretly made a few more bricks—Mei Li saw him do so. She could hardly blame him as she was a tad nervous with their plan as well. But he said nothing when they packed up and left the inn the next morning.

The rain, impossibly, was even more pervasive. It came down harder, sheets and sheets of rain that blinded a person's vision and soaked them straight down to the bone. Mei Li had heard of the phrase 'raining cats and dogs' before but felt it inadequate to the storm raging. Maybe wolves and tigers would be more accurate. Or wolves and elephants. For heaven's sake, they were partway into a city before she could make out the shapes of buildings, that's how badly the storm raged!

Hawes paused and waited for Shunlei to come abreast of him before leaning in to shout the question, "Can you fly ahead and get sight of it?"

Shunlei shook his head before Hawes could get the full question out. "I can't fly in this weather! No visibility."

Seeming to expect this answer, Hawes just nodded.

They kept riding. Nord pulled at Hawes' sleeve, then

pointed, and they changed direction. Mei Li wasn't sure what that was about or where they were now heading. Thibault might be the now modern city of Tanguay, but nothing about this city looked remotely familiar. That could be due to the storm. Mei Li doubted it, though. Either way, she had nothing in the way of landmarks and might as well be lost.

A large, dominating building sat at the end of the street. Nord seemed excited to see it, as he immediately hopped down from his gelding and strode right through the main doors. Hawes led them to the side, where a large overhang straddled the road, giving them shelter from the pounding rain. It was still loud, drops of rain bouncing off the cobblestone streets, but it was a relief to not be under the deluge.

Mei Li took the chance to get out of the saddle and stand for a bit. Shunlei slid down first, then gave her a hand down, which she appreciated. Twisting her torso, she stretched her back before leaning forward, stretching out her thighs as well. "I vote, when we head back south, we do so by ship."

Groaning, Shunlei flopped forward and let his arms and head dangle. "Ship sounds blissful."

"Doesn't it?"

Melchior casually joined them. "I can guarantee Hawes won't go for it. If we're on a ship, we can't hear rumors about things going wrong, or easily change direction."

Mei Li lifted her head to pout at him. "You're an utter killjoy. You could have at least let me fantasize."

Melchior just shrugged. "Warning you now. Oh my, that was quick."

"What is—oh." Mei Li straightened abruptly, hope rising. Nord had three people in tow, all of them mages themselves. She'd not seen another mage since her arrival. Mages were not common, no matter what era of time you were in. She understood that intellectually, but Mei Li was so accustomed to working with groups of mages that not seeing anyone aside from her own team had felt strange.

The three men carried umbrellas that they closed as they stopped under the stone awning. Nord introduced them with a relieved smile stretched from ear to ear. "Mages Janine, Sandeep, and Liggett. My friends, this is Mages Hawes, Kiyo, Mei, the warrior Melchior, and Shunlei the Red."

Shunlei got more than one startled look, but the three in question took the rest of them in stride. Janine was fair, obviously indoors most of the day, as her mint green dress was barely wet around the hem, blonde hair in a tidy bun at the top of her head. The woman standing next to her hailed from the Southern Isles, unless Mei Li missed her guess. The traditional silk dress with exposed midriff and over-the-shoulder silk tie hailed from that region. She, too, wore her black hair in a tidy bun at the back of her head, which was really the only sensible choice in this heavy humidity.

Liggett was the first to speak, giving a respectful bow to the group as a whole. He was reed thin, like a strong wind could send him toppling, and it almost did as he bowed. "A pleasure to meet all of you. Nord's told us a little of who you are and your aim here. We've been in a dither this entire time, not sure what to do. We are a magic school, but we focus on the healing arts." He gave a respectful nod to Janine.

Janine did look to be more master than student, as she was middle-aged at least. She accepted the nod with a fond smile at him. "Indeed. And I only have three seasoned students at this stage. Hardly enough to tackle an out-of-control water deity. But this group is accustomed to fighting such battles, are they not?"

"We are," Hawes answered with simple confidence. "Not deities, normally. But trouble, yes. We work under the direction and generosity of the Prince of Horvath. Forgive me, but Nord didn't say much. How do you know each other?"

"He started here, as a child," Janine explained. "I had him for three years before I realized his talents were really best suited in a different focus of magic. But he always stops in when he's in this region. I'm glad he's come to us now. We could use your help, Mage Hawes. The water level has already become dangerously high, and the storms are only increasing in their fury. Much more of this and I fear for the lives of everyone in the city."

"It's an entirely valid fear from what I've seen. Master Janine, we're frankly here to borrow more magical help. We've a plan to subdue the water deity, but as you can see, we only have four mages. I don't think that's sufficient to handle the problem."

"For that matter, I'm not sure if seven is." Janine looked to the other two and got stubborn looks in return. Her mouth twitched up, in either a smile or a grimace, it was too quick to tell. "But I suppose we must try. Certainly, no one else has offered anything like a solution. I know precisely where Gong sits. Or I should say, madly paces."

"That helps. We weren't sure where to go."

"Allow us just a moment to fetch a few things. Then we'll go."

"Of course." Hawes waited until they'd strode away, quickly heading back inside, before asking Nord, "Does this even our odds?"

"I don't know. But it has to help." Nord chewed on his bottom lip before admitting, "Master Janine is strong. As strong as Kiyo or myself. Sandeep and Liggett are still learning, but I think their magic is up to the task. They're nearly finished with their training. She doesn't trust anyone else to help. They're too young and green."

"And shouldn't be embroiled in a fight like this. I understand. Then we'll do what we can with what we have." Hawes blew out a steady stream of air. "What a strange world we live in, that men must manage the bungled affairs of the heavens."

Mei Li felt this was not the moment to tell him it would

get much worse before it got better. They still had crazy fire demons and triple volcanoes to deal with in the future. Which, wasn't that a joyful thought?

The three were back in record time. Janine instructed them to leave their horses and just carry what they needed. The path to Gong was steep and narrow, not something a horse could pass through. Shunlei volunteered to take on the majority of the bricks and shouldered the weight easily.

It was interesting, seeing the bay of Tanguay before it became the Sea Walls of Tanguay. It was a simple bay, not deep enough to bring anything larger than a schooner inside. It wasn't a large trade hub—not yet—but established enough because it was enroute between Tri-River City and the East Sea. The streets led straight to the bay, and they followed it until they reached the docks, and only then veered off to the right. They hiked the edge of the bay, and it became a little rockier, less tended, as they went. There was once a path laid in, Mei Li could see traces of the stones, but dirt and moss had grown over it and pushed it out of pattern.

Had the water deity gone mad through neglect? Sometimes they did.

Mei Li was glad to have the guide. She would have lost all bearings without Janine. The storm was so much worse now as they closed in on the epicenter. It was like walking through a typhoon. In fact, she was pretty sure they were doing exactly that. Shunlei stepped in front of her, encouraging her to use him as a windbreaker, and she thankfully did exactly that. She felt that for every step she took forward, the wind and rain drove her two feet back. It was impossible to make any real headway. It apparently took a dragon's strength to manage it.

Then they broke through, and it was nothing but still air. Not peaceful—it felt charged and heavy, the promise of a storm not yet realized. Mei Li almost preferred the storm outside to this circle of too-calm stillness.

In a half-destroyed pagoda of white columns and stone roof sat a figure. Well, a listing figure that kept twirling one hand in the sky as if stirring up trouble. He looked more liquid than solid, humanoid in the shape of a human male, but without the skin or hair of one. Something like a loin cloth was wrapped around his hips, he wore one sandal, but he looked like the ocean trapped in the outline of a human body. He didn't stir or shift as they approached.

That, more than anything, unnerved Mei Li. Did he not care that someone was nearby? Was he not worried about it? Or was his mind so far gone that he couldn't even properly observe his surroundings?

Shunlei started quietly passing out bricks. They each took two and fanned out, casually, carefully, trying not to look suspicious or rouse his interest. Shunlei stuck tightly to Mei Li's side, and she was grateful for it, as Liggett was right in front of her, and frankly? In a fight? She wasn't sure if Liggett had the reflexes to survive. He was not battle-worn and savvy. She could tell by the nervous way he kept glancing at the pagoda, as if he had no idea what to do if things went abruptly south.

"Visitors," said Gong. If the wind, grating along the surface of an ocean wave, could make a noise, that's what Gong sounded like. It wasn't akin to anything she'd ever experienced. His words were far from pleasant on the ear. He turned his head languidly, no energy or drive in the movement. "Many visitors. How long has it been since I've had visitors, I wonder?"

Shunlei gave her shoulder a squeeze and murmured, "Keep going." Then he turned and approached the pagoda with a steady stride. "You are Gong, the water deity?"

"I am." Gong sighed. It was the sigh of oceans and tides retreating and storms whistling inland. It spoke of power and sadness. "Who are you, visitor?"

"I am Shunlei the Red."

"Shunlei the Red. A dragon. In human form? I rarely see that. You know, when our Mother created the dragons, she gave them that ability. None of us understood the point of it. Why bother? But she said it was necessary. Only that. Why do you think it was?"

"To befriend humanity," Shunlei answered promptly. "It's rather hard to do when you're so much larger. It's hard to share space, for one. I'm very thankful she gave us that ability."

"But the dragons don't use it."

"We're beginning to. I use it often. I'm more in human form than dragon, these days."

"Are you really?" Gong perked up, his manner more alert than it had been even a moment before. "Why do the rest not approach as you've done?"

Mei Li looked around and saw that not everyone was in position yet. Hawes and Janine still had several paces to go until they were on the far side of the pagoda. The brick talismans didn't have to be in *precise* alignment, but they did have to be in some semblance of a circle to activate correctly. And there could be no serious gaps.

Shunlei tried to distract him. "They've prepared something—"

"Oh, I see what you've prepared for me." Gong stood, and the ocean shook and crashed against the shore, rising in higher waves that threatened to sweep over the pagoda. "You think to diminish me? To steal my power?"

"We need you to stop the storms."

Mei Li shot him an incredulous look. Then mentally smacked herself for her own surprise. Of course Shunlei would try reasoning with him. Even though he was obviously mad.

"I'll do as I like in my own territory!" Gong roared back, and the ocean rose and crashed, harder than it had before.

Hawes was flat out running now. Everyone was,

scrambling to get into position. Mei Li lost track of what was happening, her attention focused instead on getting her own bricks into the right placement to line up with Liggett's on her right, and Nord's on her left. She got the first brick down, then went flat as a sudden wave swept her legs out from under her. Spluttering, she came up, dragging hair out of her face as the water retreated. They were going to have to do this the hard way.

Flopping onto her side, she saw that the brick she'd just placed was now a foot away and in entirely the wrong spot. Swearing, she rolled onto her knees, and just in time for a second wave to come crashing through. Braced for it, it moved her a few inches but at least didn't jerk her around as badly as the first.

A crash came from the pagoda, and she looked up to see that Shunlei had tackled Gong outright. The deity came up swinging, clipping Shunlei's jaw good, but he was in dragon form now and not easily budged. Good, that might give them a few seconds.

But only a few.

Scrambling, she got her knees under her and nearly butted heads with Liggett as he lunged for his own wayward brick. They avoided a collision at the last second before real damage could occur, fetched their bricks, and hit each other as another wave crashed through and threw Liggett against her.

"Sorry!" he gasped, struggling to right himself.

"Go, go, go!" she encouraged, untangling him and pushing him off in the right direction.

Everyone seemed to be having the same trouble. Shunlei was trying to help, but physically fighting Gong to a standstill was both challenging and not working. The water deity didn't need physical gestures to control water—that was clearly evident as the waves grew and became too powerful to ignore.

Swearing, Mei Li did the only thing she could think of. She clamped one brick between her feet and lay down, keeping the other brick in one hand with a stranglehold grip. It was six feet, more or less, and she could curve her body enough to be (mostly) in alignment. As long as she held her breath in between waves, it worked fine.

She felt like a drowned rat, but it worked.

Liggett copied her once he saw she could maintain control of the bricks. Mei Li wasn't sure what Nord did, as he was outside of her view in this position. But she could feel the magic linking up as each person got their talismans into position. She linked hers in with the rest and kept her eyes and mouth firmly closed to avoid being drowned by the waves that didn't seem to diminish as they had before.

The dirt under her body, sodden with water as it was, started to rise. It felt like a reverse mudslide as it slithered up over her feet and hands, pushing at her torso. Feeling that it had a good grip on the bricks, she let go and frantically rolled out of the way before she could be enfolded and become part of the wall. Getting up on her knees, she dared to open her eyes, panting for breath. How was everyone else?

Head jerking this way and that, she checked on them. Liggett was also free, hands on his knees as he stood and panted, only to be knocked back to his knees on the next strong wave. Nord had himself braced, somehow, managing to keep his feet. His wall of earth was also rising, faster than hers. Mei Li threw some magical effort into it. They really needed to get this up quickly before Shunlei got seriously hurt.

Perhaps everyone had the same thought. The magic doubled in strength from almost every person, the wall climbing steadily and with great force. It had much the texture of the rocks in this area, which made sense, as they were drawing upon the natural force of this very land.

Gong was past words. He howled wordlessly, enraged.

The wall in front of Mei Li was now tall enough she could no longer see him, but she heard something heavy hit the side of the pagoda and winced. That was likely Shunlei. Even if it wasn't, he needed to retreat now, or he risked being trapped inside. "Shunlei, get out!"

Another hard crash. Mei Li held her breath, anxiously scanning what she could see of the sky. Come on, Shunlei, come on....

It felt like a small eternity before a flash of red darted through the still sky. Shunlei didn't go far—probably because he had no air currents to help him get airborne here. But he cleared the wall in a leap and landed hard on the other side.

She wanted to turn and check on him but couldn't move from this spot. She still had magic to feed into the wall, and it was so close to forming the top that she didn't dare move yet. Instead, she turned her head and called to him, "Are you alright?"

"Been better," Shunlei grunted back, then groaned. "Water deities have a wicked left. For future reference."

If he was joking with her, he wasn't too badly injured.

"Shunlei, sit down, we have this," Hawes directed.

"Are you sure? Because he didn't look all that worried while I was inside."

Oh. Well, that was not reassuring.

Nothing else in the world sounded like stone cracking and breaking apart. Mei Li could feel the vibrations of it under her feet. It was all the warning she had before the earthen wall in front of her was impacted hard. A crack formed, and she swallowed around a tight throat. Mercy, but that didn't look promising.

"YOU'LL NOT CAGE ME!"

Gong did not sound subdued, either. Enraged, yes. Subdued, very much a no.

Mei Li had the sudden thought that they'd bitten off more than they could chew. Did they try and retreat and attempt this again another day? Would they even be given that chance?

The top closed, for all the good that did. Mei Li stopped feeding power into it—there was no point with the spell finished—but she hovered anxiously. What could they possibly do at this juncture?

"I say, what's all this nonsense about?"

Mei Li turned sharply and just about lost her tongue. There was no possible way the man behind her was human. His feet were fused into the earth, for one thing, and he looked more like a finely-sculpted marble statue than anything living and breathing. His body was an assortment of moss, with fingers formed like tree roots, which wrapped up and around his arms before trailing out over his torso.

Mei Li's mouth went dry. There was, apparently, an earth deity in the region as well. Someone really could have mentioned that.

Nord, being quicker on his feet, immediately gave a bow. "Gong the water deity has gone mad. He's flooding all of Thibault. We're attempting to seal him long enough to either stop his actions or gain proper help."

"Flooding?" The earth deity turned and looked about him, as if taking in the entire area. Mei Li had the sense that it was more than his immediate surroundings he saw, but the entirety of his territory in that single sweep of the eyes. "Oh. Yes, I do see. Oh dear, that isn't good at all. I was wondering what had gone on up here, as things were going off-kilter down below. But I don't want that idiot sealed in with me, either."

Mei Li cleared her throat and drew upon a whisper of courage. "Respectfully, we don't want him either. And we don't have the power to stop him."

The earth deity regarded her thoughtfully for a moment. Then he grunted. "Well. Can't argue with that. And I'm responsible, I suppose, for not investigating when I first noticed the problem. Take that down; I'll deal with him."

Turning, Nord immediately took one of the bricks out to open a path inside. The earth deity strode through—well, more like glided. His 'feet' never made an appearance. "Gong, you half-wit, what have you done now?"

"Brother! They think to cage me!"

"They think to cage you because you're flooding both them *and* me, you utter moron. And what are you even doing on my land in the first place? You're supposed to be in the ocean."

"But no one was worshipping me!"

"Well, drowning them all isn't going to help improve matters. You come with me. Mother will attend to you."

"I don't want to go home to Mother! She'll scold me."

"Why do you think I'm taking you? You need the scolding. Enough, you don't get a choice on this."

There was a tragic wail of nooooooo and then abrupt silence.

Mei Li dared to peek around the hole in their earthen wall. Neither deity was in sight, and it looked as if it was just a half-destroyed pagoda and many puddles of water. Innocuous, even.

"Well." Melchior cleared his throat. "I vote we never do that again."

A general, nervous laugh of agreement echoed among the group.

At least Mei Li now had an answer why no one recorded how to seal a mad water deity. Turns out, you couldn't. Good to know.

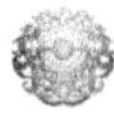

Janine invited them back to her academy to stay and rest, and they were just as happy to do it. They had many dormitory rooms available, which meant for once Mei Li didn't have to share with Kiyo. Frankly, having a room all to herself was heaven.

The next morning, they met over breakfast. The main dining hall had three tables spread out and students gathering in pockets here and there with friends. It was a wide range, the youngest being six or seven, the oldest full adults. Mei Li queued up with the rest of them in line, choosing an assortment of hot tea, baked pastries, scrambled eggs, and some sort of porridge that smelled of pumpkin. She sat down with it and ate with a smile of pleasure. They employed excellent cooks here.

Nord joined her with a clatter of a tray, sitting opposite. "Good morning."

"Good morning," Mei Li returned before swallowing a mouthful of tea. "How are you?"

"Stiff and sore from being tossed about yesterday, and glad to have a chance to rest." He eyed her as he mixed sugar into his tea with a spoon. "Lady Mei. I wonder if I might ask a favor of you."

"What?" Mei Li was intensely curious on what he'd ask for. Nord was so shy with her most of the time, after all.

"Your methods are so different from any other mage I've seen. I'd truly like it if you could pass along your knowledge to Master Janine. Sandeep, as well."

Ah. This did and didn't surprise her. Much of Mei Li's knowledge came from history, and some of the spells and invocations she knew were centuries old. A number of them even dated as far back as this very time she was in now. But of course she used 'newer' methods too. "I wouldn't mind that at all. I'd like to learn more about your methods as well."

Pleased, he ducked his head, and his hands reached for the flaky pastry on his plate. "Thank you. I didn't graduate from here—I lacked the aptitude to specialize in healing—but it's still very close to my heart."

Healing magic was strangely precise. It took a different kind of mindset when making the salves and potions for it.

Mei Li understood that not every Tomes had been good at it. She was decent, but she would never claim to specialize in the field. "I understood, truly. I'm alright with it. I'm certainly not an expert."

"Few are. Master Janine is normally in the sunroom after breakfast. I think we can meet her there and make the offer. I did speak with her about it last night, and she was keen on discussing matters with you, assuming you were amiable."

"Alright."

They finished breakfast companionably and then Nord led the way through the cool stone hallways. The sunroom was aptly named. It was basically formed of two walls of windows, all stretching from floor to ceiling and letting the morning light pour in. It was far warmer here than it had been in the hallway, and the windows framed a lovely view of the courtyard beyond with its multiple flower beds in full bloom. If Mei Li had a room like this, she'd spend most of her time in it too.

Janine and Sandeep were seated at a round table, papers and ink well spread out between them, but they both turned as the door opened.

"Ah, Nord, I see you convinced her. Good." Janine waved them forward and to the empty chairs at the table. "Do join us, Lady Mei. I'm eager to hear more about your teacher and your methods. I saw only a part of what you can do, and it intrigued me."

"I'll be happy to." Mei Li joined her, eyes taking in the pages splayed on the table. It looked like a very complex potion in the making for...snake venom? No, an antidote for it.

"Antidotes for snake venom," Sandeep answered the silent query on her face. "We do try to think of things ahead of time and have them on hand for emergencies. It's difficult to do, however. Poisons are challenging."

"Lady Mei knows how to treat a bite from a Bai Gu Jing,"

Nord informed them, taking the chair next to Mei Li. He sounded as proud of her as if he had accomplished it himself.

Mei Li found his reaction amusing and shrugged. "It's something my master taught me."

Janine leaned toward her, eyes locked on with fervor. "I didn't know that could be treated. Please, do tell me the particulars."

As that knowledge was developed in this timeframe, or thereabouts, Mei Li saw no issue with doing so. Who knew, maybe it was Janine who had spread the information to begin with? "I'd be happy to. The first thing you must know is that there's a window of opportunity in treatment. If you miss it, there's no hope for the patient—"

The door cracked open and Hawes' head popped in. "Oh, there you two are. I was told you might be here."

Janine waved him further in. "Do join us."

"Thank you," Hawes held up a hand, mouth tilted up in a sardonic fashion, "But I'll pass. It looks like you're talking magical theory, which is very much my weak point."

Janine's eyes narrowed. "You did say before that you are a battle mage."

"Quite right. If you want a shield warded for extra protection, or a keen blade with magical oomph for an attack, I'm your man. You ask me to make a complex talisman, I'll have to pass. I have excellent colleagues for a reason. In fact, I'm searching for one in particular. Lady Mei, where is Shunlei, do you know?"

How she became a dragon's keeper was a good question. "I do not. I haven't seen him yet this morning. Why?"

"I thought Melchior and I could spar with him a bit this morning." Hawes took a half-step further into the room, hand gesturing to the sunny day outside. "We really don't understand his strength. He's not used to fighting alongside humans, and that's going to get us into trouble sooner rather than later. And it's finally decent weather outside. I thought to capitalize on it."

"Oh, well, that sounds like a good idea to me." And Mei Li was of the opinion that some male bonding was precisely what Shunlei needed. Boys seemed to bond over sparring. Men didn't seem to outgrow that.

"I'll look for him. Don't let me interrupt you." Hawes ducked back out.

Mei Li left him to it. "Where were we? Ah, right, the time period for treatment." She picked up where she had left off, explaining everything she knew. As she did, the others took studious notes. Nord led that explanation into another, segueing into something else he had seen her do that he didn't know was possible. Mei Li found a way to flip the conversation, asking her own questions, as she needed a firmer grip of just what was common knowledge in this time. Right now, she only had a shaky grasp on that.

As they spoke, magical theory flying about the table, she caught a glimpse from the corner of her eye. Shunlei, Hawes, and Melchior were all in the courtyard. Melchior stood off to one side, letting Shunlei and Hawes have a go at each other. Even as she watched, Shunlei lashed out, his punch landing solidly against Hawes's shield. Even with a battle mage's protections on it, Hawes was still pushed back three feet, his shoes sliding against the slick courtyard stones. Hawes was stunned first, then he threw his head back and laughed.

Janine caught Mei Li's stare and glanced through the window. "Do we need to keep an eye on them out there?"

Mei Li waved this away. "They won't break each other."

Probably.

15

Melchior was unfortunately proven correct in his earlier assumption about their travel arrangements. Hawes did make them ride back down instead of taking the faster and easier route of a ship. He gave them all two days to relax in Thibault, and then the morning of the third day, they said their thank yous and goodbyes to everyone. By mid-morning they were back on the road heading south. Thankfully, at an easier pace and without a dark cloud following them. The roads weren't completely dried out yet from all the excessive rain, but they weren't mud anymore, either. It was well enough to travel on.

They left Thibault without incident, still following the coastal highway down. It was passing through the same territory as before, but there was no helping that. They only had so many highways to choose from. There was still Ghost General's Sword to track down once they reached Bader. Not that she could call it such aloud. People didn't name it until after it was sealed in the temple and they belatedly realized the sword was a relic from the previous war. She had to watch her mouth to make sure she didn't call it that aloud.

The sun steadily rose in the sky, crossing over their heads, then started toward the mountains on the other side. As it sank toward the horizon, the light faded with it, leaving Mei

Li wondering where they'd stay for the night. They'd passed several little towns already on the way. The fishing was plentiful here, after all—it only made sense. Maybe at the next town, they'd stop? It wasn't like there was much space off the road to camp out. The borders of the road tended to be rocky and slope at a steep incline. Had been that way for most of the day.

At her back, Shunlei abruptly went taut. "I smell something burning."

Alerted, she turned her head toward him to hear him better. "Something bigger than a hearth fire, you mean?"

"Yes. Like a town."

"Dragon?"

"Quite possibly. I've been picking up a dragon's scent off and on, but I don't think I'm in anyone's territory. I need to go ahead and look."

"Go, go," she encouraged, pulling Peanut to a halt.

Shunlei hopped off quickly and dodged to the side, where he could find open ground. He walked toward the cliff side, and she knew he was taking advantage of the wind that had buffeted them all day.

In seconds, he changed over from human to dragon, then nose-dived right off the edge. It made her heart leap in her throat—that was cutting it rather close, wasn't it?—then he soared back up, red against the sunset sky.

Hawes, of course, noticed and cupped his hand around his mouth to call back to her, "What's going on?"

"Something is on fire ahead!" Mei Li peered that way. It was a little hard to tell in the approaching twilight, but it did look like a great deal of black smoke billowing ahead. She'd not been paying it much attention. Hadn't noticed it all, in fact. "Shunlei went to see!"

Hawes clearly didn't like the sound of that and pushed his horse straight into a canter, the fastest they could go on these roads. Mei Li kept up, her eyes now anxiously fixed on the land ahead of her as she tried to see what was going on. It felt like eons, but it couldn't have been a half hour before they crested over a rise, and then she could really see the situation for what it was.

Half the town was ablaze.

To be precise, it was the dock area on fire, one of the ships in port also aflame. Settled into the valley between two rocky hilltops, the fire and smoke filled the air and made the visibility rather poor. Mei Li had to strain her eyes to get a better look at the situation. People scurried about, either children or something precious in their hands, running for safety. No one seemed to know where that was, as they scattered in different directions. Mei Li couldn't make sense of it at first, because what were they running from? The blaze itself? Shouldn't they be trying to put it out instead of just running and abandoning it all?

Then she heard the whoosh of wings and the crash of two hard bodies colliding and realized exactly what they were running from.

Her head snapped around, tracking the sounds of the fight automatically. Both dragon bodies slammed hard into a building, sending it crashing around them in broken timbers. It didn't seem to impact them much. They were up again in a moment, tails lashing as they bellowed fire at each other. Shunlei seemed to be holding his ground, but the sight of it still worried Mei Li. For once, he wasn't facing someone younger. This dragon was a much darker red, closing in on becoming a Green, perhaps. It was hard to tell in this lighting and from a distance.

Hawes turned to her immediately. "Does he stand a chance?"

"Yes." Logically, Mei Li knew Shunlei would survive this battle. Even if he didn't win it, he'd survive it. But her nerves still sang with tension as she watched because she'd never seen him so desperately hold his ground before. She winced as he was thrown, landing against another building and cracking the brick wall with his back and head. Just the sound of it made the back of her head ache in sympathy. "He'll win this, I think. We need to focus on the town!"

"Let's get this fire out." Hawes directed them with a snap of the fingers. "Lady Kiyo, you and I will make for the top part of the town, start warding it so it can't catch on fire as well. Nord, Lady Mei, Melchior, get to the docks."

Putting out fire she could do, especially when she had an ocean right there to work from. Mei Li nodded sharply and kicked Peanut back into motion. She'd work from his back as much as she could—getting off right now would only make her susceptible to being jostled in the crowd, which wouldn't do anyone any good.

Nord and Melchior were right with her as they fought their way through the panicked throngs in the streets. Mei Li pulled out talismans from her belt pouch, working with the selection she had readily available. She had two of each type of what she thought of as emergency talismans at hand: two water, two earth, two traps, and two healing spells. The rest were in the top of her bag, and she'd have to twist to reach them, but not until she had a clear line of sight to the docks. The smoke was thick in patches, making it hard to breathe, and her eyes watered from the sting of it all. Mei Li steeled herself to deal—she had no time to try to cobble together protective gear.

They finally gained an open patch of ground, the docks within range of her. "Nord, take the ship?"

"Yes."

Mei Li pulled her first water talisman and held it sharply toward the dock, activating it and directing its source at the same time. The ocean water, choppy from the wind, rose immediately at her bidding and flowed over the wooden docks and the people frantically working to put out the fire. She controlled the flow enough that it stayed low, washing over the wooden dock and piers without knocking anyone into the ocean. The flames went out within minutes, and a ragged cheer came up before they turned, spotting the trio.

The nearest man jogged to her, waving a hand over his head, splashing in the water still lingering on the docks. "My lady mage! Have you come to aid us?"

"As I can!" she called back to him. "We'll focus on putting out the fires first! If there's any grievously wounded, pull them together into one location if you can, so we can more easily attend them."

"Bless you, yes, please come. We've several heavily burned by dragon's fire. There's many trapped under that building, but we've no leverage to help pull them out!"

Swearing, she promptly kneed Peanut around. "Show us."

The man—he looked the part of a fisherman—immediately led them to the building behind one that was in absolute cinders, still smoking and raw with heat. Mei Li's eyes stung from the smoke and teared up, but she blinked past it as best she could and focused on following him.

Then she didn't need to, as she saw the problem very well indeed.

The building was still aflame, part of it burning with the intensity that only dragon fire could produce. It had destroyed the frame of the large, two-story building and warped it, collapsing the other side and trapping two different people. She saw a head there, under a pile of timber, and a pair of legs on the other side. "Melchior, can you attend me? Nord, can I leave the fire to you?"

"I can handle it," Nord assured her. He was already off his horse and heading that direction. "You can get them out?"

In the same beat, Melchior promised, "I'm on your heels."

"I have a trick up my sleeve." Only one, though, and Mei Li prayed it worked. As Nord scrambled to the other side, she rummaged through her talismans, speaking quickly and loudly to both Melchior and the fisherman still standing anxiously nearby. "I'll need both of your aid in a moment. I'm going to apply lightening spells to both of those heavy beams. It should mean we can lift them enough to haul the injured people out from underneath. Do so with care—we don't want to cause further injury, and the talismans will do their job as long as they're applied."

"But do so quickly because the fire is spreading alarmingly fast?" Melchior grimaced. "A race against time."

Yes, and those rarely fared well. Time was not usually humanity's friend.

Mei Li didn't voice that aloud. She found the two talismans she was looking for and slapped both on the heavy beams crisscrossed in a jumbled angle. The man on the left, with only his legs visible, gave a groan of what sounded like relief. Mei Li called to him, "We'll attend to you in a moment!"

"Get my wife out!" was the muffled shout in reply.

Melchior already had a hand on the beam, lifting it easily. Mei Li stooped, cradling the woman's head and torso, the fisherman on the other side, grasping hips as he could, both of them dragging her free. She was not a small woman, so it took all of Mei Li's strength to manage just this.

"Ru-Rupert," the woman gasped, her hands pointing to the side.

"We'll get him next," the fisherman promised, gasping and straining under her weight. "I think she's clear enough."

Mei Li agreed and carefully lowered her. As she did so, she anxiously looked at the other side of the building, where the fire was spreading at an alarming pace. "Melchior, let it down. NORD!"

"I could use some help!" Nord called, his voice high with panic. "Nothing's working against this fire!"

Had he never tried to subdue dragon's fire before?

Melchior was already waving her to the other's aid, so she lifted her skirts and darted around, anxiously looking at the magic already employed. Yes, as she thought, he was trying to fight fire with fire, so to speak. Talismans designed to subdue fire were spaced out every few steps, but it wasn't even making a dent.

Skidding to a stop next to him, she once again frantically dug through her talismans for what she needed. "You can't use fire suppressants on dragon fire, it's considered an element of its own, separate from fire itself. You have to counter it with the elemental opposite, either earth or water."

Nord quickly jammed his hand back into his pouch and came up with several water talismans. There was a look of determination on his face, as if he were not to be bested by mere fire, even if it was from a dragon. "Let's both use only one, can't flood the place."

Yes, water damage on top of fire damage wouldn't do anyone good in the long run. "On three. One, two, three!"

The ocean heeded their call, supplying a steady line of water, and they doused the flames carefully, talismans held in hand so they could move the water, panning it along the side of the building. She saw from the corner of her eye a small group of people racing toward them, calling out names in tones of relief. Friends or family to those trapped? Melchior's baritone was soothing as he reassured them, and someone ran off again to fetch a cart. To help move the injured, she assumed. Mei Li could only catch parts of what they were saying.

Nord let out a sigh and lowered the talisman. "That's out. How many of those do you have?"

"I think three altogether. Nord, I'm worried about the injured. I have more healing ointments and talismans than I do water talismans. You?"

"I have about an equal amount." He opened the pouch and rifled through, quickly counting. "A little less, it looks like. Do you want to divide and conquer? I can give you the healing talismans, and you let me handle the fire. We'll lose people if someone doesn't apply some magical healing—and quickly."

The shock a body sustained due to burns and injury was no laughing matter. Mei Li wasn't an expert in healing by any means, but she knew a great deal in theory, and she'd been able to apply some of that in practice. Even the limited assortment of things she had on her was better than nothing at all. "Let's do it."

They made the swap. Nord untied a satchel from his horse and handed it over to her, which she tied across her own chest. As soon as she had it in hand, Nord turned on his heel and rushed off, looking for any hint of flames.

The cart came, they loaded up the husband and wife, and one stocky, soot-covered man took charge by leading them quickly toward the center of the docks, into the only building (remarkably) untouched by fire. Mei Li retreated back to where Melchior stood, their horses' reins in his grip, and grabbed her bag from the back of her horse. She trusted Melchior to handle tying Peanut to a hitching post somewhere.

Inside the building was chaos. Mei Li spotted a charm engraved into the wall near the front door that was a fire prevention spell and absently realized that was why they were gathering here—probably one of the few buildings offering any protection. It was a warehouse, covered in boxes and padded bundles, most of it shoved aside to make room for the wounded.

And there were far too many of those. People lay out on blankets, some on the cold stone floor of the building itself, clothes and skin burned off, whimpering with pain even as loved ones tried to help. It enraged Mei Li to the point that she was sorely tempted to storm back out and battle that dragon herself.

"Who's touched by dragon fire?!" she called out strongly over the crowd.

"Here!" a woman called out immediately, lifting a hand. "My husband!"

"Here!"

"Here!"

"Here!"

Too many, too many. Growling, Mei Li pushed the bag into Melchior's hands without a by-your-leave and started rooting through it. "I'm going to activate several talismans; I want you to apply one each to every person burned. It will alleviate the pain until I can get there. This jar of ointment, it's for burns. Apply that in a thin coat to the more serious raw wounds."

"Got it." Melchior accepted everything she handed him and then headed in the other direction.

Finding what she needed, she pulled several things free and then hustled over in a flurry of skirts to the first woman who'd raised her hand. She took in the sight with a wince. The man lying with his head pillowed in his wife's lap looked half-raw. Dragon's fire was incredibly destructive, even a graze of it would do this.

Sinking down onto her knees, she flashed them both a smile. "I have two pieces of good news for you."

The husband gasped shallowly for breath, eyes barely tracking her, but the wife was keenly listening.

Mei Li's hands applied a healing talisman even as she spoke. "First, the dragon who did this is being fought even now. My friend Shunlei is battling him, and Shunlei normally wins his battles with other dragons, so I have faith he'll put a stop to this insanity."

The relief in the woman's haggard face was unmistakable, as much as the choked off sob. It had to be horrifying, sitting here, guarding her injured husband, not sure if it was safe enough to go back out for the supplies she would need to help him. And this place was warded for fire, certainly, but it wouldn't stop a dragon from smashing into it.

"Second, what I have here in hand is specifically made for dragon fire burns. I'm going to apply a coat of it—"

The husband shivered, and the pain lines around his mouth and eyes relaxed.

"—better already, right? Good stuff, this. I'll coat everything here, then you lay still. It'll harden, like a second skin, and stay like that until your skin knits back together again. We'll get you moved to a more comfortable location when we can, but bear with us. We're trying to keep people alive right now."

"Thank you, Lady," the woman choked, tears streaming down her face. "Will he...recover?"

"Fully." Mei Li gave her a tight smile, and then she darted to the next patient.

It became a blur after that. Mei Li kept repeating the same assurances, applying talismans, creams, bandages in a few places. Resetting broken collar bones, arms, legs, piecing together a sheared ear and stitching it back to the man's head before he lost it altogether. Mei Li was trained in medicine—all Tomes were—but she wasn't a healer. These people needed a proper healer.

They made do with her. Although she'd find a proper healer before this was over; she was determined on that point. Even if she had to go fetch him or her from another town.

Nord appeared at some point—she nearly tripped right over him—and with him came a new wave of patients. Mei Li only had time to demand if the fires were out. He nodded, but his eyes and hands were focused on the child in front of him. She gave back his bag so he had more to work with, then darted for the next patient.

Time passed in a blink, and Mei Li couldn't say if she'd been there an hour or all night when Hawes appeared and grabbed her. She was so startled by his abrupt grip on her arm that she nearly dropped everything in her hands.

"Hawes! For pity's sake, my soul nearly left my body."

"Shunlei," he told her, urging her out the door already.

Come to think of it, the sounds of battle had abruptly died off several minutes ago. A part of Mei Li's mind had made note of it. "Did he win?"

"If you can count it as a win."

16

With Hawes' guidance, Mei Li raced up to the side of the hill, just on the edge of town, where two dragon bodies lay prone. Her heart was in her throat even as she tripped over debris and splashed through ash-colored puddles. Shunlei lay with his wings in an odd, splayed out angle, his head turned from her, lying like he hadn't the breath or energy to move. Some of his claws dug into the earth, gripping in a way she'd never seen a dragon do before. She could see him breathe—his scaled sides panted for air—but that wasn't as reassuring as it should be. With the fiery red hue of his scales, it was hard to see if he was bloody, but she did see more than a few gashes. Superficial, judging by the sluggish way they were bleeding.

"Shunlei!"

He rolled his massive head to the right, turning enough to see her even as she scrambled toward him. Tears streamed from the edges of his light blue eyes, unchecked. Alarm shot through her all over again, racing like chills up and down her spine. What had happened?!

The other dragon lay nearby, still as death. He was larger than Shunlei by a good length, nearly a third longer. The size of his leg alone dwarfed her. There were more rips and gashes in his side, or at least deeper and more obvious. She thought he was in the same poor shape as Shunlei for a split second until she realized that initial impression was correct. He was dead.

Understanding swept through her, and she didn't hesitate to put an arm around Shunlei's head, touching her forehead to his brow. "Oh, Shunlei."

"I didn't want to," he whispered, voice broken. "I tried so hard to get him to surrender. To just stop. If he'd just been willing to stop... But they'd done something to anger him. I didn't understand what. He said something about territory, and rights, and he wouldn't *stop*."

"Shhh, I know, I know this isn't your fault. You had to stop him to protect us. You did the right thing, as hard as that was." She did her best to thrum at him, forcing her smoke-abused throat to mimic the sounds of comfort and affection.

He sighed, the sound nothing but grief and pain, and rolled his head further into her body. "Why wouldn't he stop?"

"When a man answers only to the base needs of anger and greed, he becomes lost. You can't reason with such people, Shunlei. Sometimes, force is the only answer." Hawes put his own hand on the other side of Shunlei's head, stroking down his neck in sympathy. "Thank you for taking on that burden. I'm sorry I left you alone to do it."

"The dragons aren't your duty, Hawes."

Hawes kept stroking, a sad smile on his face. "Perhaps, perhaps not, but I'm willing to help you shoulder the goal you've set. You're not alone in this."

"No, you're certainly not." Mei Li didn't want him to doubt that for a moment and made her voice firm. "We'll talk properly about how to handle situations like this in the future. But for now, can you change forms? I can see some terrible gashes in your side. How badly are you hurt?"

"It's not life-threatening." A visible wince shot through his frame. "I'm not sure if I can shift easily, though. It's always harder to do it when injured."

"I don't have enough medicine or bandages to cover a dragon form." Mei Li looked him over, chewing on her bottom lip in thought. "I'm not sure how much I can help you like this."

"I can—" He grunted, body shuddering again. "I can do it. I think. Give me a minute."

Mei Li stepped back to give him room. Her heartstrings tugged painfully, sympathetically. It was hard to see him in so much pain, both physically and emotionally. Knowing his goals, knowing what he accomplished in the end, it all seemed easy enough in context. Sometimes she forgot he'd had many mishaps. Like now, even when he won, he still felt it a loss.

Shunlei's true aim wasn't just harmony between the species. He wanted to save the dragons from their path of self-destruction. Picking a fight with an entire race would ensure their demise eventually. He'd realized it. It's partially why he was able to convince the other dragons to heed him, because he could convey that logic to them in rational terms.

Killing a dragon meant he'd failed to save him. Shunlei wouldn't look at it any other way.

The strongest urge to wrap him up in her arms and hold him, hug him through the worst of the guilt, came over her. But attending to the many wounds on him was the first order of business. He may think these weren't life threatening, but he was losing a great deal of blood. Too much for her peace of mind.

He shuddered, a hard shiver that racked him from head to toe. Another shudder chased after the first, and then another. Mei Li was on the cusp of looking for another alternative when he finally groaned, low in the back of his throat, and slowly changed over. It was the slowest transition she'd ever seen a dragon perform, and interesting in its own right. She could track in stages how he collapsed wings in, drew tail up, and reconfigured bones and muscle and tissue to a human body.

Then he lay in the dirt, gasping with pain.

Mei Li took what bandages she had and did a quick field dressing, trying to keep the blood locked into his body. Shunlei lay half-propped up in Hawes' arms, watching her with eyes at half-mast. He was utterly done, no energy left in him. The fight had taken much out of him—emotionally and physically. Mei Li kept her actions quick and efficient. She needed to get him to the field hospital where she had more bandages and ointments to work with.

"Alright. Up."

Hawes got under one arm, Mei Li under the other, and between them they half-carried Shunlei back down toward the warehouse. He walked as best he could, shaking with fatigue, wincing with every other step. Mei Li would get proper talismans and magical salves on him first and then pour a gallon of water down his throat before she would allow him to rest. He had to be beyond dehydrated.

Kiyo spied them coming and halted near the warehouse door, a crate of something in her arms. "There you three are! The dragon?"

"Dead," Hawes reported in a neutral tone. "Shunlei tried, but he wasn't interested in stopping."

Kiyo eyed the man hanging between them and sympathy flashed over her face. "I'm sorry to hear it. But glad he's stopped. We might be here a few days, Hawes. The damage is extensive."

"I know. I'm prepared for it."

She gave a nod, then hip-checked the warehouse door open and held it there. They went in sideways, careful to not lose their grip on Shunlei in the process. Mei Li had barely a foot inside when she looked for an open place to lay him down.

Melchior, bless him, had anticipated the need and

cleared out a space across a shipment of stacked rugs. Mei Li carefully levered Shunlei onto it, Hawes still supporting his back as they gently laid him down.

"I need bandages!" she called out.

"Here!" a woman she didn't know responded, tossing her a bundle of them.

Mei Li had to untie Shunlei's shirt again to get to the bandages. The clothes, of course, were pristine, being kept inside the pearl during the fight. They were now stained with blood from the open wounds, but it did garner some curious reactions from people as they realized the clothes were intact while the man was injured. Mei Li could hear the whispering but ignored it. This time, she had a clean(ish) space to work with. She wiped off mud, dug out broken claws from his side with tweezers, cleaned and applied poultice to the wounds.

Only when he was fully attended to did she relax and straighten her back with a groan. Her muscles twinged from bending over at that unnatural angle for so long. She caught his fingers and gave them a squeeze, smiling tiredly at him. "Fortunately, you're tough and a fast healer."

Shunlei gave her a tired smile in response. "Fortunately. Thank you, Mei."

"Mei, I could use some help!" Kiyo called from the other side of the warehouse.

"And that's my cue. Hawes, get as much water down him as you can. And put my blanket on him. He'll be chilled with the blood loss. I'll check in with you later." Even as Mei Li issued these instructions, she gathered up her bag and what was left of the bandages before racing off again.

She stayed in a flurry of activity, going from one patient to the next, then being hauled outside to help clean out several other buildings so they could move people out of the warehouse. The work would be insane putting this town back to rights again. Mei Li didn't even want to think about it.

As dawn peeked out over the ocean, she finally stumbled

into the inn someone directed her to. Her group had been removed from the warehouse at some point, shifting to a more comfortable place, and the innkeeper herself met Mei Li at the door. The woman looked done in, soot lingering in the lines around her eyes and mouth, the formerly white apron now more grey and black. But she met Mei Li's eyes with a nod of approval.

"You'd be Lady Mei, then?" the woman asked as if she full well knew the answer. Then again, Mei Li easily looked the part of a northerner. People tended toward soft brunettes and blondes down here, the innkeeper being one of the blondes. Mei Li could hardly be mistaken for anyone else. "I've got a hot meal waiting on you. There's a pitcher of warm water and a bed with your name on it, too."

"Thank you so much. Is the rest of my party here?"

"They are indeed. You're the last. Come on, now, eat and then rest. You've more than earned it."

Mei Li followed the woman into the sparse dining room, sitting down at the table with its covered plate, and lifting off the white cloth to reveal a simple breakfast of biscuits, eggs, and sausages. She consumed it without tasting, so tired that even her taste buds couldn't be bothered to wake up and function properly.

The innkeeper filled her glass with water three times, and on the third, lingered for a moment. "I heard that young man with the shocking red hair, the one they carried in here—he's a dragon? The red dragon that fought the other one and killed it?"

It sounded as if she needed only confirmation. Mei Li paused in drinking, and swallowed to answer. "Yes. Shunlei is his name."

"We're all very glad he came when he did." The innkeeper sighed. "That other dragon, we're not sure where he came from. But he appeared earlier this year, fishing out of the sea. He seemed content to go about his business and leave us to ours, so we didn't worry much about him. But then he started hassling the fishing boats, said we were in his territory. They didn't want a fight with him, so they shifted further north. But the fishing wasn't good there. They ended up coming back more toward the south. I guess they got too close to his territory—wherever that was. He'd never given us a marker to use. It set him off something fierce."

"Yes, dragons can be highly territorial. And that one wasn't very rational—Shunlei tried over and over to just get him to stop. Just to talk. In the end, he wouldn't, and it became a life-and-death battle." Mei Li shook her head sadly. "Shunlei didn't want to kill him. He hopes to tame the dragons."

"That's what the gruff-looking man said. Hawes? Yes, he said the same. Asked me to not be afraid of the red dragon. Said he's a gentle soul."

"Shunlei's very gentle-natured. He will put his foot down when he needs to, though. As you saw last night."

That seemed to satisfy the woman and she gave a nod. "The town will want to thank him properly when he's back on his feet. We'd have lost the whole town without all of you. But for now, you come upstairs. You're dead on your feet."

"You are too."

"I'll rest after I show you up."

"Fair enough." Mei Li heaved herself to her feet with a grunt of effort. She stumbled up the stairs, following the woman, then into the room pointed out to her. There was indeed a pitcher, a towel, and a bar of mint-scented soap. There was also a double bed with soft, inviting pillows and the cover turned down in an invitation Mei Li almost couldn't resist. But her skin was so encrusted with mud, blood, and soot, that she wouldn't rest well until it was cleaned off.

As she washed her hands and forearms, Hawes poked his head in around the door. "Good, you're in. How are things?"

"A lot of cleanup to do." Mei Li turned her head for a

moment to answer him. Hawes looked ready to drop where he stood as well. He was clean, though, his beard and hair damp from a wash. "But everyone's stable and in a position to rest today. Shunlei?"

"In a bed but refused to really sleep until you're back in."

Mei Li rolled her eyes in exasperation. "Go slap him for me and tell him to go to sleep."

"With pleasure." Hawes gave her a wink and closed the door.

Mei Li could hear his heavy tread lead into the room next door. The walls were thin—or perhaps the sound carried through her open window—as she could hear them converse in muted tones.

"She's in and fine," Hawes reported, exasperation heavily coloring his words. "Go to sleep."

"Knew she would be." There was a sigh to Shunlei's words, as if sleep was already reaching up to claim him even as he forced the words out. "She's the most amazing woman I've ever met. The strongest. Still, I was worried."

"That amazing, strong woman will come in here and club you over the head herself if you don't sleep."

Hawes was right there.

Shaking her head, she turned and said in a clear voice that she knew Shunlei with his dragon hearing could pick up easily. "I love you too, Shunlei, but stop being an idiot and sleep already."

"Yes, ma'am."

A beat. Two. Then snoring, soft and light but unmistakable.

"He only obeys her," Hawes grumbled, the words accompanied by the opening and closing of a door. "It's like my words are nothing more than a dog barking."

Amused, Mei Li stripped down to her shift and crawled into the bed, too tired to dig out her sleep clothes. She barely had her head on the pillow when darkness reached up and rolled her under.

17

Mei Li lost most of the day to slumber and woke up with a damp pillow where she'd drooled a little in her sleep. Embarrassing, but fortunately with no witnesses. She dragged herself out of bed, feeling more groggy than rested, and realized she had slept most of the day away. The light outside her window was definitely mid-afternoon.

Pulling on clothes, she took precisely a minute to tie her hair up in a sloppy bun, ram her hair sticks into it, and trudge next door. Shunlei was not in the bed, so he was feeling well enough to get up. Good. Next stop: food.

The dining hall was in full swing, crowded with people grabbing a quick bite before they took off again. Most didn't even sit down, just leaned in over a table. Rolls stuffed with meats and cheeses abounded, passed around with hot cups of strong tea. Mei Li could tell by the smell alone. Every man and woman she passed had smudged clothes and hands, but a sort of determined air about them.

These people weren't down. Not by a long shot.

Melchior spotted her first and hailed her with a hand lifted in the air. The warrior was also soot-spotted—in fact, it looked as if he'd hugged something, as it was even on his cheek above a half-grown beard—but there was a smile on his face. "Lady Mei! You're finally up."

"Up is correct. Thank you for not saying awake." She

slipped through a press of bodies to gain the table. The only ones sitting were Shunlei and Kiyo, with Kiyo fussing, piling food on Shunlei's plate. "Good...afternoon?"

"It's possibly that," Kiyo agreed, still fussing. "Shunlei, *eat*."

"I did eat!" he protested with a frown.

"You ate half what you normally do. Your body needs the energy. Eat!"

"I also ate before you joined the table," he riposted, rolling his eyes. "Here, Mei, sit and eat this. I'm full to the brim."

He did look a little green at the idea of eating anything else. With a shrug, Mei Li sat next to him, drawing the plate to her. Kiyo huffed a wordless protest, which she ignored. "Well, where do we stand at the moment?"

"People are picking up the pieces. We've cleaned up as we could. I understand there will be a mass funeral tomorrow. The mayor of the town came by and thanked us, made several requests too. Don't be surprised if you see her. She's overwhelmed trying to put her town back to rights." Hawes paused to drink a healthy swallow of his tea before continuing. He looked ready to get back to work at any moment, standing alongside Melchior. "We've helped the townspeople rid themselves of the dragon corpse. Gave it a watery grave."

Pushing it into the sea probably was the best decision.

"There's still some healing left to do, but time can manage most of it, I think. Right now, we're trying to repair enough buildings that people can go back home and get their businesses put together. Can you work renewal magic on anything, Lady Mei?"

"I can, with the proper setup and equipment," she replied confidently. After all, a Tomes' work was precisely that. "I can go about today, look at what needs to be done, then do the prep work to tackle it tomorrow."

Hawes gave her a nod, expression relieved. "Townspeople

will be happy to hear it. Is this something you can teach?"

In other words, neither Kiyo nor Nord was comfortable with this branch of magic? Interesting. Then again, had Mei Li seen them do any magic that wasn't either combat or healing in nature? She couldn't dredge up a single instance. "Yes, of course. It's just a matter of understanding the structure and how to apply the right elements to the spells. I can do a crash course with any magician and have them up to speed in three days or less."

"Then please do so. Our innkeeper has generously agreed to let us stay for free as long as we'd like. I'm inclined to stay a few days and help put the town back together."

Mei Li nodded around a mouthful. That was perfectly fine by her.

"Fortunately, the townspeople seem to realize that not all dragons are equal. They're aware of Shunlei's true form and are very grateful for his help. Still, I'd prefer for him to not be alone for long stretches of time. There's always one blinded by anger."

"I'll stay with Mei," Shunlei assured him. "I now know a little of how to assist her."

Hawes gave him a flat look, not at all surprised by his volunteering. "Color me surprised. Fine, alright. Don't overdo it."

Mei Li bit into the last roll, chewing thoughtfully. Swallowing, she asked, "Where do I need to focus?"

"Docks first. They were hit rather badly, and the economy will suffer if they can't get the ships in. Lady Kiyo, Nord, will you go with her?"

"We must," Nord stated, already standing, "to learn from her. Lady Mei, the foreman for the docks is just yonder. I will fetch him."

"Yes, please, we'll need him." Mei Li felt the strong tea hit her brain, waking her up. Which was just as well as she apparently needed her brains at full function today.

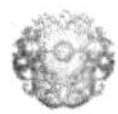

What followed was a rather grim accounting.

The docks were indeed very badly burned. What remained was either charcoal or so fragile that anything more than a person's weight on it threatened to send it to the bottom of the harbor. Mei Li, Kiyo, and Nord slapped down several strengthening spells to prevent anyone from taking an untimely dip. The foreman was thankful for the help and promised them whatever aid he could render. Mei Li issued for everything to be taken off the docks. They'd need a clean slate to rebuild with.

They spent time measuring the docks, writing it all down, and estimating how many talismans they'd need to create. Mei Li finally stopped and looked at the docks with a critical eye. "We'll need a great deal of rope."

Shunlei, sitting on a scorched crate nearby, canted his head in question. "Rope?"

"Or chalk." Mei Li frowned, not sure which would work better. "Perhaps chalk would work best. We can either write out hundreds of talismans to do the job, or write one giant one along each dock and let it do the work. I think the giant talisman will be the more efficient way to go."

"Let me shop around for it." Shunlei stood, dusting off the back of his thighs.

Mei Li turned to study him, brows beetling. "Are you up for that?"

"I'm just tender and sore," he assured her with a quick smile. "How much chalk?"

She had to trust he knew his limits. Although if he undid her hard work by being stubborn, she really would club him over the head. "However much you can acquire. This will take a lot."

Nodding, he turned and walked off. Not at his usual brisk pace, either, just a steady walk. Well, maybe he was alright after all? Dragons were sturdier than humans, and a touch faster to heal.

Shaking her head, Mei Li turned back to the other three. "Foreman Jones, this won't be a fast fix. I think we can get two docks back into working order by tomorrow."

"Just that will help, miss," Jones replied, taking his cap off and rubbing at his bald head before jamming it back on. He kept giving the harbor uncertain looks. "We've got ships out now, coming in soon. It'll take some jostling to get them in and out so people can offload."

"I quite understand. We'll work as fast as we can." To the others, she explained, "The spell isn't complicated, but magically speaking, it's draining. We'll first have to remove all remnants of dragon's fire."

Both Kiyo and Nord winced.

Foreman Jones caught this reaction and looked between them, craggy face now drawn in worry. "That's hard, I take it?"

"Difficult," Mei Li admitted. "But not impossible. Essentially, what we will do is rewind the clock on the docks. We're reminding the wood of how it was before dragon's fire touched it. But to do that, we must first remove all the dragon's fire heat lingering in the wood. Dragon's fire is magical in and of itself, you see. It will clash with the magic we bring to bear."

"What she's not telling you"—Kiyo gave her an aggravated look—"is that by removing the dragon's fire, it will flare up again. We'll have to be very careful how we control it as we draw it out."

Nord glared at the wood under his feet as if it had personally insulted him. "Ocean."

"Concisely put," Mei Li said approvingly. "Fortunately, the ocean is right here, so we have a safe place to extinguish it. But that's what will be the hardest and most draining part of this. The actual renewal spell will be a snap once we've drawn out the proper spell along the wood."

Jones only looked partially mollified by this. "Should I keep the docks entirely clear tomorrow?"

"Just in case. If you would." Mei Li cracked her neck to either side, feeling the tension in her muscles. Great magic, but this would take days. It was just as well they'd start tomorrow, too, as her magic wasn't up to it today. She felt only the dredges of magical energy at her core.

"Then I'll spread the word." Jones ducked his head at them before striding off, voice lifted as he called out to a pocket of men nearby.

Mei Li rather wanted to return to the inn but didn't want to miss Shunlei, who would return here looking for her. She assumed. Not wanting to put the time to waste, she offered, "I can apply a few safeguards here in preparation for tomorrow?"

Wearily, Kiyo bobbed her head in agreement. "Do that. We'll go survey the other burned section of town and see what else they need restored."

Since they now knew what to look for, Mei Li left them to it.

There were some anti-fire talismans in her bag, which she used sparingly along the unburned sections of the docks. Just in case that dragon's fire did get away from them. She was at it perhaps an hour or so and was frankly running out of things to do when Shunlei reappeared.

In his hands were three boxes and a wrapped bundle on top. Mei Li stopped messing with the talisman and straightened, crossing the distance to meet him halfway. At this hour, the sun was setting and few people were left on the docks. She was glad he was back so quickly. The ocean breeze had a nip to it, and she was more than ready to retreat into the inn.

"How much did you find?" she asked by way of greeting.

"Three boxes, one half-full," he answered, setting them

down carefully on the nearest flat surface—in this case, an unopened crate. "But first, this."

Mei Li accepted the bundle he handed her with absolutely no expectation of what was inside. It felt soft, like cloth, but she didn't know what to think of it. Or the expression on his face.

"It's hard catching you alone." There was a wry upturn of his mouth, but his blue eyes spoke of caution. "I'd prefer a better setting for this, but needs must. Will you accept this, Mei?"

It was on the tip of her tongue to ask what, but she didn't voice it. Mei Li didn't know what to make of his expression. It was neutral in a way—strangely so—but more as a mask that covered a much deeper emotion he wasn't willing to reveal just yet. Mei Li wanted to puzzle it out, but she had a feeling she could study that face for hours and not figure it out. Instead, she untied the plain black cloth and flicked it open on all four sides with a quick snap of her wrist. What lay in the middle, folded neatly, was a shimmering red veil. It was exquisitely done, the edges of it embroidered with yellow thread in a scrollwork pattern.

It was a bride's veil.

Mei Li's breath seized in her lungs, and she could only stare at the veil. What...was...no, she knew what it was. In a traditional courtship of this day, especially this era, a courting couple would exchange parts of a wedding outfit on a regular basis. They would give each other each piece of it, and when the full outfit was assembled, the courtship was considered complete and they were engaged.

So, she knew what this was. What she didn't understand was *why*.

Her lungs burned, reminding her to draw in air, and she sucked in a large breath, eyes still glued to the veil. Thoughts whirled and clashed in her head without any resolution of how to feel about this. For a moment, she felt weightless, as if her mind had separated from her body, leaving her in an exhilarating free fall before other emotions yanked her sharply back down. Surprise won, knocking everything else aside. Words seemed to escape her utterly. "S-Shunlei—"

"I've surprised you," he said, resigned. "I had a feeling. I courted you as a dragon would another, but the way you responded, it became clear to me you didn't understand what I was doing. Or did you?"

She shook her head frantically from side to side, because no, she had *not* picked up on that at all.

"I asked Hawes how humans would court, and he explained the customs. They sold bridal veils in the last town we stayed, so I picked it up there. I hadn't found the right moment to give it to you. I finally decided the right moment wasn't going to come magically along. I chose to just make a moment." Shunlei ducked his head an inch, still studying her cautiously. "Mei? Do you agree?"

Mei Li blurted without thinking, "You can't choose me! Our timelines don't match!"

This did not impact him as she expected it to. Instead he smiled at her a little sadly. "I know. But I've already considered that. I'll take whatever time with you I can claim."

He didn't understand. Worse, she couldn't fully explain it to him. He thought she meant that she would leave him widowed well before his time—which was certainly true—but...oh great dark magic take everything. How did she explain? To both him and her? Because for a wild, exhilarated moment, she'd been truly happy to see that veil.

Tears burned in her eyes, blinding her, and she found herself clutching the veil to her chest without meaning to. Shaking her head over and over, she protested around a constricted throat, "I can't. I'll break your heart. I can't."

Shunlei reached for her, a gentle expression on his face. "Mei—"

She couldn't even see him through the tears now.

Frustrated, heart aching, she pivoted sharply on her heel and ran. Which was cowardly, but she didn't know what to say to him, to convince him how poor of a decision this was. She was perilously close to saying something she shouldn't.

Mei Li dashed angry tears from her eyes, cursing her past self for a naïve idiot. She should have never, ever spoken that thrice-cursed time travel spell. Now look where it had landed her.

She was an utter *fool*.

18

Mei Li squirreled herself up in her room, the veil laying on the bed in front of her. With both arms wrapped around her legs, she hunkered there, glaring at the veil. She felt, in that moment, immensely frustrated. And fragile, as if one soft puff of air would shatter her heart and send it in all directions.

It took far longer than it should have to calm down enough to really think. Her emotions kept derailing her utterly before she could focus. The light outside the window disappeared entirely, leaving her in starlit gloom. Still, she didn't change her position. She felt instinctively that she was on the cusp of understanding something, if only she was calm and still enough for that realization to come.

With a deep breath in, she parsed it out slowly. Breathe in through the nostrils, out through the mouth. She still felt tenderized by emotions, but she could think now. She could put this out logically and look it over from all sides.

Maybe.

Alright, start from the beginning. She had to first consider not present Shunlei, but future. Future Shunlei must have known his younger self would fall in love with her. He'd remembered precisely where they met, for mercy's sakes—of course he'd remember how he'd felt for her.

Future Shunlei had given her instructions of precisely where to go to meet him. Words of caution, some advice, but nothing of a personal nature. No, she couldn't say that. Those last five words had been very personal, spoken in a husky, longing way from his heart.

Be safe. Return to me.

At the time, she'd been so focused on getting changed, activating the spell, going before she could be caught. She hadn't really focused on him or considered fully what he meant by that. Mei Li had assumed he meant a general well-wishing. For her to safely return to him again in the future.

But what if he hadn't meant it in a general sense?

Suspicions roused, Mei Li stared at the veil again with wide eyes. "No, surely not..."

Closing her eyes, she truly focused. Had he ever said his wife's name? Had any record made mention of it? She couldn't recall a single instance where the human bride Shunlei married and cherished had her name recorded. And that was extremely odd, now that she thought about it. She was the love of Shunlei's life, and yet no one alive knew her name? No record existed about her? Why would that be?

Unless it was deliberately erased for some reason... Mei Li wasn't suspicious by nature, but she could feel her suspicions rising. She knew for a fact that the time travel spell would alter things so no record would remain of her in the past. Even with taking precautions, Mei Li was bound to make mistakes. She'd actually been quite relieved knowing that if she did some minor slip up, the spell would nix the error later. But right now, that clause in the spell only fueled this train of thought.

Was she Shunlei's bride?

It seemed absurd on the surface. Mei Li had never once thought that. True, Shunlei's automatic acceptance of her in the future had always been a little strange, as well as his knowledge of all her quirks, habits, and sizes. But them being friends and teammates for ten years would explain much of that—Mei Li had assumed she knew the answer.

But maybe she'd made an assumption she shouldn't have.

Or was it an assumption? The records from this era were spotty, incomplete. It was understandable that records five thousand years old would be that way. So perhaps his wife's name had been recorded down, and it just hadn't survived into the future.

That seemed entirely plausible. The only reason she doubted it was because she knew the names of everyone else on the team. Why was only her name not committed?

The more she thought of this, the more suspicious it became.

Unable to come up with an answer, she set that query aside for a moment. Mei Li wouldn't be able to prove it one way or another until she returned to the future, and Shunlei's proposal could hardly hang in limbo for ten years. She needed an answer now.

How did she respond?

Mei Li could freely admit she adored Shunlei. She trusted him, considered him one of the best friends she'd ever had, and given a choice, it would always be him she chose to have at her side. Was she in love with him? She hadn't the faintest clue.

A knock sounded at the door. "Lady Mei?"

Hawes. Mei Li lifted her head and stared at the door, not sure if she wanted company at the moment or not. Grudgingly, she called out, "Come in."

He did so, head first, peeking around the door. Then upon seeing her sitting in the dark, he ducked out again, just for a moment. He next appeared with a lantern, which he sat on the table next to the bed. Mei Li shifted her legs and veil up and to the side, giving him room to sit on the mattress. He wore a kind, sympathetic half-smile as he regarded her.

"I take it you really didn't know he felt this way toward

you?"

Mei Li shook her head back and forth wordlessly.

"You don't wish for it?"

Did she? Didn't she? There were so many other thoughts and emotions complicating the question, she had no ready answer for that. "Did you know dragons can live for thousands of years?"

Hawes blinked at her, head jerking back an inch. "Can they really?"

"They age so incredibly slowly, you see. The Red stage Shunlei is in now makes him barely an adult. Like a teenager just turning eighteen for us. Even as reckless as he is, he will likely live for many thousands of years." Desperate now for advice, she explained more earnestly. "Dragons also mate for life. Even if they lose a mate, it's almost unheard of for them to take another. Do you see?"

"You're afraid of what will happen to him if you accept him." Hawes sank back with a sigh, expression filled with understanding.

"I'll leave him alone. Heartbroken. For *centuries*. Probably even longer. In the heat of the moment he can look at that possibility and say it will be fine. That he's braced for it. But can I really do that to him?" And Future Shunlei really should have given her a hint one way or another, curse him. She'd smack him for this as soon as she was back in the future.

Hawes pursed his lips and didn't immediately answer. "What it sounds like to me is that you want to accept him. That if not for that reason, you would."

Mei Li opened her mouth on a hot protest that died in a croak. Was he right?

"Lady Mei, say what you'd like, but he is a grown man. He knows all of this as well as you do. Still, he chooses you. You can't make a decision based on fear. That only leads to heartbreak."

Wise counsel, but did she heed it? Mei Li couldn't paint the full picture for him. If he knew everything she knew, would he still say the same? Or would that still be making a fear-based decision? She had a feeling it was.

"You don't have to make a decision tonight," Hawes soothed. "In fact, I encourage you to sleep on this."

"I will." Biting her bottom lip, she looked up at him hesitantly. "How is Shunlei? I sort of...ran."

"I think he more or less expected that reaction. He's being remarkably patient and only told me what happened. He said it was only fair for you to have such doubts, as he wrestled with the same. I thought he meant differences between human and dragon, but I suppose he meant the difference in aging as well."

That was true. Shunlei'd had time to really think about this, hadn't he? Of course he'd understand her knee jerk reaction—he'd no doubt gone through the same thing. Or at least a similar feeling.

With a pat on her hand, Hawes left the bed, heading for the door. "I'll leave you the lantern. Come down for dinner. Starving your belly won't solve issues of the heart."

As if on cue, her stomach rumbled petulantly. She glared downward. Really? Here she was in an emotional crisis, and her body could only focus on food? "Bodies are such inconvenient things."

"They can be." Hawes turned at the door, studying her expression carefully. "You can work tomorrow?"

"More like, I need to work tomorrow," she sighed, dragging herself off the bed. "I can't afford to sit and stew about this."

"Well enough."

Shunlei, demonstrating the sort of maturity she expected from Future Shunlei, didn't say a peep to her over breakfast or plague her for an answer. He looked her over, no doubt noting the dark circles under her eyes, but only silently offered her a cup of hot tea. It was just as well. Mei Li had spent most of the night tossing and turning, only getting snatches of rest. If he'd tried to say anything to her, she might have bitten his head off.

Kiyo seemed to pick up on it. She kept eyeing Mei Li sideways as they made their way to the docks. It wasn't until they were halfway there that Mei Li realized Nord was not with them. "Nord?"

"You are out of it," Kiyo stated, eyebrows arched in a way that construed…what? "Nord went to repair the burned ship enough that they could move it."

"Oh." Mei Li hadn't been paying attention to the conversation over breakfast. Apparently, she'd missed a few vital things.

"Just what is going on?" Kiyo dragged her to a halt next to the road, fortunately out of the way of traffic. People scurried back and forth, clearing out the burned and charred remains, kicking up ash in the process. Mei Li put her back to the ocean breeze to help keep the ash from flying into her face.

Rubbing a hand over her mouth, Mei Li debated not saying anything. But, well, they were a small group. People would figure this out sooner or later. Kiyo had already picked up on the tension, even if she didn't understand the cause. "Shunlei's proposed courtship with me."

Kiyo's jaw dropped for a split second and then gave an exaggerated sound of understanding. "Ahh, of course. Of course, he did."

Folding her arms over her chest, Mei Li glared at her. "What do you mean 'of course?'"

"This is the first time since I met the two of you that he's not somewhere nearby." Kiyo gave her an arch look of challenge. "Usually he's more faithful than your shadow.

And you really mean to tell me you haven't seen the way he looks at you when your back is turned?"

"Oddly enough, when a person's back is turned, we tend to not be able to see things happening behind us," Mei Li grumbled, growing more irritated by the second. Why did Kiyo have to act so matter-of-fact about this when it wasn't at all obvious?

Not at all deterred, Kiyo shrugged. "You said yes, I trust?"

"I didn't say anything." Mei Li was done with this conversation. She marched once again for the docks, and nearly got her foot run over by a passing wagon in the process. Swearing, she stopped short, waiting for it to fully pass.

Kiyo caught up with her in a split second. "What do you mean, you didn't say anything?"

"I mean, I don't know how to answer him, and I didn't say anything." Mei Li now regretted saying anything from the dark cockles of her soul. She should have let her wonder.

Doggedly, Kiyo lengthened her stride to stay in pace with her, weaving her way around a dockman carrying a box on his shoulder. "But you love him too! Don't pretend otherwise, you can't miss it."

"You can love someone and not be *in* love with them, Kiyo," Mei Li gritted out. She eyed the ocean longingly, sorely tempted to jump into it. Would Kiyo follow her even there to continue the argument? Was it worth being doused in seawater to escape? Mei Li still had nightmares about being brutally thrown into the ocean and truthfully, she never wanted to be in it again for as long as she lived. But right now, it actually did look inviting.

"You're really not in love with him?" Kiyo asked this as if she'd suggested chopping off a limb.

Mei Li closed her eyes and asked all the spirits and gods for strength. It did not come. "I. Do. Not. Know. I've never— How am I supposed to—What if he—Can we please focus on the thrice-cursed docks now?"

Kiyo gave her that look again, like a parent indulging a slow-witted child. Which grated. Mei Li wanted to smack her in the face for it. "Sure. We'll focus on the docks. Oh look, there's a box of chalk right here waiting on us. The chalk that Shunlei thoughtfully went to find last night. Sweet of him, wasn't it?"

Why had Mei Li's ancestors given her a tongue…?

She didn't trust her mouth not to say something she might later regret. Wordlessly, she snatched up two sticks of chalk instead and stalked toward the dock. Work first. Work, and she'd set everything else aside.

It would be waiting for her, one way or another.

19

For three days that was her mantra. Mei Li worked, ate, slept, got up in the morning, and repeated. She tried not to feel that work was an excuse, and in many ways, it wasn't. They had a lot to do. Docks, businesses, a few houses to restore because normal repair methods would mean tearing it down to the foundation and starting from scratch. People to follow up with in terms of treatment. Really, she barely had time to sit and eat, much less catch her breath.

Mei Li would have felt perfectly justified in pushing the question of courtship off to the side except for two things. One, Shunlei chose not to work with her for those three days, instead helping Hawes. Two, she felt his absence. So many times she'd turn, intending to tell him something, or ask a question, only to face empty air. Mei Li had become far too accustomed to having Shunlei right at her elbow whenever she needed him. Future or past, that habit of his hadn't changed.

His absence was very loud.

She knew very well he was giving her space in order to think about things. That he was, in his own way, trying not to pressure her. But she felt his absence like an ache, which frustrated her. There was no rational reason for it—he was in the same town. The same inn, for mercy's sake. Yet she missed him dearly.

And as much as she didn't want to think about it, she missed Future Shunlei too. Mei Li thought back to their travels a few short months ago. He had taken her under his wing immediately, welcomed her into his home, protected and aided her whenever she needed. But because she knew he still loved his wife even thousands of years later, Mei Li had always tried to keep romantic thoughts at bay, not letting unrequited love cloud their friendship.

But what if she *was* the wife... Mei Li circled back to the suspicions she'd had earlier. Was she the human woman Shunlei married, the one he had cherished even five thousand years later? It would make sense, then, why the spell had sent her back so far into the past. That had puzzled her all this time. Why do this when they had records surviving even two years before? But if she were meant to be Shunlei's wife, then of course she'd need to be in *this* time. She thought back to that first night at Dragon's Peak, to the clothes he'd given her that fit perfectly, the hair combs she now recognized as ones he had bought specifically for her.

A slow smile began to spread across her face. At the same time, doubt immediately flared up, making her stomach queasy. These emotions were a tangled knot she couldn't begin to unravel. And because that frustrated her, it fueled directly into the confusion she felt already. And then she became frustrated at her confusion, which frustrated her even further, as she should be able to figure out the answer to this. This wasn't some insane logic puzzle, like Abe used to give her, where the answer was impossible to divine in a glance. She *should* know how her own heart felt about matters.

But Mei Li had a sneaking suspicion that she *did* know how her heart felt, and that was precisely what was tearing her up so badly. Because what if she wasn't the woman destined to become Shunlei's wife, and she was messing with the timeline to be here?

Actually, now that she really thought about it...Mei Li had often wondered what sort of woman Shunlei had fallen for and married. It had always been a sort of intellectual curiosity. Thinking on it now, visualizing him married to someone, had jealousy rising so quickly she turned dizzy with it. She put a hand to her heart, trying to still its mad thumps of protest. Oh. Wow. That was...more intense of a reaction than she anticipated.

So perhaps she did love Shunlei, more than she'd ever let herself admit. Did that mean she had a ready answer to give him? No. There were too many other thoughts, doubts, and insecurities cluttering up her heart to know for sure. But Mei Li had never really let fear hem her in. She might be in emotional turmoil, but there were two facts that were rock solid.

Fact one: Shunlei married (marries?) a human bride. Whether or not it was her, he still chose a human. She couldn't use the fear of heartbreak as an excuse to avoid him, as he was headed for it one way or another.

Fact two: The idea of Shunlei with some other woman irritated her immensely. She didn't like the mental image of that one iota. Despite the timeline differences, Mei Li wanted to be that woman.

She'd told Kiyo earlier that you could love someone without being in love with them. She meant it. But apparently Mei Li was further over that line than she'd assumed herself to be. She did *not* want to share Shunlei with someone else. In fact, thinking of him giving some other woman the same thoughtful affection he'd bestowed on her made Mei Li mad enough to get up and murder something.

After three days of this emotional turmoil, she was sick of being inside her own head. She was also tired of people eyeing her sideways, like they were bracing for an explosion. And she wanted Shunlei back. Not precisely in that order.

It was nearing sunset now. People were going home, or to restaurants, looking for their dinners. There were still scorched buildings and empty lots here and there with homes that had been burned to the ground. She passed tents that sheltered people, and at one point, sadly, a series of new graves. As quickly as they'd reacted, they hadn't been in time to save everyone.

Mei Li shook the thought off. She had no time for thoughts of that nature. She was on a mission. More specifically, she had a decision to make.

She set out for the side of town not burned, the half that had escaped damage. The market was still up and hopefully open at this hour. She was going to put her own heart to the test. Maybe that way she'd get a clear enough answer to hand to Shunlei. And to herself.

The market wasn't as stocked as she imagined it normally was. With people replacing possessions lost, of course it would be bought out and leave empty shelves behind. The stores kept their doors open, though, and even at this late hour people were darting in and out, making purchases. Mostly food, clothes, and bedding from what she could tell.

She wandered down the road, looking through windows and open doorways, until she found the right shop. On the far edge of the road, just off the main strip, was a small store tucked in next to the shrine. The window display was of a woman's wedding outfit hanging by wires.

Mei Li stared at it for a long moment, the beauty of the red cloth with its golden thread embroidery. The symbolism of the lotus flowers stitched into the hem. She took it all in, top to bottom, then closed her eyes and imagined herself in it.

All of her intellectual reasonings aside, did she want this man for herself? Despite all the pitfalls, all the cons, the many years he'd face without her, never knowing when she would be ripped back to the future—was she still willing to take that leap with him?

The answer that came back to her was a resounding *yes*.

Which meant she had to properly face him.

And yes, that made her intensely nervous, because these feelings might not be new, but she was new to them. New to the realization they were there, at least. She wasn't comfortable with them yet, and they jittered under her skin. Perhaps she should have slept on it, but Mei Li didn't want to sit on them now that she'd finally accepted what she felt for him was love.

With a deep breath for courage, she stepped inside the shop. If she was really going to do this, then she needed something first. She could hardly go to Shunlei empty-handed.

Purchase made, Mei Li searched first the inn, and upon not finding her quarry, went further out and through the town. She had the bundle tucked securely under her arm, but it wouldn't do her any good if she couldn't find him. Urgency drove her forward, searching for the man she needed more than anything.

Ah, there he was. Shunlei sat on the edge of the newly refurbished docks, perched on top of one of the pillars, his head turned so that he stared out over the sea. With the sun setting slowly toward the horizon, the sky was awash with golds and purples and reds. He looked part of the painting, his red skin and hair sun-kissed with golds.

Mei Li could feel the sight of him sitting there burning into her memory and knew she'd never forget this moment until her grave. Seeing him like this, with her heart open to him, made her question how she'd ever managed to keep these feelings at bay.

"Shunlei."

He turned, slowly, head coming around to face her. Hope and trepidation warred across his face. "Hello, Mei."

Blowing out a breath, she told him frankly, "I still think

you're crazy. But I suppose I'm also crazy." Taking the bundle out, she held it toward him with both hands. "Let's court."

A wild, ecstatic smile bloomed over his face. In a split second, he was off the pillar and had both arms around her, ignoring the bundle altogether as he lifted her off her feet with his embrace. Mei Li gasped in surprise, equilibrium thrown when her feet left the ground, but wiggled an arm free to put it around his shoulders, hugging him back. Relief threatened to swamp her. In the end, she felt pleased at her decision.

"You won't regret this," Shunlei swore against her hair.

Poor, dear man. He thought her hesitation had been because she didn't want him. Curse her for taking so long to make a decision. "I'm afraid *you're* going to regret this."

He made an instinctive noise of protest.

"Yes, yes, you've thought it through, you're sure of the decision. Still."

Shunlei sat her back on her feet, gently, but kept both arms around her. It felt a little strange to Mei Li to be held so. Shunlei had embraced her and held her many times, but usually in the course of protecting her. Or transporting her. This was something new, a dimension of the relationship they were just starting. It was...nice.

She liked the way he looked at her, too, with such warmth and affection. It was clear in those never-changing blue eyes. "But you're sure of your own heart?"

"I'm sure of me, worried about you. Because I think this will be incredibly hard on you," she admitted honestly. "But I'm willing to try walking this road you've put us on."

He took her doubts in stride, nodding. "Alright. That's more than I expected after you stewed for three days. You looked very unhappy."

"Frustrated," Mei Li corrected with a grimace. "I honestly didn't know what to do or how to feel about it. I came to the conclusion that my heart wants you. It was only doubt of how you'll handle the future that kept tripping me up. Am I being too honest?"

"No. I want to know how you're feeling. I ruminated over this for weeks. The wisdom of it, and my chances, before I made a decision. You're not saying anything I haven't thought myself."

She felt a sense of relief hearing this. "Good, good. Here, open yours."

Shunlei let go of her enough to accept the bundle still pressed up against his chest and opened it with obvious glee. Mei Li had chosen to buy the belt first, as it was the easiest thing to get without knowing his exact measurements. The belt was tie-on, a dark crimson red with gold threads decorating the front in an elaborate scroll of vines. He ran gentle fingers over its folds, nearly incandescent with joy. It almost hurt to look at him, he was so bright.

"We'll need to know each other's measurements before we can continue to buy anything else," Mei Li noted.

"Yes, but that's a problem for tomorrow." With a smug grin, he offered his arm. "Have dinner with me?"

Finally, she had him back. "I'd love to."

They walked to the inn arm in arm, easy and lighthearted. They chose to have dinner there, as it was one of the few restaurants that could offer variety at the moment. Shunlei darted up to his room to carefully put the belt away before rejoining her in the main dining room. Mei Li, in an effort to have some one-on-one time with him, chose a back corner table with no sight lines of the doors.

As soon as Shunlei came back, they ordered food, and Mei Li had a chance to ask the question that had plagued her. "What was the first attempt? You said you'd tried a few times before realizing I hadn't caught on to your intentions."

Shunlei took her hand, taking it into his own lap in a light grip as he answered. His mouth kicked up in a wry twist. "Well, do you remember the deer I brought you shortly after we left Crimson Lake?"

Oh dear. She'd immediately shared it with the entire camp.

"And then the pillow I bought for you. I could tell you liked it, but you didn't seem to attach any significance to it."

Oops.

"My last attempt was the combs. You liked those too, but still I saw no comprehension from you." Shunlei seemed amused by this, and he only shrugged. "For dragons, we first prove we can be a spouse that provides. Then, that we can offer comforts. Our third gift is something that shows we know the other's tastes."

"Hence deer, pillow, then combs. Oh dear." Mei Li winced. "Sorry?"

"It's so strange for me sometimes." Shunlei's fingers played idly with hers in gentle strokes, sending little sparks of pleasure along her fingertips. "There's so much you know of my people. You speak our language impeccably, you even know how to thrum—and do a passable job of it despite your limited vocal chords—but you have odd gaps where you don't have any knowledge."

"Like courting customs," Mei Li acknowledged, still kicking herself for missing the three times he'd tried. Then again, she'd been sure he married someone else. "To be fair, every dragon I've ever met was either already mated, or hadn't found someone they wanted to court. I never saw this in progress or knew someone who was."

"Ah. And everything else you know of us, you learned by observation?"

"Well, my master taught me quite a bit too. The language, I learned from him."

"How interesting."

Wanting to move him past that, she quickly added, "The thrumming, and how to preen dragon wings, that I learned from a dragon."

"I would imagine those would be hard skills to teach, one human to another. At least without a dragon present."

Head canted, she thought about it. "I'm trying to imagine how that would be possible. It's not working well, even in my head."

"You can practice on me more often," he offered generously.

Mei Li snorted. "Is that a hint?"

"You can interpret it that way." Shunlei waggled his eyebrows at her in an outrageous manner.

Mei Li had a perfect retort on the tip of her tongue when she saw Hawes carefully approaching the table, expression hopeful. They really had worried their team leader, hadn't they? In a bout of charity, she waved him over. Hawes promptly did so, not missing their clasped hands. Then he went all shades of relieved.

"I take it you've decided to court?"

Shunlei outright gloated. "We have."

Hawes put a hand to his chest, heaving an exaggerated sigh. "I'm glad to hear it. I didn't want to take that tension out on the road."

Dipping his head, Shunlei agreed, but there was a puzzled frown, brows drawn together. "Are we leaving soon?"

"I hoped to do so in the next two days or so. We've done most of the work here that we can, and we still have a troublesome sword to track down." Hawes looked between the two of them, now uncertain. "Why?"

"I'd hoped to find enough time to create a harness." Shunlei turned to Mei Li, biting his bottom lip uncertainly. "Courting couples normally fly together."

She hadn't known that, but it didn't surprise Mei Li in the least. "I can tell you how to design it. It's basically a box that will strap to your chest."

"You can't do something like a saddle?" Hawes asked in interest. "Wait, you've had dragons fly you before? I know

Shunlei did that short flight, but I mean longer stretches."

"Yes. Not often, but yes. And a saddle is rather impractical for me. There's nothing to keep me in it, you see." Mei Li's free hand lifted in illustration, moving it back and forth as she mimicked a dragon's flight. "Dragons bank to the right and left, sometimes doing insane dives and upthrusts into the air. It isn't a stable, smooth ride all of the time, not like on a horse's back. If they twist and turn, even with me gripping the saddle with legs and hands, there's no guarantee I can hang on."

Shunlei blew out a deflated air. "She's unfortunately correct. I can try making a rope harness, but those don't tend to hold up for very long. Our scales wear away the rope rather quickly."

Hawes glanced between them, brows beetled in bemusement. "You've flown together before, though."

"That was an extremely short flight," she pointed out. "In calm weather. Otherwise we wouldn't have been able to."

Shunlei deflated even more, shoulders hunched, a pout on his lips. "But I won't be able to talk much to you if you're strapped to my chest."

"I can talk out of the top. And Long-go is loud, you know that."

His shoulders came up a bit as he cottoned onto her meaning. "That's true, isn't it?"

"We'll work it out." Mei Li squeezed his fingers before turning her attention back to Hawes. "Two days might be enough, but you'll need to let Shunlei focus on it."

Shunlei made a noise of protest. "I don't know how to do leatherworking like that."

Oh. Uh...was this a skill he'd picked up later? Future Shunlei hadn't hesitated to make it himself. Mei Li eyed him sideways. "I'm not an expert leatherworker either. Um. I can draw it out for someone to make for us?"

"That seems the saner way to go."

Mei Li took this plan further and frowned. The carrier wasn't what anyone would call small, not at the size that a grown person could fit comfortably inside. Which hadn't mattered in the future, as it was constantly in use. But here, where it would be used sparingly, it meant hauling it about for the most part. That would take up valuable room on the pack horses. "Actually, I'm not sure that's wise. We won't be able to use it much, and it's bulky. It will take up space on the pack horses we can ill afford to use."

Shunlei let out a huff. "You're right. Maybe short flights with you?"

"That's probably the best approach. We can't do long flights anyway, not right now."

Hawes gave them a smile. "I'll let you two work that out. I'm glad for you both."

"Thank you," she answered with her own smile. "So am I."

20

Being back on the road was something of a relief. The people in Haslett had picked up on their courtship—easily done with how they were acting and the purchases they made—and while some of them were indulgent, others found it to be taboo. A human and a dragon had no business being together. Especially with the aftermath of a dragon's rampage in the town, there were more than a few mixed feelings on the matter. It might have come to a more obvious tension if not for the good grace they'd all earned by putting the town back to rights.

Still, Mei Li was glad to have Haslett at her back. They rode out early in the morning, Shunlei riding double with her as usual. They capitalized on the proximity more than usual by talking constantly.

By late afternoon, they all agreed to find a good place to camp. It didn't appear they'd arrive at a town before night fell, and this was the first patch of semi-flat land they'd seen all day. They went through the usual camp chores, including putting up tents. It smelled like rain although they didn't see any signs of clouds yet.

Shunlei surprised her by snaking an arm around her waist and whispering against her ear, "Fly with me?"

They had barely any light left, but she didn't want to

refuse him. With a smile, she nodded.

Turning his head, Shunlei called, "Hawes! We'll be gone an hour or so."

Kiyo waved them on. "It'll take me that long to make dinner, go ahead."

Going further out, he found an open spot and shifted forms. Mei Li followed him, putting both arms around his neck as he cradled her up against his chest. The updraft sent chills along her skin but she ignored those. It might be a bit too cold still for a night flight, true, as summer was still a month away. But the heat pouring off Shunlei's skin would keep her warm enough.

And the skies were glorious.

A smile lit her face as she looked all around her even as Shunlei gained altitude. The stars shone in full force tonight, bright spots of light against inky darkness. She enjoyed the view immensely, as well as the feeling that if she just reached out a hand, she could touch one of them.

He banked a little, the wind rustling her hair and sending it flying in multiple directions. Mei Li dragged several strands out of her mouth and asked, "Do you have a spot in mind?"

"There." His head turned to indicate a grassy slope that overlooked the ocean.

It looked a pretty spot to relax in, certainly. And it wasn't too far from camp, which was even better.

Shunlei slowed and carefully descended with her, setting feet to earth first. She let go so he could land a short distance away, and avoided his tail with practiced ease. Dragons were like puppies when it came to tails—they often lost all awareness of where the tail was going.

Only once he was switched to human form did she approach, sinking down onto the grass next to him and snuggling against his side. They lay there with her head pillowed on his arm, stargazing.

"It's such a clear night," she said, her eyes panning the

heavens. "Normally you can't see the constellations like this."

"Really? I see them often."

Oh. Right. The atmosphere changed in the future. Mei Li cursed her tongue and rephrased, "At least, I'm usually in an area that normally has a lot of cloud cover."

"Ah, I see. Then it's even better I chose tonight to fly with you. It's the perfect night for it."

"It really is." They lay like that for several minutes, content in each other's company. It felt intimate to her, a moment just for them, and Mei Li almost didn't ask some of the questions burning on the tip of her tongue. But there were so many basic things she didn't know about him. It seemed a shame to not try and learn more. "Shunlei...as long as I've known you, I've never heard you mention your parents."

"My parents, eh?"

"You've mentioned a broodmother, but no one else."

"Ah, I can see how you'd question it, then. Well, our society is a little different from human culture. Typically, we have our own territories, and we only really cross those lines to either hunt or mate, but there's one exception. Broodmothers. These are older dragons, ones who have had younglings of their own, and they can cross territories freely. It's understood that if a broodmother is nearby, and you have a youngling you can't care for easily, you can go to her for help. Or if you find a young one, for instance, you can track down a broodmother. They'll take any and all children."

Mei Li had been aware of about half of that. "Which were you?"

"My mother took me to a broodmother for help. At least, at first. I never knew my father, and she wouldn't speak of him, so I'm not sure why she was alone. The broodmother helped look after me while my mother hunted for all of us. That's typically how the arrangement works. But one day, my mother just didn't come back. I assumed her lost for several weeks until we finally got word she'd been caught in a bad storm and didn't make it through."

Mei Li turned, putting her forehead against the side of his face. "I'm sorry."

"It's an old scar on the heart now." His arms around her waist squeezed for a moment in silent thanks. "I was very young then. I barely remember her at all. My broodmother is really the only mother I remember. I still see her whenever I pass through the right area. She's more or less claimed territory and has no intention of moving."

"Well, if she's comfortable and safe, why move?"

"Her sentiments exactly. Come to think of it, you've not mentioned parents?"

"I was given to the temple when I was very young. I barely remember my parents as well. My master came and adopted me when I was six. I was with him until the shipwreck."

"So, he's your family."

"Yes. My absent-minded father figure who can, and has, nearly burned the house down on several memorable occasions." Mei Li snorted at the memory. Then sighed, as of course she still had no idea if he was alright.

"You're worried for him."

"He's just such a careless man when it comes to taking care of himself. I took on so much of the household chores even as a child because he was inept with them. It's easy to get lost in this world—it's so vast, after all—so it's understandable I haven't found him yet. I'm just worried about what state he's in now."

"I'll help you," he promised in a low voice.

"I know you will." Now and in the future. A spark caught her eye and she gasped. "Shooting star! Quick, make a wish!"

"Does making a wish on a falling star really come true?"

"It will as—too late." She sighed, aggravated. Mei Li rarely saw shooting stars. She really should have made a wish and *then* tried to explain it to Shunlei. Oh well. "You have to make your wish before it disappears."

"Hmm. I have a feeling I can realize my own wish, though." Turning his head, he caught her chin and lifted up enough to press a chaste kiss against her mouth.

Mei Li blinked, not expecting this. She'd never been kissed before, but that was a pleasant sensation. She smiled against his mouth, and that was the only encouragement he needed to do it again.

Then once more, with sweet heat.

They parted with a soft sigh. Mei Li's hand brushed up his chest slowly, and she relished the way his eyes darkened. "Shunlei, dearest. I think we're going to be late getting back to camp."

"Are we?" he murmured, already leaning back down.

"Very, very late."

They were, indeed, very late. By about three hours. Mei Li's hair was a scattered mess any bird would love to nest in—and that was only partially due to the windy conditions of the sky. Neither of their clothing was precisely straight or tidy. It was rather obvious in a glance what they had been doing.

The only one still up was Melchior, and he gave them an indulgent smile as they strolled back into camp. "How was your flight?"

"Lovely," Mei Li answered forthrightly. "I take it you have first watch?"

"I do."

"I can turn dragon and sleep near the camp, keep predators at bay," Shunlei offered. "There's no need for people to lose sleep."

Melchior bit the inside of his cheek and looked sorely tempted. "Will you be comfortable out here? I think it'll rain."

Shunlei shrugged, not at all bothered by the possibility. "Rain won't bother me any. It doesn't smell like it'll hit anytime soon. I think we're going to be riding in it tomorrow."

"Oh, now doesn't that sound pleasant," Mei Li grumbled. Then sighed. There was no way to avoid weather while traveling. "On that lovely note, let's eat. Someone saved dinner for us?"

"We did. Tempting though it was to not." Melchior gave her a wink before nodding to the soup pot resting near the fire. "Should still be warm."

"Thank you." Mei Li dished up some for Shunlei, then herself, and sat with the men companionably as she ate. Then it was a quick wash of the dishes in a nearby brook before kissing Shunlei goodnight and turning in.

She thought Kiyo asleep in their tent and tried to be quiet as she got ready for bed, but the woman turned over, eyes open.

"How was your flight?"

"Entirely romantic." Mei Li sat on the bedroll and took a comb to her hair. She'd get out the worst of the knots for tonight and plait her hair, then have Shunlei finish the job in the morning. He pouted now if he didn't get to arrange her hair.

Kiyo only hummed thoughtfully.

Not sure what that reaction meant, Mei Li looked at her askance. "What?"

"I've been thinking about it, why Shunlei fell for you. Really, it might have been inevitable. From the beginning you've accepted him fully, with absolutely no doubts. You're confident in whatever goal he sets. I suppose that level of adoration is impossible to resist."

Mei Li certainly reacted that way to him, she couldn't deny that. "I'm not disagreeing, but...I'm not sure if that explains why he's attracted to me, though."

"Oh, I'm not saying that's all it is. I just think that's why he grew close enough to you for this attachment to form. I can't imagine he'd pay close attention to most human women on a day to day basis. It was your reaction to him that encouraged him to take a closer look." Kiyo seemed quite confident in her theory. Also tired, as she ended her declaration with a soft sigh. "I don't think this was his intention, either. When he originally set the goal for humanity and dragons to be friends, I mean."

Snorting, Mei Li agreed dryly, "Likely not."

"I bet you're glad he came up with that goal."

"I am. For entirely selfish reasons."

Curious, Kiyo pried open an eyelid to regard her. "Do you really think the two of you will marry, then?"

"Oh, of that I'm quite sure."

21

Riding, riding, riding. Laborde seemed peaceful still, at least. Mei Li was grateful for small favors. The only thing that broke up the monotony of traveling was her talks with Shunlei.

At night, he often took her on short flights so they could spend a little time alone with each other. Mei Li loved those stolen moments more than words could express. Having his undivided attention wasn't precisely new to her, but knowing she carried part of this man's heart with her somehow made it new. His patience and affection were quelling her fears and slowly giving her confidence. He really had thought this through. The best she could do was to be with him *now* and make their time worth it.

They exchanged the second piece of the wedding outfit—the shoes—and Mei Li did it with complete confidence. Seeing her confidence overjoyed Shunlei. She had no idea where or when they'd be able to buy the next piece, but she looked forward to the moment they could exchange the next garment.

The long days of riding and the short, sweet moments eventually carried them through the main leg of their journey. They passed through the rolling, golden foothills north of the Summer Wind Mountains, continuing along the coastal highway that bordered on the East Sea. When they crossed into the flat plains south of the foothills, Mei Li knew they'd just crossed into the border of Bader.

Which meant they were, at least, finally in the right country. Now that they were in Bader, they stood a far better chance of finding and stopping Ghost General's Sword—and whoever was unlucky enough to wield it.

They were in sight of Bader's border when a dragon flew overhead. It caught all of their attention, and they stilled, waiting to see what it would do. This one was a Green, quite dark in tone, so heading for Blue stage shortly. It spied them, banked, and did a lazy circle around the group before calling down in Long-go, "I seek Shunlei the Red!"

Shunlei immediately called back, "I am he!"

"I would speak words with you!"

"Then come down, we will speak as friends."

This seemed amiable to Green, as he (she?) turned and found a good stretch of road to land in. Shunlei hopped off as the other dragon landed, loping ahead several paces and changing forms until he was in dragon mode as well. Mei Li assumed some sort of etiquette was in place and didn't ask.

Green turned, settling down with wings tucked in along the sides. With a duck of the head, the dragon greeted them all. "I am Kalei the Green."

"Well met, Kalei. You've words you wish to tell me?" Shunlei settled down opposite of her, also relaxed on the road, for all the world as if they had oodles of time.

"Yes. I have heard of you, and your goals. Many that I met have spoken of you. Enlai is such a one. He said you brokered a deal for him so he may claim human territory as his own?"

To Mei Li's ears, this sounded hopeful, as if Kalei wanted the same for herself.

Carefully, Shunlei answered, "He claims it as home, yes. It still belongs to humans, but he can hunt and live there. In return, he helps them."

Kalei nodded, as if she already knew this. "Yes, he explained how the deal was made. It was a good deal. I wanted to meet with you and ask you to help me do the same. My mate and I search for a good place to settle and have eggs. But there's no place that offers good hunting that isn't already taken."

This sounded especially good to Mei Li. She approached from the side, so both dragons could easily track her, and offered a bow. "Kalei, I am Mei."

Kalei gave her a duck of the head, a startled sort of smile on the dragon's face. "You speak Long-go?"

"I do. I know of a place you and your mate would be welcome."

Kalei's tail gave a happy thump on the ground. "Where is this place? Is it good for hatchlings?"

"It is." To Shunlei, Mei suggested, "Lady Ilona's?"

"Ah." Remembrance flashed through his eyes. "Yes, of course, that's perfect. Kalei, we were visiting in Laborde not far from here. The city that is surrounded by orchards and grapes, you know of it?"

"Yes, I pass it often."

"The lady that governs the city is keen to have dragons live there. For protection, mostly. She offers the same deal Enlai now enjoys. If you tell her I sent you, she will happily give you a home."

Kalei thrummed, a happy, excited sound. "This is good. You've directed me to a good place. I thank you, Shunlei, Mei. I will find my mate, and we will go there. It is good I found you on the way. We are leaving our old territory. It is too dangerous there."

Uh-oh. That didn't sound good. Mei pressed, "Why, what happened there?"

"There is a sword, a magical sword, that is causing havoc. It made men fight us even when we tried to avoid them." Kalei shook her head in disapproval. "It became too dangerous for hatchlings. We chose to leave and find another place. I would not go further south. It is only trouble."

Ghost General's Sword. Check. Mei tried not to sound too eager as she questioned. "Where was it precisely, do you know?"

"It moved often. We kept waiting, thinking it would leave our territory. But it does not, just changes hands. We grew frustrated." Kalei canted her head, thinking. "Near the mountains was where we saw it last."

"That gives us something of an idea. Thank you."

"Thank you," Shunlei echoed. "Safe journey. Ask for Lady Ilona or the Lady of the Fields."

"I will do so." With another duck of the head, Kalei shook her wings out and did a powerful upthrust, springing herself back into the sky.

Hawes approached, still in the saddle and asked, "What was that?"

Turning to him, Mei Li gave him the succinct version. "That was a dragon looking for Shunlei. She wanted to get the same deal Enlai now has at Crimson Lake. We told her to go to Lady Ilona's."

Hawes smiled, quick and pleased. "That's wonderful. She'll be excited to see her."

"Them," Shunlei corrected, changing back to human form in an easy transition. "Kalei is mated. They want to start having children, so they've been on the lookout for safer territory. They said they had to abandon their old territory, as there was a dangerous magical sword on the loose."

"Dangerous magical sword, eh? And where was their old territory?"

Mei Li pointed dead behind her. "South, at the base of the mountains, is where she saw it last."

"Well, then, sounds like we're heading the right direction." Hawes got that grim look on his face that suggested he was already planning ahead. "Right. You two mount up. Let's go hunt down a sword."

They did so, resuming their southern trek, but with a steadier purpose this time instead of a vague idea of where to go.

The Divided River was a natural barrier they had to cross in order to reach the southern coast. Fortunately, there was many a ferry set up for travelers, and since they were on a major highway, the ferry was more than just one man with a flat barge. They had a small ticket office, several flat boats, and even a holding pen for cattle and sheep off to the side.

It was a bit busy, with more than a few people wanting to cross, and a line formed up to the side. Hawes went ahead of the group to buy them a ticket, and everyone took the chance to get out of the saddle and stretch their legs a little. Mei Li felt practically bow-legged after so much time in the saddle and was thankful to be on her own two feet. Even if it was only for a few minutes.

As she stood there, she heard whispers from ahead and behind.

"—not sure if it's a good idea to go west—"

"—they say no one can stop him—"

"—looks mad—"

Shunlei turned, apparently hearing the same, and gave a bow of the head. "Excuse me for eavesdropping, but what are you speaking of?"

The two behind them in line looked to be farmers and likely brothers—the pronounced high brow made them very similar in appearance. The taller of the two cleared his throat, giving a quick bow in return.

"Master, it's just that we've heard stories from our uncle. He's a trader, always brings word up to us about all that goes on. He said it's not safe to go near the mountains right now. Said there's some madman north of Bader's capital who's destroying anything and everything in his path. Our uncle claims he got a glimpse of the man and said he was holding a sword and looked mad, absolutely mad. He was laughing even as he was killing."

Mei Li grimly listened. So. Ghost General's Sword was nearby and active. "Did he give you a firmer location than that?"

"Well, he was passing through the capital and on the way back to here," the shorter, and likely younger, of the two offered. He scratched at his shaggy brown hair and gave her a shrug. "I don't remember him saying precisely where. But it would have been somewhere along that route."

"Just that tells me a great deal. Thank you." Mei Li turned immediately and moved past the horses, searching for the rest of her team.

Hawes spotted her and stopped mid-sentence, cutting his conversation with Melchior short upon seeing her face. It must have said something, and certainly she felt very determined and grim. "Lady Mei, is there an issue?"

"I think I've just found the cursed sword we were looking for. At least, from the description, I'm fairly sure it's the sword. The man who passed the information along said his uncle had seen a mad, sword-wielding lunatic slaughtering people and laughing. He's somewhere just north of the capital."

Hawes' brows drew together in a dark frown. "If it's somewhere north of the capital..." He trailed off, thinking hard. "That could be anywhere between a day or two days ahead of us on the road."

"Yes, I know." She could tell what he was thinking, as the words were practically written across the man's face. "You want to send Shunlei ahead."

With a grimace, Hawes shifted uneasily on his feet. "I'm not in the habit of separating a courting couple, but..."

"No, this only makes sense. With the proper rope talisman, he might be able to hook the host of the sword and stop him long enough for us to catch up." Mei Li didn't like the idea of Shunlei going ahead either, but for an entirely different reason. Humanity didn't think of dragons as allies, not yet. If he was seen attacking another human, odds weren't in his favor. Someone might try and stop him—or do worse than just try and stop him.

A hand settled at her back as Shunlei joined the conversation. "I think it's best to at least try it. I hate to think of how many innocents he's killing. And if someone else stops him before I can get there, that's something you need to know. If nothing else, I can go and scout out the situation."

Mei Li bit her bottom lip. All of that was true. So why did she have this uneasy feeling in her gut? In terms of flying, he could get there well ahead of them. It might take her a full two days just to catch up. At the same time, it was too far of a distance for her to perch in his arm like she normally did. Was it the distance that bothered her? Sending him ahead without any backup?

Shunlei kissed her temple in reassurance. "It's fine."

"I'd feel better if you went, even if it's to scout ahead and report back," Hawes admitted with splayed hands.

"I would as well," Melchior agreed with a nod.

Shunlei seemed to expect those answers. To Mei Li, he requested, "Give me the rope, just in case."

"Let me re-spell it. I can change the spell so that when it's within a certain range of the cursed sword, it will activate on its own. You'll just need to release it." Mei Li turned toward Peanut, already re-designing the spell in her head. This would take several minutes, but they had time until it was their turn for the ferry.

Upon reaching her horse, she found that Kiyo had already retrieved the rope and was re-working the talisman woven into the fibers.

"She heard you," Nord explained quietly. "She wants to give it a boost, just in case."

Since Kiyo's magic was more powerful, Mei Li let her

work without a qualm. Instead, she focused on Shunlei. "You'll be careful? It's alright to drop the rope around the target and then retreat. You don't need to stay and keep an eye on him. It'll hold for twenty-four hours, which should give us the time we need to reach you."

"It'll be fine, my love," Shunlei assured her. "It's not the first time I've tangled with magic."

"It's the first time you've tangled with magic without a mage being nearby," she countered. "And you promise me that if it reaches twenty hours, and we're still not there, you'll come fetch me. We should be on the highway heading that direction, I'm sure you'll be able to find me. I don't want you trying to tackle that thing on your own."

His head canted to the side, blue eyes narrowed. "But the magic you worked on me should protect me from the curse on the sword, correct?"

Mei Li shook her head in frustration. "I don't know. I've never studied the sword in person, and the one record I read of it didn't give much in the way of details. It's a very insidious magic. It speaks to a man's weaker nature or promises him great power to achieve his goals. The shield I gave you was meant for more direct attacks."

His mouth pursed. "Well. That gives this problem an entirely new dimension. I'll strive to keep my distance. I might well stay and guard the sword so it can't tempt any other human."

That was not what she wanted to hear. "No, Shunlei, it would be better to drop the trap and then retreat—"

"Doing so, and then leaving it unguarded, only leaves the possibility open for the sword to switch hosts. I do not think it wise." Seeing her worry, he smoothed a hand down her hair, smile gentle. "Do not worry, I will guard it, but keep my distance as well. I will take human form as soon as I can to prevent people from thinking this is some nefarious work of a dragon."

She really wished he wouldn't, but Shunlei did precisely what he wished. He'd always been that way. "Alright, fine, but be careful."

Mei Li regretted those words immensely. Twenty-three hours they'd been on the road, and still no sign of Shunlei. They pushed themselves and the horses hard, barely resting for four hours before re-saddling and getting back on the road. Still, through the exhaustion, worry ate at the back of her mind. She didn't understand what had happened or why he'd not come back to her. They'd been traveling along the road, just as she'd said they would. Shunlei should have been able to find her.

If he'd left looking for her at all.

One scenario after another crashed through her mind. Mei Li really hoped none of them were true, but her mind seemed to fixate on them. Had he not been able to stop Ghost General's Sword and was forced to battle it? Was he hurt? Was he stopped from fighting it by other people and was now chained down? Had Ghost General's Sword somehow latched onto him? Was he at the curse's mercy?

It could be any of that, or none of it—she had no way of knowing.

But she knew they were going in the right direction. That was very obvious. They passed bodies strewn off to the side of the road, numerous injured being tended to by loved ones, and it killed Mei Li that they couldn't stop. Couldn't offer aid. But they did not have the time. They *had* to get to Shunlei before the rope's magic wore off. As it stood, the magic was already dangerously weak and was probably incapable of caging Ghost General's Sword for much longer.

A town rose in front of them, and even from here, she could see the smoke still rising in tendrils from between the roofs. It looked as if a small army had crashed through here.

There were slash marks on every possible surface—even one through a stone corner of a building. The damage was incredible, especially considering it was just one sword that had caused it all.

The town wasn't large, more of a stop for traders and merchants on the way to the capital. Barely fifty buildings in all, and Mei Li blessed that. It meant less possible casualties, for one, and she couldn't get turned around in the streets while searching for Shunlei. Her seeking spell could only show a direction, much like a compass.

It took no time at all to get off the highway and through the main street, into the center of town. Clearing the last corner, she finally laid eyes on Shunlei.

For a second, a split second, relief threatened to overwhelm her. Shunlei sat on an upturned barrel in the center of an open courtyard. Damage had clearly been done here, as there were great rends in the paving stones, and the water fountain nearby spurted water at random through the ruined stones. A prone man wrapped in the rope lay not far from Shunlei's feet. He lay with his back to her, so she couldn't get a clear look at him. The sword was tangled up with him, though—she could see it half-tucked under his body.

Shunlei, for the first time ever, didn't immediately greet her. He stared hard at the sword instead, his body unnaturally still.

"That," Hawes said with a grunt, "does not look good. Shunlei?"

No response. Shunlei didn't even twitch.

Mei Li saw from the corner of her eye that people watched warily from open windows and peeked out from behind their doors. They were clearly aware that this situation was a bad one and had no interest in getting any closer. She didn't have that to contend with, at least.

It was a very small silver lining at the moment.

"I don't know what's going on here." Melchior dropped out of the saddle with a grunt. "Lady Mei, what's your opinion? Is Shunlei enthralled by the sword?"

"No." She meant to say that with confidence, but it came out a trifle weak. "If he was really enthralled, it would be in his hand and he'd be swinging it around."

"I'd say he's on his way to being enthralled," Kiyo put in. She was already reaching for her bag, readying talismans. "Mei, do we dare approach him?"

"I wouldn't suggest it. But can you be ready to slap a quick seal on the sword?"

"Yes."

That left her to handle Shunlei. Mei Li sucked in a deep breath and dismounted from Peanut. She had to approach this carefully, otherwise she'd upset whatever delicate balance was hanging right now. Right now, it looked to her as if Shunlei had stayed, as he said he would, to guard the sword from being picked up by someone else. After twenty-something hours, it might have found a way inside his head.

She stopped ten feet from him, to the side and away from the sword. "Shunlei?"

He half-turned toward her. "It calls to me, Mei."

"I'm sure it does." Oh, thank all the gods, he was still rational. "Can you ignore it and come to me? Let Kiyo seal it."

"I've been trying to move for the past several hours. I wanted to go to you. I don't trust my will right now. I'm barely keeping myself from lunging for it."

Oh. Hence why he sat so very, very still. She cast her mind about for a solution.

His voice turned sing-song, eyes glazing over. "It wants me to wield it. It promises me great power if I wield it. Do you think I can tame the dragons if I do so?"

Chills raced over her skin. That was not her Shunlei. Whatever restraint held him in check was quickly fading.

"No, I don't think so. Shunlei? Dearest, can you focus on me?"

His eyes didn't leave the sword. "It says I'll need its power to attain all my goals. Do you think it's right?"

She was losing him. A wave of terror hit her like nothing she had experienced before. Her hands shook, desperate to latch onto him, but she didn't dare make any sudden moves. Swallowing around a dry throat, she cast her mind desperately for some way to draw his attention from the sword. "Beloved. Look at me."

By degrees, Shunlei's eyes came up to meet hers. An absent quality lingered there, as if his attention was still not wholly where he looked.

"You want to marry me, don't you?"

"Yes," he answered without hesitation.

"And I want to marry you. Why don't you come to me so we can talk about it."

A light flickered in his eyes before they glazed over again. "You have doubts, though. Doubts that we should court. You think I'll regret things in the future. The sword keeps promising you'll have no doubts once I use it. It promises that it will keep us together for eternity."

Mei Li cursed her past self a thousandfold and aimed a mental kick that direction. She mentally cursed the sword, and its maker, while she was at it. Of course it latched onto every doubt and weakness lurking in the shadows of Shunlei's mind. Mei Li paid no attention to their audience as she used every bit of honesty and sincerity to disarm the sword's grasp on her man. "That's nonsense. I've left all of those doubts behind."

A bit more of himself came back into his face so he looked a little less like a puppet. "You have?"

"We have now. Shouldn't we fully live in the present, before we worry over a future we have no control over? I want you now. You said you want to marry me. I want to marry you, too. Why depend on a sword for that when you can have me right this very moment? Come to me."

She held out both hands, smiling at him, a silent plea.

Shunlei stared at her hands in something like awe. "We really can?"

"Yes." It was working, but not enough to move him. And then she realized what she had been missing, the words she had been too afraid, too inexperienced, to say before. "You know, I love you a great deal. I love your intelligence, and your warm hands, and the sweet affection in your eyes when you look at me. I love it when I fly with you because it feels like we're the only two people in the world in that moment."

The corners of his mouth tilted up and a little more of himself came back to his face. "Yes, I love that too. You really feel that way?"

"Of course." And she thought she knew how to prove it, one more thing that would appeal to the dragon side of him. Her throat was dry—this would be harder than usual to manage—but she put her heart and soul into it.

Mei Li thrummed. She mimicked the sounds of affection, of safety, but mostly of love. A deep, unparalleled love that knew no restrictions, no boundaries. Pushing aside all worries of the future, she thrummed to him as loudly as she could, desperate to reach him.

His eyes closed for a moment before re-opening. The fight was visible on his face, the war between what he wanted and what the sword said to him. Hesitantly, he stood gingerly, like an aging man with bad joints. Mei Li almost caught her breath, afraid he'd go for the sword after all, but she didn't dare stop thrumming. She doubled her efforts, keeping her hands out and steady.

With both hands, he grasped hers, then took that last step in to rest his head against hers. With a sigh, he settled there, and for the first time, thrummed back. It was a richer, deeper tone that vibrated against the top of her head.

Kiyo lost not a second as she leapt forward and slapped not one, but two sealing talismans on the sword directly. Doing so had a direct reaction on Shunlei, who toppled forward like a marionette with its strings cut. Mei Li caught him by the shoulders, then dug in her heels when his body weight threatened to topple her.

Shunlei's arms came up weakly to hold her to him and he sighed, his head pillowed against her shoulder. "Thank you."

Stroking his head, she promised him, "You're not going ahead alone ever again."

He gave a content hum, pleased at this promise, and passed out.

22

The mayor of the town was immensely grateful for their aid in stopping the rampage caused by Ghost General's Sword. He especially had nothing but kind things to say for Shunlei, praising the man's willpower and stalwart defense of the sword from any other careless hand. He offered them rooms not only in his house, but his daughter's next door, and they accepted immediately. All of them were exhausted and barely functional.

Mei Li stayed with Shunlei, afraid of any aftereffects of that sword messing with his mind. She curled up next to him on the wide bed, the door cracked so that if something did happen, she could call out to either Nord or Hawes. But even though she intended to watch over him, her body betrayed her. She slept with the same soundness as a drowned log. Even her dreams were of sleeping.

A hand gently stroking hair from her face woke her. Mei Li blinked slowly awake, then smiled at the scene that greeted her. Shunlei lay on his side, watching her with a gentle smile on his face.

"Good morning," he greeted softly.

Sighing, she caught his hand and pressed a kiss into the palm. "You're well?"

"I'm fine. Mentally tired, still. I had no idea that a battle of wills for twenty hours could be so exhausting."

She blinked at him, her mind tripping to full wakefulness. "Was it really twenty hours?"

"Something like it. Maybe not a full twenty." Shunlei frowned a little, eyes going distant. "When I left you, it took me a few hours to find him. Then several frustrating minutes as he dodged in and out of buildings. I couldn't just drop the rope as you'd told me to. Finally, he crossed the square and it was open enough ground. I dropped the rope, and it entangled him firmly. I was set to land, just watch for a while, with the thought I'd leave once I explained things to the people nearby. But after I landed, I saw the sword glowing still. I was afraid it might ensnare people once I left. I was right—it would have. It worked very hard to convince me to wield it."

Mei Li stared at him, absolutely gobsmacked. "I knew you had a strong will but great deities, man! Your will is indomitable. Anyone else in that position would have been seduced."

This amused him. But pleased him, too, she could see it in the smug tilt of his mouth. "Really, for most of that time, it was easy to ignore the sword. I only want two things in life. For the dragons and humanity to be friends, and you. It couldn't give me either."

Still...Mei Li was reeling from the idea that he could face that sort of temptation head on and not bow to it. "But when I reached you, you said it was very hard to ignore it?"

"Toward the end, it was. It wasn't so much that I believed its lies. I was just tired. My will was reaching the point that I wanted to pick up the sword and end matters. I didn't for the simple reason that I wasn't going to let a thrice-cursed sword get the better of me."

"Ahh, stubbornness," she acknowledged with a soft laugh. "Now that I believe."

"Of course. Stubbornness has worked out well for me so

far."

"I suppose it has." Mei Li was starving, and thirsty, but she still didn't want to get out of bed just yet. She was comfortable where she was, for one thing. And this was a peaceful moment. Those were hard to come by.

She snuggled in closer, wrapping an arm around his waist, and settled again with a happy sigh. Shunlei pulled her in closer still, hand idly stroking her back.

"I worried you, didn't I?" he murmured apologetically against the top of her head.

"I was frantic to get to you. I didn't know what had happened, only that my seeking spell insisted the trap had been used. But it's alright. We'll never do this again. I'm going with you from now on."

"So, you're saying we'll really need to design a harness for you."

"That's exactly what I'm saying."

"I'll get to fly with you more often. I'm alright with this plan."

"I didn't think I'd get an argument." Feeling a little mischievous, she tacked on, "I have another plan you'll like."

"Oh?"

"I vote we go to Summer Winds Temple after this and rest for a while."

"Why there, specifically?"

"They have natural hot springs on the grounds." She waited for that to click. Three, two, one...

"In other words," Shunlei said with rising excitement, "they have open-air baths?"

"They do," Mei Li purred.

"Big enough for my natural form?"

"Maybe not on the temple grounds themselves, but there's plenty of springs in the area. I'm sure we can find one." Or make one. Mei Li would throw magic at the problem if that was Shunlei's wish. He'd certainly earned the privilege. And she liked making him happy.

Shunlei vibrated as if he were tempted to spring up right this second and dash out the door. "Let's go."

Snickering, she reminded him, "We need to convince everyone else, too."

"Bah," he dismissed. "We'll tell them we're eloping. They can come or not as they please."

That sounded half teasing, but also half serious. "Eloping?"

"Well, it's a temple, after all." Shunlei's tone indicated this was obvious, and she should have already realized what he meant without him having to spell it out. "Hawes explained that humans have to be married in a ceremony with a person of power officiating. A priest at a temple would be able to do it, right?"

Mei Li felt a cultural gap coming on. "Shun, dearest, tell me something. How long do dragons normally court before they marry?"

He went still again, and his tone was cautious. "Normally a week or two? I'm afraid to ask. How long do humans court?"

"A year is pretty standard."

He made a noise like a duck choking on a cracker. "Why would you wait so long?!"

"The thought is, it gives the couple time to really know how well they're going to work together. And most wedding ceremonies are pretty elaborate and take a while to plan out. But dragons normally do a mating flight, right?"

"Right. No ceremony with us. And really, we should know in the first two weeks if we'll be a good match or not. We go hunting together many times during a courtship, and work through challenges, so it's obvious quickly." Shunlei hummed, one of those deep-chested thrums that indicated thought on his part. It vibrated Mei Li's body in a pleasant way. "Do we...need to court a year?"

The reluctance in him was obvious even though she

wasn't looking at his face. Mei Li, perhaps, should have said yes. Convention urged her to do that. In truth, it wasn't necessary. She'd worked and fought alongside this man for many months. She'd shared sorrows and triumphs with him. She knew him now better than she knew herself, in some ways.

And she knew, without a shadow of a doubt, that she loved him.

With complete confidence, she tilted her head back to look him in the eye. "No. As far as I'm concerned, we can elope today."

The joy that came over him was practically incandescent. Shunlei kissed her fiercely, vibrating with joy, and then pulled back to demand, "Can we really go today?"

Mei Li almost said yes, then belatedly remembered a certain sword. Not to mention a half-completed wedding outfit. "Well—"

"I hear them talking," Hawes said from the hallway, voice a little muted. "I think they're up."

"Uh-oh, we're caught." Mei Li lifted up enough to swing her legs off the mattress, sitting up. Shunlei followed her example, although he seemed grumpier about the interruption.

Seconds later, Hawes rapped lightly on the door before sticking his head in. "Ah, good, you are up. How are you feeling, Shunlei?"

"Hungry, but victorious," he answered brightly. "Hawes, Mei and I are going to elope, alright?"

Their illustrious leader blinked, taking a second to turn that over. Then he gave Shunlei the same look any parent would an overexuberant child. "No, you may not elope. You have people who want to celebrate with you. And a cursed sword that has to be safely dealt with first."

Shunlei actually pouted. Openly pouted.

Mei Li had to bite the inside of her cheek to keep from

snickering. She kissed him lightly to erase the pout. "We have half-completed wedding outfits, remember?"

Growling, Shunlei slouched a little. "I knew I was forgetting something."

Shaking his head, Hawes focused on her. "I'm glad you're up. We've been discussing what to do with the sword."

"Ah. I think I have the answer to that. Is everyone gathered?"

"More or less. Nord's still sleeping, but everyone else is in the dining room. Our hostess, as it turns out, is a very good cook."

"Then let's go down and talk this over." Mei Li would like to steal a minute to wash her face and change clothes, but it could wait until after she'd filled her belly. Her stomach threatened mayhem if she didn't feed it soon.

They followed Hawes downstairs, Shunlei still pouting a little, which amused Mei Li to no end. She'd like to be married sooner rather than later, but it also felt inevitable to her. That it would definitely happen. It took some of the urgency off. Shunlei clearly didn't share that opinion.

The dining room was rather plain for a mayor's house, with white walls and polished dark floors and barely any furniture other than the table and chairs. A single china cabinet lurked in one corner, a landscape of the sea on the wall, and that was about it. Mei Li barely noticed the decoration; in truth, her eyes and appetite solely focused on the spread of food along the table.

Melchior grunted a greeting, halfway through his own plate. Hawes apparently had eaten before getting up to check on them, as he resumed a seat but didn't reach for any of the dishes. Kiyo, fixing herself another cup of tea, greeted them.

"Well, good afternoon, you two."

Was it really? Actually, the sun was rather high in the sky. Oops. Understandable they'd slept so late, though. Mei Li wasn't bothered. "Yes, good afternoon. Pass me the tea, please."

Kiyo spoke as she passed the white porcelain pot over. "The sword is safely sealed and under tight lock in a room right now. The mayor's son is standing guard over it. We're not sure what to do with it at the moment. I don't think it's possible to break it."

Mei Li shook her head in agreement but didn't speak around the roll in her mouth.

"Everything else we've tackled, we've been able to either destroy or seal in place. But the sword shouldn't be left here. For one thing, no one in the town wants it here. For another, they hardly have the defenses to keep it protected if someone decides to come after it. And I really feel that someone with magical abilities should be nearby, in case our seal comes undone for whatever reason."

Mei Li nodded in support of this.

"Swallow so you can tell us where to go," Hawes ordered her in exasperation. "You said you have an idea of what to do with it?"

Shunlei actually answered for her. "She said the Summer Winds Temple would be the best place to go next."

With a thankful smile at him, she paused in eating long enough to give a brief explanation. "There's a few reasons for my rationale. First, there's magic users in training there and likely always will be. Second, the hot springs in the area means there's a constant and steady source of fire element— if we use a fire-based seal around the sword, then it should be able to maintain itself for many generations." She didn't tell them how she knew this. "Third, *I* want to be up there."

"So we can get married," Shunlei filled in, excited all over again and practically bouncing in his chair. "And then have a honeymoon afterward in the hot springs."

Pointing to him, Mei Li agreed, "What he said."

Kiyo and Melchior looked at both of them as if they had lost their minds.

"You haven't been courting that long!" Kiyo objected.

Shunlei shrugged this off. "We've spent plenty of time together by dragon standards."

When their eyes went to her, Mei Li also shrugged. "We haven't been officially courting that long, true. But we've spent months together at this point. I'm sure of my decision. We'll spend maybe a day or two here, rest up? Order the rest of our wedding clothes. Then we can go to Summer Winds Temple. Hawes, I think it best to send a message ahead and explain what we're bringing to them."

"It's only polite." Hawes stroked at his half-grown beard. "Assuming they'll agree to host it at all."

"I'm quite confident they will." Mei Li knew it for a fact. The sword had always been guarded by that temple since the day it was brought to them. It was a point of pride now.

Kiyo did not look ready to move past the argument of them marrying already. She had that bullish expression of someone who was going to argue this point to death.

Mei Li decided to ignore her for now. No doubt Kiyo would corner her about this later.

If Hawes saw their silent exchange, he chose to ignore it as well. "Alright. I'll craft up a letter to send ahead. Lady Kiyo, if you'll help me write up the magical particulars of the sword and what will be required of the temple to host it, I feel that would smooth matters ahead of us. Even if they're not willing to host it long-term, they might be willing to hold it for now until we have a better idea of what to do with it. You're quite sure we can't destroy it?"

Kiyo grimaced, side-tracked from the marriage topic, and faced Hawes as she explained, "It's incredibly powerful. Normally, I'd say we could counter its magical force by drawing upon Shunlei's dragon fire. But in this case, it won't work. It was forged in fire and earth, so using dragon fire against it will only fuel it. I assume Mei suggests the hot springs not only because a fire-based seal will last longer, but because submerging it in water will help keep the sword in check."

Mei Li gave her a salute with her tea cup for a well-educated guess.

Kiyo gave her a nod in return. "I thought as much. So, the answer is no, we have no chance of destroying it now. Our best option is to seal it and wait for it to weaken. A future generation will have to attempt it."

The future generation being Mei Li herself. Now there was a glum thought.

"I see. Pity, that. I'd rather have that nuisance destroyed. Alright, we'll explain that in the letter as well. Lady Mei, Shunlei, I assume you'll clean up and then go do some shopping? I'll give you some funds before you go. Take an hour or so and see if you can commission that flying harness to be made." Hawes shot Shunlei an enigmatic look. "I, for one, don't want to repeat what we just did with you. And I know you'd rather fly with her."

"That I do," Shunlei agreed calmly. "We'll look for someone. But I doubt it can be finished before we leave for the mountains."

"No, we'll likely need to come back this direction and pick it up. We're sitting on the main road going up into the mountains, so we'll come back this way regardless." Hawes gave a weary sigh, showing his own exhaustion for a moment. "I hope they agree. I could use a bit of relaxing in hot springs myself."

Mei Li gave a mental cheer. She knew they'd get their way. All she had to worry about today was shopping.

Today was looking up already.

23

The shopping, not to mention the harness making, ended up taking three days. No one in the town was very happy at the delay in getting the sword out of their domain. They pitched in and helped with the harness, rushing the job and making it in a fraction of the time. Even with their unease, they did seem to understand that negotiations were in progress with their local temple and were willing to wait. Uneasy, but willing.

To offset their unease, Mei Li offered to fly the sword up with Shunlei, going ahead of the group. They needed to do a proper flight to test the harness, anyway, and the temple was only a day and a half trip up by horse. A half a day's flight, more or less. It seemed the most sensible suggestion.

The only downside to it was that Mei Li had to be in very close proximity to the sword for several hours. Which frankly, no.

Shunlei picked up on this, of course, and as she gingerly slid into the harness strapped to his chest, he asked in concern, "Are you alright?"

"You ever have those moments where you say something, and then you have instant regret? That's me right now." Mei Li sucked in a breath, psyching herself up. The sword was already in place, lightly strapped to the inside, and faintly glowing. Like it was laughing at her.

Hawes offered a shoulder to steady her as she slid in. "We can go back to the original plan?"

"Even if you ride it up, it will still mean someone has to be in close proximity to it," she grunted, getting her legs properly in and sliding the rest of the way. "And it's better for that to happen for only a few hours instead of two days."

"Which is why I agreed to it, but you look very uneasy right now." Hawes stared at her with outright concern on his tanned face.

"It feels like I'm next to lightning trapped in a bottle."

Shunlei's head turned so that he could look at her. "A charged, electrifying sort of feeling?"

"That, and stupidity. I can't imagine why anyone would want to try and catch lightning in a glass bottle."

"I can carry it in my claw?" he offered.

"You absolute mung bean." Early stages, inventing curses. "No. Not after yesterday, you're not getting in direct contact with it. It's fine, let's go and get this over with."

Shunlei did not look convinced. Neither did Hawes.

Mei Li growled mentally and pointedly said the one thing she knew would get Shunlei immediately into the air. "If we go now, we'll have time to make arrangements with the temple for a marriage ceremony."

Shunlei immediately snapped back around. "Safe journey up, Hawes. See you in a few days."

Shaking his head in exasperation, Hawes backed up. They were on the highway, as it was the only place with enough open space for Shunlei to stretch his wings out. With a flap of his wings, Shunlei started running, getting enough lift to leave the ground. Jostled, Mei Li gritted her teeth until she could feel his body leave the ground. Her stomach dropped out as he gained altitude, then the flight steadied.

After several minutes, she dared to open the top and stick her head out enough to talk to him. Switching to Long-go, she asked, "After we get things settled, should we do a preening session?"

"It's like you read minds," he sighed, tone dreamy with anticipation.

"No, I just find you very predictable."

He let out a rolling laugh, like muted thunder. "I suppose I am in that sense. Mei, there is something that bothers me."

"Oh? What's that?"

"It feels very odd that we'll be mated but have no home of our own. Normally, we'd be building something together. But it's not something we can really do right now, either."

"We'll need to settle on a place to stay during the winter, though. I, for one, am not about to tramp about in the ice and snow. Even the worst of the troublemakers tend to hunker down and wait for winter to pass."

"That's a good point. Somewhere with hot springs?" he asked hopefully.

"Ooh, that's a lovely idea. Horvath has a natural hot spring in it, too. I wonder if we could stay there?"

"If we ask very nicely, I'm sure they will let us."

She lay on her stomach, speaking of the future with him, letting the wind rustle past her face. It was easy to ignore the sword lying at her side. Mei Li idly played with the two rings on a necklace around her neck. She'd crafted them herself yesterday, fitting the simple gold bands to both of their fingers. Shunlei had found the tradition of wearing wedding bands to be charming and had cooperated perfectly. Mei Li hoped to have them properly engraved at some point. There just wasn't a goldsmith in town, so she'd had to whip up something with a gold ingot, magic, and some determination.

The flight seemed to last minutes instead of hours, and they arrived at the Summer Winds Temple before Mei Li properly realized it.

The Summer Winds Mountains were vast, with primeval forests that stretched far past what the eye could see, even from the air. The temple was easy to spot among all of the green trees, the red fencing and gates eye-catching. The main building soared four stories up, and she could see little dots of people as they moved about in the open courtyard. Shunlei banked right, and she had to close the flap to keep herself properly in the box and not accidentally thrown free.

Even inside the harness, she could hear an alarm sound, the gong of a bell being struck repeatedly as people spotted an incoming dragon. Then they stopped and milled about in confusion as they saw something strapped to his chest. Mei Li wanted to call out assurances to them but didn't dare open the flap until Shunlei had all feet on the ground.

"Hello," Shunlei called out in greeting, sounding cheerful. "I'm with Hawes' party."

"Shunlei the Red, correct?" an ancient voice greeted. "I am Iram, head priest here."

Mei Li got the flap undone and flipped herself out of the box, not entirely gracefully. She never would get used to dismounting from that thing. Brushing her hair back from her face, she turned and got her bearings.

A dozen or so young priests-in-training stood in a wide circle, spears in hand, although only a few were pointing them. The rest seemed to have caught on that this was not an intruder, but guest. Directly ahead of Shunlei was an elderly man stooped with age and a white beard trailing down his chest. He eyed them both with thick white brows pulled down over his eyes.

"Greetings." Mei Li walked to him and gave a bow. "I am Mei, a mage, and Shunlei's betrothed. We've brought a cursed sword for your keeping."

Iram's brows shot up at hearing 'betrothed.' "Yes, your leader spoke of the sword. We are prepared to receive it, although I would like to sit and counsel with you on the best way to guard it. Hawes said you would know best how to handle the matter. But a human betrothed to a dragon?"

Iram didn't seem to know how to react to such a pairing. Mei Li chose not to take it personally, as it probably did look odd from his stance. As far as most of humanity knew, the dragons were beasts. Unreasonable beasts, at that. They had no idea dragons also possessed a human form. Her choice in spouse probably looked strange from his shoes.

"It hopefully won't be the last such pairing." Mei Li shot Shunlei a smile. "He's determined to make dragons and humans allies."

"Are you, now." Iram was at least trying to be diplomatic about it.

"I think my odds are good. At least, my efforts have succeeded for the most part." Shunlei gave a shake from head to tail and then shifted smoothly to human form. That startled their onlookers even further. Iram actually skittered back a step. Shunlei took hold of the strap of the carrier, keeping it from toppling over. "At any rate, Priest Iram, after the sword is dealt with, we have a personal matter to confer with you about."

"We'd like to get married and hoped you would do the honors," Mei Li said with a hopeful smile. Her amusement at their reactions she tried to keep to herself.

Iram looked between the two of them, torn between surprise and some other emotion threatening to topple him over. "I—well, yes, we should definitely talk about that. Um."

Bailing him out, Mei Li added with a jerk of her thumb toward the carrier, "But let's deal with the troublemaker first."

Recovering, Iram acknowledged it with a nod. "Yes. Quite."

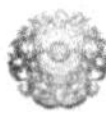

Mei Li was able to borrow several of the mages and mages-in-training at the temple to help her seal the sword and build a barrier over it. It was better that way, really, because now they all had hands-on experience with it and knew precisely what to do if either the barrier or seal failed. The seal would eventually fail—no human magic was infallible. She knew from very personal experience she'd have to deal with this thing in the future. She wrote a very concise report of how everything was done and then sent it ahead to the Prince of Horvath.

Writing the report felt both nostalgic and strange to her. She knew very well that in this time period, this shouldn't be her responsibility. The first Tomes would take over this duty once they found him. Or met up with him, however one should phrase it. According to Mei Li's count, that was still almost two years into the future, though. It did no harm for her to write the records now.

She knew good and well they'd get lost before the first Tomes managed to get things organized.

Mei Li was now of two minds about the shoddy record keeping of this era. And the lack of back-up copies in general. The organized part of her that wanted things neatly lined up in a row still bristled that no one had planned ahead. Or thought of what-if's. She'd been forced to time travel, for mercy's sakes, because of people's poor planning. It made her want to time travel to each generation so she could smack them for such a grievous goof.

And yet.

The part of her that wasn't task-oriented was so relieved she'd needed to travel back in time. If she had not done so, would she have ever realized what she and Shunlei were to each other?

Mei Li traveled through the room she'd been given to stay in. Her room and Shunlei's both opened up to some of the open-air baths. This was the largest of the lot, and Shunlei was even now testing whether or not it could hold him in dragon form. The answer: yes. But barely.

He was stretched out, the tip of his tail hanging out on

the far end and twitching with idle happiness, his large head on the other side, pillowed on two towels. He reminded her so strongly of a cat in a sunny spot that she had to bite back a laugh. Stopping in the doorway, she stood and watched him for a while.

The Shunlei of the future was so much more contained, his emotions not easily displayed. But she now wondered how much of that was him trying not to give everything away. How hard must it have been for him to see his wife in front of him and know she had no memory yet of their life together? To be forced to wait until the timing was right? If their positions had been reversed, Mei Li had no faith she would have exercised the necessary patience.

Five thousand years alone...the thought rent her heart to pieces. It seemed entirely unfair that only he would suffer from that. And it would be so much worse because the spell dictated that she would suddenly disappear from his side without warning. He'd have no way of knowing what happened to her.

No. Wait. Shunlei the Black was very aware she time traveled. How had he known that? Mei Li had been very careful to not let anything slip or give the impression she was not from this time. Granted, her soon-to-be husband was beyond clever, so perhaps he'd figured it out on his own.

Or was there some way for her to tell him? At least give him an explanation of what would happen to her so he wouldn't be left wondering? Disappearing without warning from his side was too cruel. If there was a way to work around the loopholes in the spell...

She had time to figure this out. Ten years, in fact. Mei Li silently swore to herself to do so. There must be a way.

"Are you going to join me or not?"

Snapped out of her ruminations, she blinked at him for a moment before the sentence sunk in. "I was going to preen you, but you look entirely too comfortable just now."

"Hmm," he hummed, not disagreeing. "Come join me."

She'd put on the dark grey bathing robe before coming out, so it was an easy matter of slipping off the straw sandals and sliding into the narrow area not taken up by his body. The water was deliciously hot, and she sighed with pleasure as she slid in. Shunlei's shoulder proved a good place to lounge against, and she promptly did so without a by-your-leave.

"Let's stay here for the rest of the year," Shunlei murmured. He lightly thrummed with contentment.

"I'm perfectly alright with that. You think everyone will let us?"

"We can at least steal a few days. We're owed a honeymoon."

"That we are." Oh dear. Now that she was warm and relaxed, she felt sleepy. It was hard to focus enough to speak. "In two days, you'll be an old married man."

"With the most beautiful, intelligent woman at my side."

"Oh, you *are* smooth." She laughed and lightly smacked him on the shoulder. "I think Priest Iram suspected we were jesting with him at first. He kept watching us like a man waiting for the other leg to be pulled."

"He did, didn't he? But now I think he's just as excited as we are."

"Darling, I think everyone would prefer dragons marrying humans over fighting with them."

"*I'd* certainly prefer it. I suspect we'll get quite the feast with our wedding, even though we told him twice we only need a modest celebration."

"I suspect you're right." Mei Li smiled. She didn't mind either way. "I have no doubt we'll achieve your goal in time. I think mine we'll achieve in a few years."

He canted his head to look at her out of one eye. "Your goal of having a dedicated record keeper? That goal?"

"Yes, that goal."

Shunlei blinked at her, the motion a little lazy. The heat was making him sleepy too, apparently. "You really think we can find someone to do that?"

"It might take a few years," she allowed. "But I do. Just wait. In the future, you'll see how vital this really is."

He gave a soft sigh, head settling again. "I don't doubt you're right."

"You're not allowed to fall asleep in the bath. I'm not hauling you out."

"Five more minutes."

Mei Li allowed this, as she didn't want to move yet either.

"You're not allowed to fall asleep either."

"But you *can* carry me out," she objected, mouth curling up in a grin.

"Nope. Fair's fair."

"Awww."

24

Mei Li might have been a bit nervous.

She was dressed fully in the red wedding outfit except for the gauzy, thin veil. Kiyo was behind her, carefully arranging her hair even as Mei Li slipped elaborate golden earrings into her ears.

"Stop fidgeting." Kiyo gave her a light whack with the hairbrush.

"I'm not fidgeting, I'm putting in earrings. You think the men are doing alright?" Mei Li knew Hawes, Nord, and Melchior were doing their best to support Shunlei in his own preparations. And she appreciated it beyond words. Still, a part of her heart felt that this was entirely unfair to the friends and family they had in the future, who'd never see this day. Abe, for one. Rone, especially, would have loved to have been here. As irrational as it was, she did wish she could have them here today, too.

"You are fidgeting, and they're fine. I'm almost done. Hawes will be here any moment to get you."

They'd spent most of yesterday afternoon discussing how to do the wedding and making decisions. The temple had been very generous with matters. This room, for instance. It was an airy courtyard right off the garden, normally reserved for the most elite guests, but now turned into a bridal chamber just for her. They'd blocked off all sight lines with several screens and even had both wine and a tray of snacks on hand just in case she needed something to settle her stomach. Or her nerves.

The wine, admittedly, looked tempting. "I'm not nervous."

Kiyo gave an inelegant snort. She clearly didn't agree.

"I'm marrying a man I'm madly in love with, why should I be nervous?"

"Because you're entering into a different chapter of your life," Kiyo informed her promptly. "One that you didn't properly prepare for, no less. And you're trail blazing by doing the first interspecies marriage to ever be recorded in history."

"Oh. Said like that, I have plenty of reasons to be nervous."

"Nervous or not, *stop fidgeting*."

Mei Li tried to sit still, but it proved hard. She was antsy and wanted to move. Part of her brain was convinced that as soon as the ceremony was done, she'd settle right down again. It was the anticipation that was undoing her control right now.

Someone cleared their throat right outside of the screen. "Ready to go?"

"No, because she keeps *squirming*." Kiyo jammed one more pin in her hair, then sighed. "Finally. Alright, give me the veil."

Mei Li was just as relieved to be done and promptly handed it over. She didn't move her head as Kiyo draped it over her hair, resting just so, allowing it to drape elegantly over her face and down her back.

"Perfect." Kiyo straightened and gave her a pleased nod. "I'll leave you to Hawes and go take my place."

"Thank you, Kiyo. I'll return the favor if ever it comes about."

Kiyo shook her head even as she headed for the screen. "Let's worry about today first. Hawes, she's all yours. She can't see well through that veil, remember, so watch out for her feet."

"I will." Hawes stepped through and then stopped dead. He looked a little wistful as he took her in from head to toe. "Well. Aren't you a vision."

Mei Li smiled up at him. "Thank you, Hawes. How is Shunlei?"

"Beside himself, he's so excited. I almost had to sit on him." Striding to her, he extended a hand. "Let's get you to him."

Mei Li accepted the hand and squeezed it. "I'm glad you're with us today."

"I strangely feel like I'm giving two children away today. Which, considering my own unmarried state, is rather odd." Hawes gave a soft chuckle. "Nice, though."

She wanted to kiss his cheek so badly but the veil blocked her from doing so. "You're the best father figure I could ask for."

"Stop that. I'm perilously close to tears as it is."

Snickering, she just squeezed his hand again and let him lead her into the gardens.

Mei Li kept her hand on Hawes' as he led her forward at a stately pace. The formal gardens in the temple were in full bloom in this summer season, and someone had taken the care necessary to clean all the sidewalks and paths so not even a single flower petal touched the grey paving stones. In the center, directly in front of a koi pond, a red carpet stretched out in front of a low altar where incense burned, along with a bowl of earth and a bowl of water.

There had been some confusion yesterday about how to do the full ceremony, as part of it required bowing to ancestors and/or parents, but neither Mei Li nor Shunlei had any portraits of relatives living. In the end, they'd created a wooden memorial to those people and let that suffice.

Her eyes skipped over the arrangements, her mind

automatically cataloging all of it, double-checking that everything was there and correct. It was hard to see through the red veil covering her face, but she trusted Hawes to guide her footsteps. She passed friends and curious onlookers, all with smiles on their faces. It was a silent well-wishing, and she smiled back, not sure if they could see her expression through the veil.

From the opposite side, Shunlei approached. With his thick red hair, red skin, and the red wedding clothes, he was bright and very attention-grabbing. The beads of his headpiece masked some of his face—all but those penetrating blue eyes that were locked on her. There was an irrepressible smile on his face as well, matching her own.

Until this moment, Mei Li had been so focused on the logistics of this day that she'd not properly felt it. But now, as she walked to him, and he walked to her, her heart threatened to bloom right out of her chest.

In the time she'd known this remarkable man, she'd worried over him, fought beside him, protected and been protected by him, supported, laughed with, and depended on him. She'd come to love him as a friend first.

And now, as a husband.

The full magnitude hadn't hit her until this moment. It seemed to fill her from head to toe, the promises she was about to make. Her mind ran in circles for a moment, desperately rooting around looking for guilt or panic. It bowled over the intense relief she felt, elbowed happiness out of the way, upset hope to no end, took a worried peek at her libido (which was starting to stir and ask some interesting questions), and rooted through all the reasons this was going to end in disaster, looking for something to hit her with.

It found only firm resolve. Perhaps this would bring about heartbreak for both of them. Perhaps she was making a mistake. All Mei Li could do was love him to the fullest and hope those memories would be enough to carry him through until she could reunite with him in the future.

They met in the center of the red carpet and with a smile at each other, turned to face Priest Iram. He was arrayed in pure white, and gave them a sort of puzzled smile, as if he still wasn't sure how this had happened.

"Mei of Demarest. Shunlei the Red. You have come before us today to exchange vows of marriage. Shunlei, you are willing to marry Mei as your wife, in sacred marriage together for life? Whether she has sickness or health, poverty or wealth, has beauty or is plain, in good times and in bad, you are willing to love her, comfort her, to respect her, and protect her?"

"I am," Shunlei answered firmly.

"Mei, you are willing to marry Shunlei as your husband, in sacred marriage together for life? Whether he has sickness or health, poverty or wealth, has beauty or is plain, in good times and in bad, you are willing to love him, comfort him, to respect him, and protect him?"

"I am," Mei Li echoed.

"Bow once to heaven and earth," Iram instructed.

They bowed toward the bowl of dirt and water on the low table.

"Bow twice to your ancestors."

Mei Li and Shunlei altered their stance a few inches and bowed to the wooden memorial tablet standing in the center of the table.

"Bow three times to each other."

Mei Li did so, hands clasped in front of her stomach. This was it. After she did this, she'd be married to Shunlei. Her stomach clenched and jittered with emotion, some tangle of excitement and nerves that she couldn't begin to unravel. Then she lifted her head, caught his eyes, and saw everything she felt reflected back to her.

Iram intoned formally, "I present husband and wife. May they have health, happiness, and long life."

The watching crowd clapped, Melchior even letting out a whistle, and Mei Li laughed in pure delight. Shunlei's hand found hers, and she could feel the wedding band on his finger, much as he probably felt hers. Doing the Baderian version of the wedding ceremony hadn't allowed for the exchange of rings with the vows, so they'd slipped them on beforehand. Mei Li found that she didn't mind it.

They were drawn away from the garden and back inside, where a feast was laid out along the tables. They were placed at the head table, which overlooked the room on a slightly raised platform, the other tables moved down on a winch and pulley system to the correct height for the rest of the guests. The aromatic scent of all the foods made Mei Li's stomach rumble. She'd barely eaten, as it had taken forever to be officially washed, blessed, and dressed. It was mid-afternoon now, and she was nearly faint from hunger.

Only after they were seated did Shunlei turn to her and whisper, "I forget, when can we remove the headpieces and veils?"

There had been some confusion on that. Mei Li's homeland held firmly that the veil stayed on until the couple reached their honeymoon suite. Bader, apparently, had different rules on that score. "I don't remember either? But I don't want to eat while fighting the veil."

A passing young priest heard them and leaned in long enough to whisper, "Wait until the wedding cake is served to you. Then you can lift and remove each other's veils."

"Thank you," Shunlei whispered back. There was a twinkle in his eyes as he confessed to her, "Your human traditions are elaborate and confusing."

"You're telling me."

On light feet, a young girl in a pure white smock approached with a flat cake balanced carefully in her hands. She set it down between them on the table with a look of intense concentration on her face that only eased once the cake was safely delivered. Then she stepped back with a relieved smile. "May this cake bring you full bellies through all seasons."

"Thank you," Mei Li responded. She turned to Shunlei and carefully pulled the headpiece off, holding the beads still so they didn't smack him in the eye in the process. She set it aside and then stayed still as he did the same to her, carefully lifting the veil off her face and away so it trailed decoratively down her back.

Then finally, finally they could eat. Mei Li ate a bite of the cake, letting the fluffy layers of moist, sweet heaven melt in her mouth. She wasn't sure how, but somehow half the cake disappeared in a minute flat. Magic, perhaps?

Well-wishers appeared, coming to the table and offering their congratulations. Mei Li paused in eating, greeting each in return, side-stepping some of the lewder hints from the people who were already too far into the wine.

Melchior proved to be the last of them, and he had a wide smile on his face as he spoke. "I'd never have thought when you stumbled across us, Mei, that this day would come. That I'd have a sister of my heart marrying a brother-in-arms. I'm both pleased and perplexed on how this came about."

She truly did adore this man. "I feel the same way about it, in truth."

Melchior leaned in to confide in a lower tone, "We'll understand if you want to take a season off and rest."

"We'll do so this winter," Shunlei answered with a quick glance at her. "My wife is determined not to leave you shorthanded, and truthfully, I feel the same. We hope to find a good place as we travel where we can retreat when the snows hit."

"Horvath will welcome you with open arms," Melchior promised. "I'm not saying any airy promises. The Prince of Horvath has guaranteed us all places to stay this winter."

Something Mei Li had not known. "Thank you, Melchior.

We might very well take him up on that."

"Good, good. Also, I understand a keg of wine is coming this direction shortly. If you escape now, you'll miss the rowdier after-party."

Mei Li was very much in favor of that. She'd been to some wedding celebrations that went straight until dawn. No, thank you. She had other plans for her wedding night. "Warning taken."

With a wink, Melchior retreated back to his table.

Shunlei leaned in to her side to whisper, "Should we leave now?"

"In the next minute or less, yes."

He popped the last bit of cake in his mouth and then stood, offering her a hand. Mei Li took it, waving to the few people that called out to them, and beat a retreat outside. She thought they were going to the suite but instead Shunlei led her out to the wider temple courtyard. No one was there, everyone at the feast, and it was honestly nice to stand there and let the mountain air stream through her hair for a moment.

Shunlei stepped several paces off to the side and shifted to dragon in a smooth transition. Mei Li had a split second to wonder what he was doing before it hit her—of course, the flight. She'd been so focused on the human ceremony that she'd almost forgotten their plan to do the dragon ceremony afterwards.

He extended a claw to her, and she folded in against his chest. This would necessarily be a short flight, but the length of it didn't matter. Flying together did. Tucked up against his chest, he thrust hard and lifted them both into the air. She clung as tight as she could, enjoying the wind as it swirled around her. A smile lingered on her face as they flew in a lazy circle around the temple.

Flying with Shunlei was always a pleasure. Today, it meant something more. It meant everything. She tried to take it all in at once, sure that her mind would retain the way the sunlight splayed over the mountain and the way the temple glistened against the dark green trees ringing it. Hopefully, she'd remember the feelings as well as the visuals. This wasn't a day that she wanted to fade in any way.

Shunlei did several laps before silently taking them back down, using a side entrance this time. He must have asked ahead, as he knew precisely where to go once they landed to reach the suite set aside for the two of them. It was a perfectly lovely room, with its own attached miniature garden and a fenced-off hot spring for their private use. The canopy bed had a light netting that went around it to fend off the bugs and give them the option of leaving the windows and doors open, enjoying the night air.

Mei Li had every intention of taking advantage of all those things. But first things first. She closed the door firmly behind them then spun about, catching her husband by the waist and tugging him firmly toward her. "Come here."

Shunlei obediently came, tilting his head down to meet hers in a kiss. Mei Li loved every second of that kiss, but tonight she wanted more than this. She tugged at the outer jacket, letting it spill to the floor.

Lifting his head, Shunlei asked hopefully, "It is tradition for a husband and wife to come together on their wedding night, correct?"

"Yes," she answered firmly. Then mischievously tacked on, "And even if it wasn't, I want you."

In a rush, he confessed, "Thank all deities, me too, why are you wearing so many *layers*?"

"You too," Mei Li fussed. "Off. All of it, off!"

They pulled at each other's clothes and then fell to the bed, laughing and squirming, enjoying the exploration as they learned how they liked to be touched. The intimacy went deeper than the physical touches they exchanged, reaching down to the heart and binding them together in a different way. It didn't distract from anything but rather added another level. By the end of it, Mei Li finally understood why people were all a bit fixated on love making. She fetched up against Shunlei's side, tucked in against him with her head pillowed on his chest.

He turned his head enough to kiss her softly on the forehead. "I love you."

She smiled against his skin. "Love you, too."

"Thank you."

"For what?"

"Not letting fear make the decision for you."

"I almost did. In the end, I want all of the time with you I can possibly steal."

"Good. Me as well."

Teasing him, she poked him in the ribs. "Just remember, you promised today to love me when I'm old and wrinkly."

"Love is blind, remember? I won't see any wrinkles."

"Oh, you *are* smooth. Good husband, good husband."

"Are you...are you patting me like I'm a dog?"

"Maaaybe."

Shunlei immediately started tickling her for that. Mei Li laughed and squirmed and tried to catch his hands, but he was decidedly quicker than her reflexes. She ended up flat on her back and begging for mercy, breathing hard.

Maybe her wedding vows should have included no tickling.

Well, no. She wouldn't change a single moment of today for anything.

25

Two years later

Mei Li ducked behind Shunlei's back, using her fire-proof husband as a shield long enough to grab the next talisman she needed. This fire imp had caused all sorts of trouble in this land of drought and dry grassland, setting two different towns on fire and seemingly intent on continuing. Shunlei and Mei Li had been sent ahead to scout the area to see if they could spot it, with every intention of reporting back and leading the rest of their party toward it.

Well, you know what they say about intentions.

Now here she was, frantically trying to do the job of three people, running around and dodging the imp's fireballs while Shunlei tried to battle it to a standstill. It was alarmingly quick on its feet and slick. Shunlei had put a claw on it twice, only for it to wriggle free at the last possible second. She had no rope traps on her—curse the luck—and was instead trying to create a make-shift trap to keep it still long enough to vanquish it entirely.

Of course, it knew what she was doing, and kept shifting areas. Mei Li would swear, but couldn't think of any words strong enough off the top of her head.

Shunlei's tail whipped about and sliced through the air. He broke off the attack with a yelp and growled, "He just bit me."

"Bite him back," Mei Li suggested around a pant. She was really getting winded with all of this sprinting about.

"Oh, you're so funny."

"I do try." Finding the three talismans she needed, she darted out again, slamming two talismans to the earth before sprinting again to the other quarter. Her calves and thighs screamed in protest, but she didn't let it slow her down any.

The imp was an ugly thing, barely the size of a child, pot-bellied and with a mouth full of teeth. It snarled at her, then snapped against Shunlei before darting forward, only to be checked by Shunlei's wing. They would have been able to defeat this thing much faster if Shunlei had been able to use dragon fire. But in this dry, arid grassland they didn't dare. The fire would get away from them far too quickly.

From behind her, she could hear a horse's hooves thundering against the hard soil. She didn't spare even a glance, trying to get into the right position to block the imp. It failed before she was only half-way there as he managed to squeak through Shunlei's guard and out to the other side. Not far, though. Shunlei whirled and blocked him.

Still, it was just enough that her placed talismans wouldn't link up with each other properly. Mei Li seriously felt like crying out of frustration.

The horse skidded to a stop and she risked a glance this time. The rider was a fit man, probably near her age, and he had the obvious power of a mage. Her hopes rose, and she called out to him, "I'm trying to do a trapping spell!"

"Earth based?" he called back, already flinging himself free of the saddle. "Which variation?"

"Nine pins!"

"Got it!" His hand dove into the bag strapped to his waist and he came out with a handful of talismans, written not on yellow paper like hers, but a thicker, white parchment. "Take dragon side."

That seemed best, as he was no doubt uneasy with her dragon-husband. Well, that would change later once proper introductions could be carried out. Mei Li retreated toward Shunlei but gave him plenty of room to maneuver. Shunlei, after two years, knew very well what a nine pin trapping spell involved and where *not* to stand while mages were throwing it about.

The new mage was stalwart in his stance, not giving any ground, and deft with his hands as he quickly placed the four talismans down. Mei Li was quick to do the same, and it was a race between them on who could put the final talisman down. In the end, he beat her to it, and then they both clapped their hands, spreading magic into each talisman and activating them. With a snap, the trapping spell flared into existence like bars surrounding their quarry.

Whirling, the imp looked in every direction and then snarled viciously upon seeing itself trapped. It flung itself at the bars only to be shot back as the magic reacted. With a whimper it spun and fell to the ground, curling into itself with pain.

Mei Li had no sympathy for it. She stood there panting for breath, sweat pouring down her temples and the back of her neck.

"Thank you ever so much," Shunlei said to the mage. "We've been struggling with this thing for the past hour."

Surprised at being so cordially addressed, the mage stared at Shunlei for a full second before finding his voice. "I'd heard the imp was here from the last town I was in. When I saw you battling it, I thought to lend a hand."

"We do appreciate it." Mei Li straightened, feeling like she finally had her breath back. "Archery is *not* in my skillset, even using magic. And we didn't think it wise to use dragon fire under these conditions. It became a game of tag. Which

I don't appreciate."

"I can imagine." Extending a hand to her, he introduced himself. "I'm Kare Tamu, mage and scholar."

Mei Li's hand found his on automatic, which was just as well, because her mind had gone perfectly blank for a moment. Kare Tamu. Kare Tamu?! Ye little deities! The first Tomes had finally arrived. She lit up in a smile that might have come out a little demented. "Mage Kare, you have no idea how happy I am to meet you. I'm Mei. This is my husband, Shunlei."

Kare blinked at her, then stared uncertainly at Shunlei. "Ah, a pleasure. I heard that right? You're married?"

This reaction never got old for Shunlei, and he chuckled for a moment before switching forms. In his human form, he took a moment to settle his sleeves before calmly crossing to Kare. "Indeed, we are. Well met, Mage Kare."

Kare had obviously not been aware dragons could shift forms, and he seemed utterly flabbergasted, his jaw dangling for several seconds. With a hand, he slotted it back into position and croaked, "Well met. Heavens above, but you two really are a bundle of surprises, aren't you?"

"We get that often," Mei Li answered cheerfully. She really couldn't have been happier with how today turned out even if she'd planned it herself. Aching, sore muscles included. "Mage Kare, you said you'd heard of the imp from the townspeople and came out to hunt it down? You do that often?"

"Ah, well, not really on purpose. It's more that I've been studying the change in magical patterns over the past few years, and I keep stumbling into situations." Kare had an affable sort of look to him, like the boy next door, and he rubbed at his short, wiry black hair in a rasp of his hand. "I understand there's a group dedicated to magical problems, funded by the Prince of Horvath, and I keep hoping I'll run into them. They're sure to have many answers for me."

"Congratulations," Mei Li informed him, practically bouncing on her toes. "You've found them. Well, two of us, at any rate."

A blinding white smile lit up Kare's face, his white teeth in high contrast with his dark mahogany skin. "Have I really?"

"You have," Shunlei assured him. "And we'll be glad to take you back to the rest of our party and make introductions. We came ahead to scout the area, see if we couldn't locate the imp. And we did, but didn't have time to fetch everyone else."

"Yes, I can see how that would be the case. Well." Kare looked one second from hugging them. "Today is a very good day, indeed. Um, we should deal with the imp first?"

Mei Li nodded in perfect accordance with this. "Yes, imp first. Let's drag it back to the town. There's a bounty on its head that we'll happily split with you. Then we'll regroup with our party."

"Sounds splendid."

They killed the imp without fanfare, then took down the nine pins spell. Shunlei picked up the corpse like a high lady would a dirty dishrag and carried it as far away from himself as he could manage as they walked back to the town. She felt a little sorry for him as Mei Li wouldn't have wanted to carry that stinking carcass back either.

She walked alongside Kare, answering the many, many questions that the man had. Mei Li wasn't even surprised that he'd been making notes on his findings as he'd traveled and had a journal full already. It took effort. It took discipline. But she didn't cackle like a demented soul.

First of Tomes: Acquired.

Finally.

Guide

Dragon Ages

Cream – newborn
Yellow – 5-10 years
Orange – 10-20 years
Red – 20-100 years
Green – 100-300 years
Blue – 300-1000 years
Purple – 1000-3000 years
Black – over 3000 years

Name Pronunciations

Abe – AH-bay
Acala – ah-CAW-la
Bader – BAY-der
Bai – bye
Bohai – boh-hi
Budworth – BUD-worth
Cavanaugh – kaa-vuh-nuh
Chen – chen
Dolan – doh-lin

Edan – AY-din
Elora – EE-lore-ah
Enlai – EN-lie
Ernest – er-nest
Gen – g-en
Giselle – JI-zelle
Hawes – haw-z
Horvath – hor-vath
Huan – h'wan
Hui – h'wee
Iram – ee-rahm
Janine – ja-NEEN
Ji Lin – JEE lin
Jingfei – JING-fay
Kalei – kay-lee
Kare Tamu – KAH-ray TAH-moo
Kiyo – KEE-yo
Kovel – co-vell
Laborde – la-BOARD
Leah – lee-ah
Liasa – lee-ah-sa
Liggett – le-get
Ling Ling – LING ling
Llona – l-ah-na
Lothar – low-thar
Mei Li – may LEE
Melchior – mel-kee-or
Nord - nord
Odom – OH-duhm
Pari – pa-ree
Preston – PRESS-tuhn
Rabarbra – rah-bar-bra
Rone – rone
Sandeep – san-deep
Scott - scott

Shunlei – Shoon-lay
Simeon – si-mee-on
Sotejo – so-TAY-jo
Tanguay – TAN-gway
Tengfei – TENG-fay
Teoh – TEE-oh
Voas – VO-as
Wightkin – WHITE-kin
Yu Yan – you yahn
Zaffi – zah-fee

Other books by Honor Raconteur
Published by Raconteur House
♫ Available in Audiobook! ♫

ADVENT MAGE NOVELS
Jaunten♫
Magus ♫
Advent ♫
Balancer ♫

ADVENT MAGE NOVELS
Advent Mage Compendium
The Dragon's Mage ♫
The Lost Mage

WARLORDS (ADVENT MAGE)
Warlords Rising
Warlords Ascending
Warlords Reigning

THE ARTIFACTOR SERIES
The Child Prince ♫
The Dreamer's Curse ♫
The Scofflaw Magician♫
The Canard Case
The Fae Artifactor

THE CASE FILES OF HENRI DAVENFORTH
Magic and the Shinigami Detective
Charms and Death and Explosions (oh my)
Magic Outside the Box
Breaking and Entering 101

DEEPWOODS SAGA
Deepwoods♫
Blackstone
Fallen Ward
Origins

FAMILIAR AND THE MAGE
The Human Familiar
The Void Mage
yttRemnants
Echoes

GÆLDORCRÆFT FORCES
Call to Quarters

IMAGINEERS
Imagineer

KINGMAKERS
Arrows of Change ♫
Arrows of Promise
Arrows of Revolution

KINGSLAYER
Kingslayer ♫
Sovran at War ♫

SINGLE TITLES
Special Forces 01
Midnight Quest

THE TOMES OF KALERIA
Tomes Apprentice
First of Tomes

Author

Dear Reader,

Your reviews are very important. Reviews directly impact sales and book visibility, and the more reviews we have, the more sales we see. The more sales there are, the longer I get to keep writing the books you love full time. The best possible support you can provide is to give an honest review, even if it's just clicking those stars to rate the book!

Thank you for all your support! See you in the next world.

~Honor

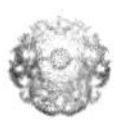

Honor Raconteur is a sucker for a good fantasy. Despite reading it for decades now, she's never grown tired of the magical world. She likely never will. In between writing books, she trains and plays with her dogs, eats far too much chocolate, and attempts insane things like aerial dance.

If you'd like to join her newsletter to be notified when books are released, and get behind the scenes about upcoming books, you can click here: NEWSLETTER or email directly to <u>honorraconteur.news@raconteurhouse.com</u> and you'll be added to the mailing list. If you'd like to interact with Honor more directly, you can socialize with her on various sites. Each platform offers something different and fun!

www.ingramcontent.com/pod-product-compliance
Lightning Source LLC
Chambersburg PA
CBHW050320160726
48002CB00001B/119